T0070250

Strength of Living

Strength of Living

By

Bright Avwoghoke Okoro

Malthouse Press Limited

Lagos, Benin, Ibadan, Jos, Port-Harcourt, Zaria

© Bright Avwoghoke Okoro 2019
First Published 2019
ISBN: 978-978-57397-6-3

Published and manufactured in Nigeria by

Malthouse Press Limited
43 Onitana Street, Off Stadium Hotel Road,
Off Western Avenue, Lagos Mainland
E-mail: malthouselagos@gmail.com
Facebook:@malthouselagos
Twitter:@malthouselagos
Istagram:@malthouselagos
Tel: 0802 600 3203

All rights reserved. No part of this publication may be reproduced, transmitted, transcribed, stored in a retrieval system or translated into any language or computer language, in any form or by any means, electronic, mechanical, magnetic, chemical, thermal, manual or otherwise, without the prior consent in writing of Malthouse Press Limited, Lagos, Nigeria.

This book is sold subject to the condition that it shall not by way of trade, or otherwise, be lent, re-sold, hired out, or otherwise circulated without the publisher's prior consent in writing, in any form of binding or cover other than in which it is published and without a similar condition, including this condition, being imposed on the subsequent purchaser.

All glory comes from daring to begin.

- Eugene F. Ware

CHAPTER ONE

Robert was awaiting daybreak in his living room, while reflecting on a sermon for his family's morning devotion to God. It was customary for him to wake up to study and reflect deeply on the morning devotion and patterned it clearly in his mind before beginning the morning worship with his family every morning. Left with him, he would prefer the devotion much earlier as he liked the period for praise-worship to be longer. But he appreciated the fact that not everybody in the family would like it, especially his children who were hurried into the devotion and followed it willy nilly, as they struggled to keep awake during the session. Robert knew that his children had not been able to appreciate the morning devotion, the way it should be. But he thought the children must of necessity be made to imbibe Christian values as early as possible and get used to its lifestyle and had their lives patterned after it. He had always had his mind fixed on the biblical saying. *Train up a child in the way he should go and when he is old he will not depart from it (Proverb 22:6).* Be that as it may, he would not want to disturb them too earlier in the morning, so that they would not see the early morning worship as a burden and develop wrong attitude towards it. At 5.20 am, the devotion began. Oro, his first child who was in her final class in primary school led the praise worship. Most cases she led the praise-worship session, and always did so in the same order by regularly repeating the same songs successively each day and they all had become so used to it that each of them could easily predict the song that would follow every song in the praise-worship. In this way, the whole praise-singing had become so mechanical that, apart from Robert, no other person among them was meditating upon the wordings of each rhythm, in appreciation of God's benevolence towards mankind, especially the faithful. But that was not to bother the head of the family who was a devout Christian. Ensuring that his children embraced Christian life as early as possible was all that mattered to him.

Agnes, Robert's wife, appreciated her husband's devotion to the faith. As a daughter of a Reverend, she had gone through the same regimented Christian upbringing as a child and was used to her husband's insistence on strict observance of biblical principles in the family, which sometimes reminded her of her own father. At times she saw her husband exactly in the mould of her father. But with the hindsight of a pastor's daughter, she knew that the casting of children into the Christian mould regimentally might not always lead to true Christian life in adulthood. In some cases, it might be counter-productive. But as a wife in the Christian faith, she knew her place in the family. She was only an adviser, who must not push her ideas too strongly lest she would be reminded of Ephesians 5:22 in the scripture: *Wives submit yourselves unto your own husband, as unto the Lord.* But from time to time, she had told her husband that, all that the children needed was a guide and a close monitoring while allowing them to express their natural tendencies where there would be opportunities for corrections. Robert was often reluctant to make his feeling known to his wife whenever this issue of how to raise their children came up. He believed very strongly that children should be properly brought up in the fear of the Lord and the only way to do that was to make them see life and everything from the prism of the Bible. He saw the Bible as all-encompassing, touching every aspect of life. And to make the children thorough Christians they had to study the Bible thoroughly and commit every word in it to their hearts, so that, every of their actions and conduct was regulated by the word of God. In this way, they would be in good standing with the Lord. Robert placed great emphasis on Bible-reading in the family, as he always ensured that his children read the Bible in their spare time, and he had been getting encouragement from the children, Ovo, his son, had won the Bible quiz, twice in the church. Oro had also made him proud when she came out first in memory verse recitation last year. These occasions were his proudest moments in the church.

As usual, the praise–singing that morning was followed by Bible study. That week Robert had scheduled the 'Ten Commandments' for the family study which he believed was the foundation of children's moral upbringing. Oro read the 'Ten Commandments' in Exodus Chapter 20, to the hearing of everyone in the house. But as usual with Robert, he considered the first reading as preparing the ground for a thorough study. Robert always considered it his duty to re-read the Bible passage of every morning 'devotion' slowly and resonantly to bring out the spiritual meaning of the word. As he was doing so, he expected each of his children to pay absolute attention with all his mind and soul to what he was saying. It would be most unfortunate for any of the children to be seen dozing or not paying absolute attention during the period. The children knew their father's attitude towards the devotion so they always tried to maintain absolute quiet and undivided visible attention as expected.

After Robert had re-read the Scripture passage and had done all the pontifications, bringing out all the moral implications in his thorough and exhaustive analysis, they would prayer. Most times, the prayer session could be so long and boring that after sometime, the children would only be waiting for their father's final word to say their Amen, without really listening. In this way, nevertheless, Robert was able to carry his family through the morning devotion successfully always. Once the devotion was over, Agnes, his wife, with the children would go about the domestic chores like bees, knowing that the devotion had taken much of the time, in order for the children to be in school on time. On several occasions, she had appealed to her husband to be time conscious, during the morning devotion. But she always heard the rebuffing refrain, 'Allow the Holy Spirit to lead.' And after sometime, she stopped complaining.

Robert was a disciplinarian and strict adherent to work ethics. He was the Site Engineer of Ansco Construction Company Limited. He coordinated and supervised the company's construction projects. At work, Robert did not only emphasize strong work ethics among the workers under him, he also ensured that project works were carried out strictly to specifications, in compliance with their engineering designs and he was an exemplar of what he averred. Because of this, he was highly respected in the company. His diligent and thorough supervision had earned his company a good reputation. He had won 'the best worker of the year' award twice in the company. But some of the workers under his supervision disliked him because they felt he made them to work like donkeys.   Also, the company's suppliers of construction materials often had problems with him, as he always insisted on the highest qualities of materials. He had rejected a good number of materials supplied by them. No supplier of Ansco Company had his peace until Robert had approved his supplies for use. Robert's approval of their supplied materials was like passing with distinction in a highly competitive examination. Once a supplier had been given 'Local Purchase Order' after approving his quotations, his next fervent prayer was for the Site Engineer to approve his supplied materials, as Robert would never listen to any entreaty after his disqualification.   He was generally called in the company as, 'Mr. No Nonsense.' So, to some of these workers and suppliers, Robert was their albatross. They wished something would happen to get him out of their way.

But as far as the Site Engineer was concerned, he was doing his job in the fear of the lord, and was not interested in whatever views some persons might hold about him.   As long as he believed what he had done was consistent with the word of God, it was satisfactory. Nevertheless, he was not unaware of some negative image several of the workers and suppliers had of him. He had always encouraged himself with the saying, 'Whose voice will I obey? Is it the voice of human or the voice of God?' So he had this I-don't-care attitude to whatever negative impression some persons had of him. Because of this stoic posture of his, his detractors thought he was heartless and incorrigible.

Robert was always engrossed with his work. He seldom talked at his workplace. He never welcomed an idle visit at work. He saw such visits as a distraction and he firmly believed that the work place was meant only for work and not for fiddling around. In their shift work, workers assigned to work under Robert were sometimes derided by their other colleagues, not in that group, for their hard luck. But in the innermost minds of these workers, they knew that Robert was an exemplary worker, even Robert's most virulent critic among them knew this – when they were not self-seeking, they knew that Robert represented excellence and they could not do what he was doing, as human being naturally avoids discomfort if he can afford it. That is why the likes of Robert are rare in the society.

In his church, Robert was well known. He was one of the active members. He and his family were always participating in every church activity, including all-night revivals. Besides this, he was the chairman of the 'charity committee' of the church. One of the main functions of the committee was to identify and attend to the needy within and outside the church. Sometimes, they would visit the hospitals to pray for the sick and offer them some basic items like toiletries, juice, milk and other consumables, assuring them of the abiding presence of the good lord. The prisons were not left out, in their charity efforts. They used to visit a prison once every month to preach the 'good news' and sometimes offered free Bibles to prisoners. Robert was able to influence his church's council to realize his desire of raising offering for charity, once every month, usually after his brief remark on the pitiable and pathetic conditions they often found in the hospitals and prisons, and, he would call for more humanitarian intervention. He was also thinking of extending their succour to some orphanage homes. The charity organization of the church had become a very prominent ministry under his leadership. Hitherto, it was one of the organizations that had been in the background in the church, with little significant attention. But Robert had ballooned it up. He was very committed to it, which attracted the overwhelming support of the church; church members had been well sensitized to realize that besides absolute faith in God, charity means almost every other thing to Christian living. At every opportune time on the pulpit, to talk about his committee's activities, Robert would present a huge humanitarian challenge that the church still needed to address. After every of such briefing to acquaint members of how their good offerings to charity in the church had brought succour to a good number of the needy in the hospitals and prisons, and had won many souls for the lord, he would further inspire and encourage members to do more.

"Brethren, you need to be there and see things for yourselves. The challenge is huge. We really need to do more. Brethren, the lord is depending on you. We can do it by His Grace." He would encourage members.

This was usually followed by a resounding applause from the congregation. Robert was a happy Christian. All his effort and commitment to the work of God in the church was quite inspiring and was duly recognized and appreciated by the church, which had encouraged him to do more. He saw the charity organization of the church as his personal concern that needed all his attention. Where money and personal effort were required for it, Robert would not hold anything back. Sometimes, his selfless effort in the church strained his family financially as Robert would always give precedence to the church over his home. His wife, Agnes sometimes, would want to express her disapproval of her husband's church priority at his family's expense. But she had come to understand the kind of husband she had and all that he stood for. So it was pointless to express her displeasure. In such moments of extreme frustration and distress resulting from Robert inability to meet some of the financial needs of the family, she preferred to go to their bedroom and try to force herself to sleep, but in the process, she would find herself crying there. The cry sometimes helped to relieve her of the distress. In one of such frustrating moments, she saw herself and her children as the biblical lamb, taken to the altar, for sacrifice, without the least resistance. But in her indignation she asked, 'Has our Saviour not done that for us who believe? Why must we then pass that forlorn journey again?' She hoped to put the question to her husband that night. Instead, she eventually found herself that night, praying that God should have mercy on her and grant her the grace to adjust fully to her husband's full devotion to His work. Robert understood his wife silent disapproval of the family's sacrifice for God's service, even though she had not said it in any of their private discussions in the home. He certainly saw it in her forlorn and subdued agitated look, which she expressed in her cold and listless attitude to him in the home at such times. Robert expected Agnes to express her feelings, which he thought would give him the opportunity to explain things clearly to her as they stand in the scripture, on such occasions. Disappointedly, he would find his darling wife taking refuge in the bedroom, agonizing herself. Only to return to him later so full of life, as if she had never been in any kind of distress earlier, oftentimes, expressing exceeding and passionate interest in the children and every other thing in the home. In some cases, she would be singing joyfully, praising the good lord for his mercy and loving kindness in her life. And joy, love and understanding would return to the home again, as if there had never been any silent difference in how the finances of the family were handled.

CHAPTER TWO

'Dear, you looked like a real super model in that your new designer suit this morning. Seeing you in that suit, gave me a great joy, of being the lucky winner of the super model that I saw in you this morning. My only regret is that, you were too much in a hurry to have my kiss and hug; that'd have made my day,' enthused Agnes.

'Oh, my darling, I'm very delighted to hear this gratifying remark from you, I feel highly puffed up. My love, that's one quality that makes you so special and engaging. I'm really sorry that I was too concerned with my arriving punctually at the meeting, to look at my dearest, this morning. That would have made me sensed your desire to give me a kiss and a hug, before leaving. Certainly, that'd have made my day more fulfilling. But is it too late now?' Robert beamed with a smile as he looked expectantly towards his lovely wife, and they both had a snappy kiss, packed with romantic delight and laughter.

'Will it not be nice complementing the mirth with glasses clicking!' smiled Robert.

'Absolutely!' returned Agnes hilariously as it was desiring.

Immediately, a wine was brought from the refrigerator to perfect their evening delight.

'My dearest, if you were to contest with all the fashion models of this world, you would certainly beat all of them to it, this morning,' Agnes re-emphasized enthusiastically, in her continuation to blow her husband's mind with compliments, over his new designer suit.

Expectedly, Robert reeled with laughter.

'But how come, I wasn't even aware of the designer suit? Robert, when did you start keeping secret in this house?' added Agnes with some mild accusation in her voice.

Robert laughed repeatedly almost without end. 'Really, I wanted to make it a surprise to you. The designer suit was a gift from my Australian co-project supervisor at Ansco Company. He bought the designer suit in Paris on his way back from a summer holiday with his family there recently.'

'That's very kind of Lea. Dearest, but you should have told me. I ought to have thanked him very much for being so generous to you!' continued Agnes in a fluttered voice, though trying not to spoil their evening relaxation with any unkind remark.

'I think that wouldn't have been necessary my love, I've already done that,' answered Robert calmly.

'Appreciation is never too much,' returned Agnes.

'Well, that's true; said Robert thoughtfully.

'How was your meeting with the minister today?' inquired Agnes.

The Minister of Works had earlier invited all the firms handling his ministry's major construction works for a briefing that day. Robert who was Ansco company's project supervising engineer and its Area General Manager were at the meeting to represent Ansco Company. That was why Robert had to put on a special suit that morning.

'Well, it went well, only that it was rather too brief. We expected a special and elaborate interaction with the minister, as we thought, it was an opportunity to impress our client with the challenge we're facing with our project execution, which of course, was delay of funds. But the minister came to the meeting like a school teacher, to instruct us to execute their projects within specified time, saying that government is concerned to have its prime projects executed without further delay,' narrated Robert.

'You mean the minister did not give you people the chance to express your constraints?' said Agnes, expressing surprise.

'He just breezed in like a man who had an urgent message to deliver and leave. He was actually not prepared to entertain questions and excuses. He simply came to hand his instruction to us and we were expected to obey it without any hesitation. You know soldiers obsessively flaunt their authorities like their military uniform. That is why I don't like them being in public offices. I think it goes with their training, so we came back very disappointed. But my dear, you have made my day. Your compliments have lifted my spirit from the damn outing of today,' Robert turned his face towards Agnes cheerfully and patted her on the back, in a manner that suggested that they should drop the uninteresting encounter with the minister.

Just then, their children ran into the living room with great excitement to announce that they had completed their school home-works for the day. And their parents were quite happy to hear that, and commended them for doing so. This heart-warming compliment for their school performance by their parents which they earnestly craved for was the overall object of their dashing to their parents in the living room – it was a morale booster to them. And their parents understood this.

'Oro how was your school today? Hope everything went well?' probed Robert.

Oro nodded her head in a radiating smile.

'What was your score in Maths?'

'Ten over ten,' Oro said excitedly.

'And your English language?' asked Robert again, beaming with a smile of high expectation.

'Got all, too,' enthused Oro.

'That's my daughter! Come and hug me. You are a true daughter of your father.'

Robert happily spread out his arms and Oro dashed into her father's warm embrace.

'My daughter, that was very good of you, do keep it up.'

Next, was Ovo. Ovo's performances in Mathematics and English language were equally very good. As attention was shifting from Ovo, it was discovered that Oke the last child had disappeared. Oke's performance in school was extremely poor and was the odd one out of the three children. Knowing that she would be the butt of everyone in the family and probably fearing that her father might go beyond rebuke, and might cane her, she decided to go into hiding in the toilet.

'Where's Oke?' shouted Robert, pretending to be very serious. 'She was here, just now,' he added, and the other two children and Agnes, their mother, burst into hilarious laughter, knowing why Oke had suddenly disappeared.

'Oro and Ovo, go and bring her from inside. Why must she go into hiding?' said Robert, pretending to be very offended by Oke's action. But immediately he saw Oke being dragged into the living room by her two siblings, who obviously were overzealous and excited as they were wont to, while Oke was resisting them vehemently with all her strength and was crying, Robert was completely overwhelmed with pity and affection.

'That's all right! Oro and Ovo, please leave her alone,' he shouted pretending to be angry with Oro and Ovo for dragging her. 'My darling daughter, don't mind them, please come.' Robert beckoned to Oke with persuasive smile. But she remained where her two siblings left her, raising her voice the more crying. Robert went to her and cuddled her fondly to the sofa where he had been sitting and continued patting her on her head, while Oke was sobbing in her effort to stop her cry.

'That's okay, my daughter. I know you're a very intelligent girl. You just watch and see,' he turned to the rest of them. 'This my beautiful daughter — my shining star— she'll soon be outstanding in her class, and turn out to be the envy among her peers, you just wait,' Robert started patting Oke softly again. 'Ovo, please bring one mineral drink from the fridge,' instructed Robert, which was opened for Oke, all in an effort to make her happy.

Oke eventually became calm, and was quietly gloating over how she had successfully turned her unimpressed performance at school to her advantage. But one needed to see the faces of Oro and Ovo, the other two children, who thought they were to have the place of Oke that evening, for doing very well at school. Their faces were immediately clouded with extreme jealousy and anger, and were totally unhappy with the reverse of situations.

'My dear, it isn't fair,' noted Agnes sharply, after a glance over Oro and Ovo.

'What's not fair?' returned her husband, who was surprised to hear such an angry remark from his wife, with whom he had been having a delightful companionship in the living room and was afraid that the whole evening relaxation might just turn sour.

'The other two children deserve a drink more than Oke. They did very well at school and should be encouraged,' answered Agnes.

'Oh yes my dear. You're right; I was carried away in my effort to pacify Oke. At times, it happens like that,' Robert said, and laughed.

'Please, don't be carried away with your fondness for Oke. It could make the other two jealous of her and that can be very dangerous, darling,' said Agnes accusingly.

Immediately, Oro and Ovo were told to take a mineral drink each from the refrigerator. On hearing this, they became excited and ran to the refrigerator as if they were in a competition. It was true that Robert had a special attachment to Oke, and Agnes had observed that the other two children had also become aware of it. She equally realized that they were inadvertently becoming sensitive to and resentful of it, so she considered this occasion quite apt to bring it to the consciousness of her husband before it became unhealthy in the family.

When the children had all got their drinks, the atmosphere became relaxed and lively again. A time like this when the entire family were in a happy mood together was the children's best time. It was a time they always looked forward to because their father would not be in his usual hard and firm disposition of a strict disciplinarian, but genial and complaisant. That was the time the children would feel at ease to ventilate their nagging concerns over issues they had not had the courage to express to their father. It was the time to resolve them, and the children knew that when their father was in this mood, he was always tolerant, considerate and understanding, so they made maximum use of such moments, to say many things on their minds as they could remember.

'Dad, you haven't bought me the boots you promised me when I came second, in my last exam,' said Ovo grudgingly.

'Oh yes,' Robert nodded his head repeatedly in remembrance, as he had forgotten. 'You should have reminded me. Your daddy has so many things in his head to think about, you know,' he smiled mildly, throwing the accusation back to Ovo and Ovo became silent and did not say anything again. Not that he actually forgot to remind his father as children never forget promises made to them. They are always there on their minds. In most cases they are afraid to express it as they wish, especially when such promises are parried after one or two reminders, because they know, contrary to adults' belief that one is no longer willing or unable to keep the promise. They also know that further repeated reminders might provoke pestering anger in such adults. In that understanding, they pretend to forget.

'My dear, please remind me about it next Saturday, when we go to the market for our monthly shopping,' Robert said to Agnes.

Agnes betrayed a doubtful smile.

'Why are you smiling like that?' asked her husband.

'Why won't I smile? You are promising again, raising Ovo's hope. I just hope you'll keep that promise, if not, you'd better tell him there isn't any money now. Remember, you haven't paid their school fees, and there are other financial challenges to contend with. The children don't know your problems but they could be offended when promises made to them are not kept. Though, it is not deliberate, they can't understand. So make them understand when you cannot keep your promises to them, rather than raise their hopes and dash them again,' cautioned Agnes.

'No, no, I'll keep this,' argued Robert, becoming very sensitive to his wife's subtle accusation.

'Daddy, you also promised to buy me a special dress in my last birthday but you haven't,' remembered Oro accusingly.

'Ssh! that's over,' said Agnes. 'Your daddy is doing his best for you children. You're privileged! There are children who hawk during school and sleep in open markets and under fly-over bridges at night – they have parents – but nobody cares for them: No more of such talk again,' declared their mother and that silenced the children from saying more, as Agnes knew, there were still other promises to them that had not been fulfilled by their father.

The truth was that, Robert was quick at making promises to his children on the spur of the moment, in his effort to make them imbibe the right values and perform very well in their studies. In most cases, he bit off more than he could chew, that made some of those promises to the children unfulfilled. But instead of bombarding their father for the fulfilment of those unfulfilled promises, the children put the heat on their mother because they lacked the boldness to tell their father, so Agnes was more informed about the children's feelings than their father. This is quite natural, mothers are more intimate with their children than fathers, as they spend more time with them, hence mothers exercise greater influence on them, though with lesser authority over them. Authority resides more in the father that is why the mother will have to recourse to the child's father when her own authority over her child is failing.

While the children were happily enjoying their drinks in a warm atmosphere with their parents, it occurred to Robert to expound the holy Scripture to the children, in a way of learning to appreciate the goodness of God in their lives.

'Children, I can see that you're all happy now.'

'Yes, we're, daddy,' they all answered.

'Do you like to be happy every day?' smiled their father.

'Yes, of course,' chorused the children excitedly.

'Then, what must you do daily to be happy?' said Robert.

The children became silent and began to think.

'We must obey our parents,' shouted Oke quickly, trying to be the first to answer.

'Yes, that's true but it goes beyond that,' replied Robert.

'Perform well at school,' Ovo chipped in quickly and excitedly, thinking he had got it.

'Of course, that's good and necessary, but there's something more important!' returned Robert and the three children began to think again.

'Read the Scripture and pray daily?' Oro said excitedly at once.

'That's a must but it is still beyond that,' answered their father.

They began exerting their brains much harder, as the question which appeared simple initially, was becoming a poser.

'Love our neighbours as ourselves,' tried Oro again.'

'That's amazing,' answered Robert excitedly and Oro jumped up with excitement, thinking she had got the answer.

'Yet, it isn't the answer,' their father said calmly, and the children felt they would not be able to provide the answer, after all, and they were becoming discouraged. It then occurred to Robert to provide the answer. He wanted them to come to the end of their brain power, so that they would be very serious with the lesson he wanted to impart on them.

'One vital habit you must acquire is the appreciation of God's goodness in your lives, every day,' started Robert. 'It is our duty to acknowledge His loving kindness and tender mercies that sustain each of us daily in this troubled world we live in. He is our all-sufficient God - there is nothing anyone can do without his divine support. That's why we must learn to thank Him every day and acknowledge His infinite grace upon our lives. Every individual upon the earth is at his mercy. He provides us with intelligence and wisdom to explore and exploit His unlimited resources for our sustenance. He gives us strength, great and special abilities, to do things that are unthinkable! Whatever we are at any moments of our lives, is by His Grace and He expects each and every one of us to appreciate and give Him praise for his goodness towards each of us in the universe. If we do that He is pleased and more inclined to grant us our heart desires. Not to do that, is to limit His blessings upon our lives as individuals. Giving Him praise always is the most important duty to our Creator, the owner of our souls and the entire universe,' expounded Robert.

For some time, the children remained very quiet as they were reflecting upon the message which was quite unclear in their minds.

'So God provides everything that we need every day?' said Ovo who was very inquisitive.

'Yes, of course,' replied his father warmly.

'But dad, you're the one providing our needs,' answered Oke doubtfully.

The other two older children smiled somewhat in agreement.

'Yes, I do, it is God that favours me with a job that makes it possible to provide for you all. There are some fathers who have no jobs to support their families and their families suffer. I may not be more intelligent and hard-working than such unfortunate fathers. There're also fathers that are bedridden in the hospitals, so can't provide for their families. Can you see now that we are highly favoured by God,' added Robert.

'Our teacher says that many people are sick because they do not tidy and make where they live clean,' said Oke.

Their father was now beginning to feel that the children could not understand what he was saying.

'Yes, that may be true,' he said, 'but not in all cases. There are sicknesses that just come to some persons, no matter how careful and neat they are. Let us not overstress the matter, but know this: God loves and cares for us, especially when we obey His words. That is why we must study the Bible very carefully to know how he wants us to behave in every giving situation. And absolute obedience to His word must be our watch word,' he stated emphatically.

Agnes later went about the evening meal while the children began to take their baths. Robert was left alone in the living room as it were, waiting for the news of the day on the television.

CHAPTER THREE

At the project site, workers were busy at the task of raising a gigantic office complex of nine storeys. A huge heap of granites stood in front of the building project, which some of the workmen were fetching with their wheel barrows for concrete mixing with cement. Piles of iron rods were also lying by, for the immediate laying of the foundations of the building. Some of the workmen had the task of pouring the mixed concrete on the foundation lines for the casting of the project foundations. Robert was the Site Engineer; he had been darting here and there to see that the concrete mixing and its pouring on the foundations were done to specifications. He had earlier studied the architectural design of the building project and had observed some structural defects. The architect of the project design was quite mindful of his distinct profession by telling Robert that the design could not be faulted by a non-professional.

'Engineer, listen, just do your work as specified in the design. You're not to question it. Before the project was given to your firm, experts in the Ministry of Urban Development had looked at it carefully and approved it. Who're you then to question it? If you don't understand the structural design let us know, we'll guide you. I'm not here for argument,' said the architect.

'Just take a careful look at this point of the structure. Don't you see that this spot,' Robert pointed at a point in the design, 'and the other angle are not exact,' pointing at both ends of a spot in the project design.

And the architect took a closer look at the disputed area and observed too that both ends were not exact, and he nodded his head in acknowledgement.

'I think you're right there,' conceded the architect with some remorse.

They both began to adjust the measurement to correct the defect. Since then, the architect had come to see Robert as a thoroughly trained engineer with an uncommon diligence.

Robert was a painstaking professional who believed that a task worthy of effort, was worthy of all attention, so he did not play with his job. Because of this, he did his engineering supervision with all devotion, without betraying any sign of fatigue. Every worker in the company knew him for his high sense of duty and thoroughness. He worked very hard with his workers as if there would be no other day. But only few of his workmen liked him for his devotion to work, as they believed that they would be much better workers under his strict supervision, and were rather encouraged by his indefatigability.

As the work was going on, Robert would examine the operation of each activity to ascertain whether it fitted squarely with the project design of the entire structure. Sometimes, he tried to picture in his mind how the construction would eventually be in its final completion. In such instances of musing on the project work, he might see the need for some cosmetic adjustments to the original design that would dramatically enhance the aesthetic appeal of the project, beyond the architect's imagination. One's perception of a thing determines one's attitude towards it. Robert believed that the Site Engineer was personally responsible for the final physiognomy of his construction, so he must accept the flaks or the accolades that attend the outcome of his building project. With this in mind, he believed that the Site Engineer must give extra attention to every structural design with the hindsight of his previous experiences to add more value to the construction. Robert also believed that the architect needed the inputs of the Site Engineer in his project design for an excellent work, as he thought the Site Engineer being the one on the field, knew the challenges involved in all the stages of construction. In his opinion, the Site Engineer was the one to observe the topography of the land on which the building would stand, in the absence of proper assessment. He would also deal with the client's interest vis-à-vis his financial limitation, besides labour and other social issues involved. So when Robert was assessing a building plan, he kept all these variables in perspective: he was never in a hurry to jump to site and begin construction. He took his time to think carefully about the execution. That was why those clients who were too excited to see their building projects commence became impatient with him and accused him of being too slow. But such an accusation never bothered Robert, as he knew that at the end of such a project, the client would appreciate him better and be happier for having him to handle the project, which was always the case.

One person who had truly appreciated Robert as a skilful and diligent Site Engineer was Lea. Lea was a structural engineer from Australia. He was recruited as an expatriate engineer in Ansco Company. He did not find it easy initially working with Robert in the company, for he had had reasons to disagree with Robert over some technical details several times on the job. Later on, Robert would always be proved right. After sometime Lea found out that Robert was a very organized and thorough engineer who did not play with his work and his knowledge of the job was deep and extensive, especially when the factor of locality was involved, and they had been working smoothly together after understanding each other. The more they worked together the more they understood each other. This had also improved their personal relationship. At times, they shared their personal matters together. But they knew their limits very clearly as both of them were far from each other in matters of religion. Lea was an atheist. He did not believe in celestial authority to whom humans must submit and worship. He accepted life the way he saw it and handled every situation of life the way he could, without recourse to any spiritual authority. For him, the belief that there was an omnipotent supreme being who created and controlled the universe was a silly idea, conceptualized by some clever people, to deceive others to follow a pattern of blind reasoning, so that their 'captives' could be under their permanent control.

There was a day both of them had a good chance on the matter. That was when Robert had not really known Lea; it was the first time they had the opportunity of taking their lunch together, in a hotel where they lodged, while on a field work. That day they went back to the hotel for lunch after a very tiring and exhaustive task. When they were on a field assignment like this, they usually worked the entire day, only to return to their hotel late in the evening, as they needed to complete the work as quickly as possible and return to their base. So the only time they had a break was at lunch time. At night they would study the project design for some time, and plan the next day's task, before retiring. They began by taking some drink while they were waiting for their meal that afternoon.

'Lea, we've a special revival at my church next Sunday, I'd like you to be there with me,' started Robert.

Lea raised his eyes at him and lowered them again without saying a word.

'Many people are expected to be there. Our guest preacher is a very well-known servant of the Lord. His sermon touches people easily. You can never leave his presence without being blessed. He has the grace of impacting the Word on his audience. Just be there and experience Jesus, the Saviour,' persuaded Robert. Robert was naturally a man of few words, but he was always very passionate about the word of God.

'The waitress is delaying in bringing our meals. I'm so hungry,' returned Lea.

'Well, we have to be patient a little, you know, they don't get the meals ready before request. But what do you think of the revival next Sunday?' continued Robert.

'I'm very hungry,' just thinking of food, right now,' answered Lea reluctantly after a sip of his drink which he had almost emptied.

'Maybe we talk about it later,' returned Robert.

'Better,' said Lea uninterestedly.

Not long, their meals were brought readily, wafting good aroma. Lea did not spare any further time while Robert blessed his fried rice and chicken with prayer, appreciating God for the provision as usual, before beginning his. They ate without talking to each other until they finished eating. Robert looked towards Lea and saw that he was relaxed after the meal. He reminded him of the Revival again. Lea wiped his mouth with a napkin and began to watch the movie on the cable television in the restaurant.

'Going with me next Sunday?' asked Robert with a patronizing smile.

Lea knew that Robert was not a talker and was just wondering why he was in this talkative mood on an issue he considered trivial and personal. He began to think whether Robert was one of those religious bigots who were bent on forcing others to accept their faith.

'I thought we would be going back to site after some rest,' answered Lea without losing his attention on the television.

'Have we rested?' said Robert.

'Not really,' answered Lea.

'Hope I'm not troubling you by inviting you to my church revival?'

'Not exactly, but I think religion should be personal,' smiled Lea, trying to show that he was not offended by Robert's persuasion.

'Yes, you're right. But does that stop me from telling my friend about something I consider very good for him, just as we do talk about other things personal, sometimes?' answered Robert. 'I know you've been stonewalling on this matter. Jesus Christ is good news to everybody on this planet earth. Lea, you need His salvation,' urged Robert, looking at Lea for a positive response.

Lea looked at Robert for a while and shook his head.

'Robert, I don't believe things like that and don't waste your precious time – I'm not so impressionable,' he replied.

'Then, what do you believe?'

'Nothing,' answered Lea, shrugging his shoulders.

'I don't believe you. Every responsible person must be guided by a set of principles which he believes in. If not, such a person is open to all manner of obnoxious behaviours and can easily be tossed about by any wind of influence, so cannot be trusted. Hope you're not such a person,' asserted Robert.

Lea had respect for Robert for his usual percipient comments on their job and this statement made him to be direct.

'Have you heard about Charles Darwin and Jean Sarte Paul? I believe in their philosophies.'

He used the opportunity to ventilate on the philosophy which he learnt in school, thinking he could influence Robert with it.

'I don't know whether you audited some courses in the social sciences and philosophy. In my university, it was compulsory for all engineering students to register one elective course, either from the Arts or Social Sciences in first and second years. I took in Sociology and Philosophy. We were made to understand that, as engineers, we were not only going to handle equipment in our career, we were also going to deal with humans, and live among people and that requires understanding the society and human behaviour, so that we can also fit and mix well in our work environment and in the society generally. And today I'm quite happy I took courses in the two areas which have actually deepened my understanding of life and society. Two theories really influence me in these two courses; "Evolutionism" and "Existentialism". And what I see of this world, these two ideas are real. But religion is different. Religion is in the realm of imagination, an abstract thing, you know. "Nobody can be exact about such transcendental matters", in the word of Prof. Bike, my Sociology lecturer, and that's why you have all manner of religious beliefs today. We still have not been able to understand very well this physical earth we all live in, why should we bother ourselves about things that are beyond us? Is it not funny to you?' affirmed Lea.

'I understand your premise very well. I was privileged also to have studied the two concepts. Evolutionism is the most profane, misleading and satanic theory ever propounded in the world. Such dangerous idea which believes that modern humans evolved in their genetic composition from *homo sapiens* believed to have appeared in Eastern part of Africa in pre-history and subsequently spread into North Africa, then Middle East and ultimately to the rest of the world is a calculated deception from the pit of hell. This dangerous idea till this moment we speak remains speculative. It's not a proven theory. Yet the idea continues to penetrate the hearts of many, so don't be a victim of such primitive speculation,' cautioned Robert.

'It is not a primitive speculation. I've seen raw pictures of the fossils showing the various stages of human development from prehistory to the time we are now. Besides, the homo sapiens found then, had the clear rough figure of human and they are no longer in existence, which is a clear proof that the metamorphosis is true,' argued Lea.

'But there are several other mammals that have also become extinct. If not for the efforts of conservationists, there would have been several other animals we might equally be seeing only in pictures today, so extinction is not peculiar to *homo sapiens* alone. The biblical account of the creation is very authentic. How did the so-called ape-humans cross the ocean to America without a ship then?' asked Robert. 'Darwin's Evolution is a mere flight of fancy. You're too intelligent to be taken in by such a silly idea,' Robert concluded, laughing.

'Well, it is more worth believing than one that has no basis of proof in the first instance,' retorted Lea calmly.

'On the contrary, Christianity has clear evidence that it is true,' asserted Robert.

'What is the proof?' retorted Lea.

'First, the natural occurrences like the day, the night, the different seasons, the stars, the moon and the sun, are all occurring in fixed order of time. These are things beyond human understanding, and they show clearly that a supernatural being is in charge of our existence. Have you ever imagined where all the waters in the seas and oceans flow into? Does that not convince you that there is a supernatural being that can do the impossible, beyond the imagination of human? That is the Almighty God we Christians talk about. Do you ever spare a thought on human life? You see someone grows from childhood to adulthood, carrying out all manner of actions. One day, the person ceases to live and eventually turn to earth. Have you ever imagined where that force which used to activate the dead person goes? Of course, he goes to his maker, the Almighty God, the owner of all our souls,' averred Robert. 'You can't ignore all these realities, Lea. I thought you said you were a realist. All these evidences make God real! Believe in the Almighty God through Jesus Christ our Lord,' continued Robert,

'There, you go again,' laughed Lea. 'Almighty God, then Jesus Christ, a go-between, heh? You may also want to talk about the Holy Spirit, which I have also heard of, in your faith. You have to go through this complex maze in your worship? Quite a great deal of devotion, I must say,' Lea shook his head.

'You get it all wrong, Lea. I know what you mean – the trinity – there's nothing complex about it. Just one God, the Creator of the whole universe. 'Cause of his infinite power, he has three manifest forms. God-the-father, God-the-son, and God-the-Holy Spirit, in exercising His powers and authorities in the universe, and each of these three powers has specific authorities. God-the-father is the supreme power, followed by God-the-son- the Lord Himself whom the supreme God-the-father had given all powers and authorities over the whole universe - the Saviour and Redeemer of humankind, God-the-holy-spirit is God's Spirit that administers His power and will to us, His faithful. The three are one, one God,' asserted Robert.

'Does that sound intelligent to you?' retorted Lea.

'That's the problem with humans,' said Robert. 'Things of God are mysterious; you can never understand them until they are revealed to you spiritually.'

'Why then do we strive to be Christians when we know that we cannot be without being initiated by these powers?' returned Lea sarcastically.

'Yes, it is not by human effort, but if you can just believe in Jesus Christ as the redeemer and saviour of humanity and accept Him as your Lord and personal saviour, He opens your mind's eyes to know the truth,' asserted Robert.

'Why should I look up to him? Those of you who are his followers should do so, not I!.'

'Whether you accept Him or not, He remains the lord over heaven and earth. Humans were once disobedient to God – Adam and Eve – under the influence of Satan, who was guilty also of disobedience and rebellion against God when he was one of God's arch-angels and had already been condemned. This sin of disobedience we all inherited from our first forebears. But Jesus Christ, the son of God has redeemed us humans back to God as His children, by dying for all our sins. Once you believe this and surrender your life to Him as your lord and saviour, you shall come under the redeeming grace of Jesus and you shall be free from Satan's evil influence, and you shall live a life of abundant grace as promised by the saviour himself. He shall give you the powers to put Satan and his influence underfoot. But if you refuse, you are giving Satan dominion over your life, because he has spiritual powers which manipulate you to do wrong and rob you of your blessings and will eventually lead you to destruction, to which he has been condemned.'

'I know if I allow you, you will spend the whole day talking about your faith. I don't espouse such belief and don't need further push, please. I think we should be back to site,' said Lea as he rose from his seat with some air of finality.

'I won't bother you further. But one thing is sure, whether you accept the lord Jesus or not, a day is coming when everyone including you will give account of his life here on earth to Him. Lea, don't allow that day to come before you believe, which conforms with your existential idea that one must be responsible for one's own actions. Then, it'll be too late.'

'I've heard you,' laughed Lea as they were leaving. Since then, Robert did not visit the issue of religion with Lea again.

CHAPTER FOUR

'Today, I bring you good news of salvation. You may be lying on your sick beds with pains of sicknesses in your bodies, eagerly waiting for doctor's treatments. Some of you might have been told that you have terminal diseases beyond cure. You might have given up hope – Just waiting for the end with a confused mind, reflecting on things not yet accomplished and you wish that you could still live much longer to fulfil one or two aspirations. In some cases, there are nobody to look after your children after you are gone – so many worries on your minds. There are also some of you here who have nobody to care for you. The cost of your medical treatment is above what you can afford, and your relatives and friends have abandoned you, so there is nobody to care for you. Your fate is already known to you. You feel lonesome and abandoned and your mind is filled with bitterness, frustration and disappointment. On the other hand, there are some of you here who have good attention from relatives and friends but you are tired of being in the hospital - you are homesick, you see the hospital not a place to be. But I bring you all good news from our lord and saviour, Jesus Christ, the one who has solution to every problem of life and can do all things. He has great hope for the hopeless. We are from Glorious Baptist Church at Market Road. We are here to bring you salvation news,' announced Robert who led the charity committee of his church to a public hospital in the town.'

This was at the male ward. Robert and his charity committee members had come to distribute some provisions – milk, tea, sugar and toiletries - to the sick there. The nurses and the doctors of the hospital knew them because they had been coming to the hospital regularly to render charity services. The hospital management had arranged with them it would be convenient to carry out their supports in each of the wards at weekends. Before the handing out of the items, Robert would preach to them. First, he would take them through praise-worship to prepare them spiritually. Many patients in the hospital eagerly looked forward to this kind of ministrations as it was a great succour and morale booster to their low spirits. Some had testified that they received their healings through such spiritual ministrations. So once Robert and his group appeared in the wards, many of the patients would brighten up and get ready to hear him speak. Those who had their Bibles would immediately get their Bibles ready for the Word. The exhortation from the Scripture always lifted their spirits and they would be filled with joy and hope, believing that they would survive their sicknesses, as they had been made to believe, by putting all their faith in the good lord. In this way, the exhortation had become great nourishment for their souls. And to make their joy full, a package of provisions and toiletries would be handed out to every patient in the ward at the end. They were so excited in receiving these gifts that they forgot their pains and sicknesses momentarily, as they prayerfully bowed their heads as a token of their appreciation and reverence to the good Lord and His messengers. Seeing the profundity of their appreciation and excitement, Robert and his committee members would wish that they could do more each time they came.

Today, Robert was taking his sermon from Matthew 28: 20b: *I'm with you always.*

'My brothers and sisters listen to the great saviour, Jesus Christ, who has the power of all things both in heaven and on earth,' started Robert. 'He is assuring you that he is with you always, the Almighty Healer is with you presently. He is the Comfort to all those in discomfort. He is here to heal you. All you need to do to receive his perfect healing is to believe that he can heal you now. Do you believe?' said Robert with an assuring smile.

Many of the patients nodded their heads in the affirmative.

'Today, the salvation of the good Lord has come to you. Believe it! Don't doubt and you shall receive your healing.'

Robert narrated the story of how the Saviour healed the ten lepers in the Bible and later crowned his story with how He raised Lazarus from death as recorded in John 11 in the Bible.

'If He did it then, He can still do it now, 'cos he is the eternal saviour, He changes not, just believe!' he urged, 'and you shall receive your miraculous healing. Just believe!' he shouted with all the strength in him. Thereafter, Robert led the patients in his regular song at the hospital.

> Everywhere He went He was doing good.
> Almighty healer, he healed thy leapers
> When thy cripples saw Him they started walking.
> Everywhere He went, My lord was doing good, was doing good

His committee members and all the patients in the ward repeated the song with him several times for about ten minutes. They clapped their hands as they sang. After this, prayer began. The singing and the preaching were to prepare the patients for the prayer session, which was believed would do the healing.

'Pray, pray for forgiveness of your sins. It can stand against your prayers,' Robert exhorted the patients as they began to pray. 'Anyone who says he is not a sinner is a liar. Pray, pray for forgiveness.'

And every patient began to pray with fervent spirit.

'Pray for God's mercy upon your lives, pray!' said Robert and they intensified their prayers. 'Pray for his healing power to come upon you and heal you now. Pray, pray...'

And they prayed with much fighting spirit, believing that the moment had come for their healings. Some began to bind the powers of the devil that might be responsible for their ailments.

'Pray now! Don't allow this moment of healing to pass you by. Pray with strong spirit, pray with all your strength and power. It is a passionate prayer of groaning spirit and faith that receives instant answer. Pray, pray brethren, pray like Hannah in the Bible!'

And the fervency of their prayers was felt in the entire ward.

'Jesus, Jesus, Saviour, save me!' One of the patients cried out. 'Son of David, have mercy on me. Have mercy and heal me! I pray thee O lord,' and he began to cry. 'Have mercy, have mercy, O lord. I can't help myself,' he cried louder and he broke down in tears.

When the prayer session was over with the final amen, the man was still praying with so much effusion and crying, seemed not even aware that the prayer session had ended. He was completely absorbed in his own spiritual rescue and was lost in his supplication. At a point, he broke into complete hysteria, and began to wail in his frantic supplication, calling for God's help. He became the attention of everyone in the male ward. Robert took particular note of him and observed that the man had a deep spiritual distress, deeper than his physical health challenge and needed a special and closer attention.

After they had distributed the provisions and toiletries they brought, Robert went to the man after the man had finished praying. When the man saw that Robert with his group came to him his eyes lit with great interest.

'Man of God, thank you very much for your word. Your preaching and your prayer have given me hope. I believe God can do what man cannot do. May God Almighty bless you for your good work,' said the man prayerfully.

'Thank you sir for your encouraging word, you appear very worried. Is it the pain of the sickness?' asked Robert with concern.

'That was before you came in. But your word and prayer has given me hope. I believe all that you have said, man of God, 'cause the Almighty God is the only one who can deliver me from this sickness.' answered the man.

'I'm happy to hear such words from you,' said Robert. 'Miraculous healing comes from God by faith, as He has assured us in the Scripture: *That those who trust in Him shall not be put to shame,'* quoted Robert.

'I believe that, man of God, and I know that it shall be so with me,' returned the man.

'Amen,' chorused Robert and his group.

'Man of God, my case is different from the rest of the patients here. The doctor has told me that I need to go overseas for my treatment, that my sickness cannot be handled here in our country. And the money involved is so much that neither I nor my extended family can afford it.

My family and friends initially tried to see what they could do. But they could not raise much, so they have lost hope on my recovery, and I've been abandoned here waiting for the final day. But you have just said something that has given me hope. Nothing is too difficult for the saviour Jesus Christ to do. So I look up to him for my healing, bless you man of God,' said the man with a firm voice of hope.

'What is your name?' asked Robert.

'Johnson.'

'Johnson, be assured that God will be glorified in this your condition, to prove to us here that He is God, the one who can do what no man can do: The one who solves the problem when all human efforts have failed. Have your faith in Him. Now brethren,' Robert turned to his group members, 'let us join our faith with Brother Johnson's and pray.'

They all held hands together with Johnson and Robert led a long feverish prayer for the healing of Johnson, calling on the Holy Spirit to come down and do his work. After that, he shook hands with Johnson and they left.

As they stepped out of the hospital gate, they saw a madman passing by. Immediately the mad man saw them with Bibles, he looked towards them and mumbled some words to himself. Though Robert and his evangelical band did not quite understand what he muttered to himself, they could deduce from his manner of speaking that he disliked them. At once, he walked straight to them menacingly, and they began to keep their distance. When the insane man observed their attitude, he exploded in a hilarious laughter and tried to go his own way too. Unexpectedly, he ran back to tell them something he thought was very important.

'Not every Christian is a Christian,' he pointed his hand at them, particular to Robert. 'Not every Christian is a Christian. Even, not every pastor is a pastor. Some are cunny, some are cunny and wicked pretenders. I say some are cunny and wicked-pretenders. Believe me, I swear,' he raised one of his fingers up. 'I am telling you the truth, as Jesus Christ your master would say. Some are cunny like fox and snake.

Be careful, not all those who call you brother, are your brothers and sisters. Some are snakes and foxes. They are no brothers and sisters. They have daggers in their hearts for you, you don't know!'

He burst into another hilarious laughter and ran away.

Robert and his band were a bit amused with the performance of the madman. They all laughed as the madman was running away.

'The mad man has come to preach his own gospel after we have just finished preaching the gospel of salvation,' said one of the members jokingly, as the laughter was dying down.

'Well, some of these mad people on the streets have a way of telling the secret truth in their madness,' commented another member.

The women's leader in the group felt rather disappointed with the statement, especially when it was coming from one of them.

'It appears you both don't have anything to talk about, that's why the mad man's word is interesting to you. As far as I'm concerned, the mad man was only talking from his madness, so whatever he has said is rubbish,' she sounded harsh and indicting.

Robert who saw the remark of the madman as a cast of aspersions on the church and should not have been corroborated by a church member, felt compelled to add his voice to what the women's leader had said.

'Beloved, madness is of the devil and nothing good comes from it. The Bible tells us that we should be wary of the words we speak from our mouths, as every careless statement will certainly be accounted for, on Judgement Day,' he cautioned.

And all the group's members nodded their heads in the affirmative. And they all felt very disappointed by the statement of the member who gave credence to the madman's remark and thought that the statement was outrageous. Their attitude showed it clearly. The reproved member became upset and remorseful immediately and felt so ashamed for being so profane in the midst of his fellow Christians.

On arriving home that day, Robert met his elder brother who came from their village, Okah, to see him. Ovoke frequently visited Robert in Otu, for one thing or the other. Ovoke had three wives and many children, and he was a peasant farmer who could hardly support his large family, so he relied largely on his wives for the sustenance of his large family. That was when the putting his children in school had not arisen. When his first three children had grown up, fortunate for him, two of them were girls, so he simply gave the two girls out in marriage. The third, Smart, was a boy. He gave Smart to his cousin, Onose, to stay with in the city, so that he could learn bricklaying, after his primary school. But Smart was returned to Okah village when Onose noticed that he was not serious with the trade, as his trainer had made repeated complaints about his nonchalant attitude towards the work. Sometimes, Smart also ran out of the home without telling anybody his whereabout. Onose had looked for him several times and had warned him sternly in each of such instances, never to do so again. But Smart would not heed his warning. Not long after, he would run away from home again. His guardian resorted to flogging him on his return, whenever he left home. Yet that did not change him; rather Smart was getting used to the flogging. While his guardian was still thinking of the next action to take Smart came up with a more frightful behaviour. He started keeping bad company and was becoming more unruly. He had been spotted several times among street boys who were smoking cigarettes in street corners. On sober reflection, Onose's wife called his attention one night while they were in bed. 'This boy in your care that's growing more wayward daily, may turn out to be a dreadful lion in this house one day. I don't want to die now, neither do I want you to die soon. The sooner you return Smart back to the village, the better for him and us all. It is when an adder has not grown into a full snake you kill it; when it is full-grown, it becomes too dangerous to dare. Return the boy to the village. I've to talk now so that nobody will say later: "Before the boy grows so bad like this where was the woman of the home?" Because when a child is bad, it is the mother or the woman-guardian that takes the blame. But when the child is good, the credit goes to the man, the head of the family; it is so with our people. That's why I'm speaking out now before it is too late. I'll tell anyone that blames me later that I told you to stick the tendrils before they tangled up clumsily with unwanted plants. Don't say I didn't tell you,' she cautioned.

Onose heeded his wife's advice and returned Smart to his parents at Okah village. Initially, Smart appeared sober and regretful of his wayward urban lifestyle. He became a bit withdrawn. After sometime, he developed a strong attachment to his immediate younger brother, Igho. Igho became the only one he liked to be with; he was always with Igho, playing and doing other things with him. He hardly related with any other persons in the family. Their bond grew so strong that they hardly separated from each other. Their parents were very happy for the bond between them, and they thought that Smart was only using Igho to re-launch himself into full integration in the family after he had been disgracefully brought back from the city.

But one afternoon it was noticed that Smart and Igho had not been around the home and nobody in the family was aware of their whereabouts. The family searched everywhere in the village looking for them, but they could not be found. From all indications, nobody in the village saw either of them that day. Ovoke, their father, decided to break into the one room apartment assigned to them within his wives' abode, opposite his own house in the compound, after all efforts to get clues that could lead to their whereabouts had failed that evening, as it occurred to the visibly worried Ovoke that there might be a lead there. Their room was next to his third wife's one room apartment in the six-room house. Ovoke found out to his chagrin that his two son's essential belongings were no longer in the room. It immediately dawned on him that Smart and Igho had disappeared from the village. He was transfixed where he stood, gazing at the room absent-mindedly, until the other members of the family came around.

'Are their things intact?' the mother of the two brothers asked her husband as she came close with anxiety.

Ovoke did not answer her but his look gave the answer to Omote, and she dashed forward and looked in with all her sense of anxiety. As her eyes flashed here and there, looking for their essentials, she shook her head sorrowfully and tears started streaming down from the corners of her eyes.

'To where have they gone now?' she cried out in agony.

'Only God knows,' returned her husband with a saddened voice as he returned to his own abode, leaving his wives and children in their lamentation and panic.

At once, Ovoke's family members began to cry out in alarm which attracted the whole neighbourhood and beyond into their compound. Soon, a crowd had gathered in the compound. Ovoke sat in his living room, reflecting on the sudden disappearance of his two sons. He was unhappy with his wives for attracting the people's attention over the matter because he thought that there was nothing anyone could do over the matter there, in the village. He believed his two sons must have run away to the city. His instinct told him so. Early in the morning the following day, he set off to see Onose, his cousin in Yare.

Onose was surprised to see Ovoke that morning in his place. He was about leaving home for work when Ovoke arrived.

'You're just in time; I was almost on my way to work,' he smiled as he walked towards Ovoke to receive him.

After they had exchanged greetings and pleasantries, Onose hurried back to the dining table to gulp down his last tea.

'You know in the city, time is business. We work all day yet we don't have enough to spend,' said Onose as he was about to hurry off to work.

'That's the life in the city – people are always in a hurry to do one thing or the other – it's suffocating to me. I'm quite comfortable with the peaceful life in the village. Only that we also desire modern social amenities in the village,' countered Ovoke, laughing.

'You're quite early and you looked a bit worried when you came in. What's the matter?' asked Onose after a few minutes, wanting to deal with whatever issue his cousin might have come with readily and go to his work.

'Well, it's Smart. He disappeared with his brother, Igho, yesterday from Okah and I suspect he has returned to his friends here in Yare. You know the boys of these days don't like to stay in the village.'

'You mean Smart left the village?' Onose said with great surprise. 'He didn't come here,' he added thoughtfully and he had no idea of where to look for Smart. 'Well, you'll have to wait till I return from work. I believe Smart and his brother are somewhere in Yare. We'll certainly trace them, even if it means using the police,' assured Onose.

Onose told his wife to give Ovoke drink immediately and prepare him some food while he was leaving.

Onose and Ovoke both searched for Smart and Igho for three days without any trace. On the fourth day, they came across one Smart's co-apprentice, who told them that he saw Smart at a popular joint in the centre of the town two days ago. That gave them the assurance that Smart and his brother were actually in Yare.

'We know now that both of them are in the town. It may take some time to find them on our own. I think we should involve the police; they can track them down very soon,' suggested Onose and Ovoke nodded his head in agreement. 'But you must return home immediately to tell the story to our people to allay their fear. Once they're tracked down, I will let you know,' said Onose on the fifth day and Ovoke left for Okah.

At Okah, Ovoke related the story to his people with the hope that Smart and Igho would soon return home.

'I'm quite happy that they were seen by some one in Yare. My prayer is that, God should protect and bring them back to us safely. I can't wait to see them again,' said Omote, their mother, after hearing her husband's story, when he returned from Yare.

Three months later, Onose came with the shocking news that Smart and Igho were shot dead by the police in an armed robbery. They joined an armed robbery gang in Yare. In this particular robbery, they were robbing a major shopping mall in the town. Acting on a tip-off, the police ambushed them on their way out of the premises, and four of the gang members were shot dead while three others escaped with serious bullet wounds.

The sudden death of his two sons in such shameful circumstances in Yare brought disgrace and embarrassment to Ovoke, besides the pain of losing two sons at once. This incident made Ovoke to reflect deeply on his life and painfully realized the need to give his children proper upbringing and good support for a meaningful adult life. It crossed his mind at that moment that parentage was not just about bearing children; that it was a huge responsibility.

Putting his children in school to make them acquire good training became his major concern. Unfortunately, he was a peasant farmer, whose farming was hardly enough to support his large family; he had decided to be seeking Robert's assistance towards this effort.

As soon as Robert sighted Ovoke in his sitting room watching television, on entering his three-bedroom apartment that evening, his face dropped with grave concern. He knew that Ovoke had come for another financial assistance. He usually came to him when he needed assistance, which was becoming too frequent and had become a very great burden on him. At present, Robert had no money for such support. He had just paid his children's school fees and his annual rent was due for payment which he had not been able to settle, besides other sundry needs to attend to, in his home, so the natural joy of seeing a visiting relation was not in Robert. Ovoke already knew that he was gradually becoming a pest on his brother who hardly complained of his frequent financial requests, but he thought he had no choice in the circumstance. He had made his mistake of having a large family which he could not fully support on his own; he felt it was better for Robert to help him support his family to succeed, albeit with pain, than leave them to perish in misery.

'You are here?' said Robert with a forced smile when he came in that Sunday evening. He spread out his arms to embrace him.

'How were your wives and children?' added Robert as they embraced.

'What can I say my dear brother? They were fine, and can always be fine, especially with the benevolence of some persons in the family. I'm particularly grateful to you, my brother. You have been very understanding,' said Ovoke.

Ovoke had this uncanny way of disarming Robert from refusing his appeal for assistance, with his placatory attitude of dramatized gratitude.

'I don't really know how to thank you for all your care and support, only the Almighty God can truly reward you, and I pray all the time for His bountiful blessing upon you, for my sake,' continued he.

Ovoke went further to invoke blessings upon Robert as he stretched his right hand towards heavens.

'The Almighty God that maketh things happen for the goodness of humans should take the glory, not I,' smiled Robert in a mild correction.

'Yes, my brother, we thank God Almighty for everything,' concurred Ovoke as they took their seats.

'Darling, darling,' called Robert and Agnes appeared from the kitchen. 'Can we have some drinks?' said Robert.

'Oh, my brother, our dear lovely wife has already taken care of that,' Ovoke cut in before Agnes could answer.

'Oh, that's lovely,' returned Robert satisfactorily. 'What about food?' asked Robert.

'Food is on the fire. It'll soon be ready,' Agnes answered.

'Please leave our dear wife alone; she always knows what to do,' Ovoke complimented, laughing.

'I know, but I still need to ensure that the appropriate actions are taken,' returned Robert jovially as Agnes walked back to the kitchen.

After their supper that evening, the two brothers continued their conversation into the night in the sitting room while watching television. Then, Agnes and the children had gone to bed. Ovoke was never in a hurry to talk about the motive of his visit. He always waited for the right time for that – when Agnes and the children had gone to sleep. He did not like his brother's wife to hear that he had come for assistance. He believed a wife could be a huge block against her husband's goodwill towards others, as she considered first the interest of her home and she could easily do so, by reminding her husband of the needs yet to be met in their home.

It was past ten in the night, their conversation had faltered, as there was very little left to talk about. Robert was just struggling to remain attentive; he had almost dropped off to sleep twice in their conversation. Ovoke drew closer to him at that moment, to signal something very important and personal to talk about.

'Can you reduce the volume please?' he whispered, pointing to the television, and Robert pressed a button on the remote control which was on the centre table. 'My dear brother, I actually came to see you for something very urgent and important. I know you've done so much for me and I really don't like to bother you anymore for my family responsibilities. But my dear brother, who else will I turn to?' he said with a voice filled with deep emotion and was close to tears.

Robert was deeply moved. He looked at Ovoke with great concern.

'Just imagine, Omo, my daughter is in the hospital. Emma and Kelvin, my two sons, want to enrol for their school certificate examination and the deadline is next week. Here I am, my brother, with practically nothing; I've spent all my money on Omo, my sick daughter. My brother, just look at the situation!' he demonstrated dramatically with his hands. 'How do I go about it? From where do I start? Where is the money?' lamented Ovoke. 'I'm just confused; I don't just know what to do.' His voice trailed off at that moment completely and he began to sob, 'I don't know my brother; I don't know what to do with my life,' cried he.

Robert was as confused and helpless as Ovoke. He was speechless and thoughtful where he sat, listening to his brother tearful lamentation.

'Well, I don't really know what to say. There's really nothing on me now, my bank account is empty as we speak. I'm just struggling with my family to survive till I receive my salary at the end of the month,' he narrated. He thought for a moment, 'let's see what tomorrow will offer,' he added.

And Ovoke heaved a sigh of relief on hearing that.

'I pray, my brother, tomorrow will be good,' encouraged Ovoke.

Robert nodded his head.

'Let's hope so, I'll talk to one or two of my colleagues if they can lend me some money,' trying to encourage Ovoke, as his mind turned in the direction of his two reliable friends in his work place.

Ovoke nodded his head hopefully like a helpless debtor at the mercy of his benevolent creditors, and assured himself that his brother's friends would not fail him.

Robert had a strong instinct that he would be able to get the money for his brother. And they went to bed that night with some ease of mind.

Luckily, Robert returned home from work the next day with sixty thousand naira. He gave his brother forty thousand naira to take care of the problems that had brought him from Okah, while he kept the balance for contingency in his home. Although he was quite happy that he was able to raise the money for his brother, he was just wondering how he would be able to cope in the succeeding month, with that staggering amount to be repaid. He wished Ovoke would be able to cope with his family responsibilities, without having to come to him for financial assistance from time to time, as his burden was becoming too much for him to bear. He thanked God however, for giving him an understanding wife who hardly complained about his financial pressures, which often strained their own living conditions.

CHAPTER FIVE

'Hurray! The year is ending, a time for the big annual staff party in Ansco,' every staff member seemed to be saying. This was a mega party they all looked forward to having, yearly, so the staff were all in an excited mood. In a week's time, the 'best worker of the year' would be announced to all staff, in a grand ceremony of celebrating the company every year during the yuletide. A practice the company had adopted to boost workers' morale and to promote hard work and excellence among the staff of the company. The awardee always won a fabulous prize and this year's occasion promised to be exceptionally remarkable, as the company won several capital projects from the government and some blue-chip companies, so every staff member was expecting a huge profit in the company this year, which would expectedly attract end-of-year bonus for workers. And the workers might be lucky, to have a pay increase in their emoluments in the coming year, which was usually announced at the annual staff party, after the share-holders' meeting. This made this year's binge looked more special than ever before. Staff were already speculating who the winner of the big prize might be this year.

When the party started, dancing, eating and drinking featured prominently and the party lasted for a long time. The company staff and their spouses with few other guests were all in their best clothes. The few whites among them always loved to wear local dresses at the annual event to identify with the rest of the staff. They always wanted to demonstrate at the party that they enjoyed the local life-band music and they danced with several other staff members in a highly dramatized manner – it had always been a frolicking occasion for them. The award of prizes featured last at the occasion.

'Distinguished guests, staff and their invited spouses, ladies and gentlemen, it is time to give honour to our deserving staff members of the year, staff who have displayed rare attributes in their official engagements that have contributed immensely to the efficiency of our services,' began the Area General Manager of the company, Mr. Fisher, who was also the chairman of the occasion, after several hours of merry-making. 'These awards were instituted at the headquarters of Ansco in Austria, seven years ago. It is a yearly event, so there is opportunity for every staff member to strive harder and win an award,' he added.

From grapevine, the workers heard that this year's selection proved to be very tough and challenging, because many staff members did very well in their performances more than ever before.

'The way we are going, I believe in no distance future, this our company's practice will be the standard bearer for all companies in the country and beyond,' continued the chairman of the occasion. 'I am not surprised therefore that several companies are now buying into this our noble idea of rewarding excellent performances every year. Our recently held AGM particularly noted with satisfaction, our overall performance last year and has graciously approved thirty per cent pay rise across board for our workers.'

Expectedly, a cheering applause by workers interrupted Mr. Fisher.

'Well, you deserve it,' remarked the Area General Manager with a broad smile on his face.

'Management believes that the pay increase will act as a fresh impetus for higher productivity among staff. Let me at this time, call on the chairperson of the committee for this year's awards, to finally announce their outcome, chairperson of the committee please,' he signalled.

And the Area General Manager took his seat amidst applause, as the elegant-looking Public Relations Officer of the company walked down majestically to take over the micro-phone. It was the most electrifying moment the workers had been waiting for.

'Chairman Sir, fellow colleagues, distinguished guests, ladies and gentlemen,' she began with a flush of delight and a mesmerizing smile in her face, which accentuated her ritzy appearance, making her announcement most affectionately alluring to her enthusiastic audience. 'The task of selecting our annual awardees of excellence this year was not an easy one. The awards were so keenly contested for, using our well known criteria for the selection. This indicates that our general performance has improved remarkably. I think we all deserve a resounding applause,' she said excitedly and everybody stood up and clapped happily for some time. This charged the social atmosphere more than ever before.

'Without putting you in further suspense, Mr. K. K. Oni of Procurement Department is our most punctual worker of the year.'

And there was a great applause.

'Mr. Oni can you come forward for your award,' announced the Public Relations Officer (PRO).

Mr. Oni walked down majestically in the midst of ecstatic ovation and had a handshake of honour with the Area General Manager while an elegant lady was waiting to present him a bronze plaque and a medium-size television, the latest and most fancied at this time. Mr. Oni's wife was with him to assist. As Mr. Oni lifted his bronze plaque, the audience gave a joyous shout of applause.

'Ms. Ruth Okeme of Accounts Department is the most devoted staff of the year,' declared the PRO without wasting further time. Another medium-sized television and a plaque were handed to her.

'Mr. O. K. Mark of Communication Department is the best team worker of the year,' continued the Public Relations Officer.

Mark was also given a medium-sized television and a plaque. Then came the Overall Award that had all the attention.

'The overall best worker of the year is...,' the PRO decided to delay the announcement, to say a few things about the overall best worker. 'The overall best worker of the year is one that should be emulated. Using all the criteria of assessment, he was almost scoring hundred per cent. He is truly an all-round best worker, a good manager of time and resources, full of verve and savvy, which he has brought to bear on his work. Since he has been in Ansco's employ, he has introduced some brilliant ideas which have improved our services tremendously. As a result, we are among the most efficient companies in the country. Well, time will not permit me to say all about our overall best of the year.

Suffice to say, he is a model for all workers. Ladies and gentlemen, Mr. Onoyoma Robert of Project Department, is our overall best worker of the year!' announced the PRO with ecstasy.

The ovation was almost unending as Robert, followed by his pleasant-looking wife, stepped out with pride and joy to receive the award.

'Just before the presentation please,' signalled Mr. Fisher, the Area General Manager, stood up and took the microphone, 'Ladies and gentlemen, let us all stand up and give a resounding ovation to our Overall Best, for he deserves a great honour. I had been observing Mr. Onoyoma closely on his work. I tell you, all through my thirty years on this work, I have never seen a man so dedicated to his work and profession like him.'

All the staff nodded their heads in acknowledgement. On the prompting of the Area General Manager, Robert was given a prolonged standing ovation before he was given the biggest size television and a gold-rimmed bronze plague. He and his wife, Agnes, felt so elated to be so honoured. After the handshake with the Area General Manager, which was followed by a quick photograph, Robert raised his covetous plague to his enthusiastic audience who responded with great cheers and loud ovation, as he moved back to his seat. Many of the staff also shook hands with him. Some went further to hug him while few others accompanied him and his wife to their seats with hilarity. Others, who were beyond reach, gave thumbs-up for him with cheers, as he walked back to his seat. Robert became the toast of the occasion, and he really got all the attention of the day. One sometimes wishes life should always be like this – just having goodwill and happiness always—what a lovely place it will be! But no, life cannot always be! it is in most cases, a place of extreme struggle and rivalry which often involves plotting, scheming and stratagem, in the pursuit of limited possessions. This makes the world a place of fear, uncertainty and great courage, which constantly prods one to crave for more security beyond the physical realm.

Certainly, the occasion was one of the happiest moments in Robert's life. As many staff workers smiled at him and expressed pleasant words to show that they were happy with him, he and his wife, Agnes, were full of smiles and were happy to have handshakes with open, friendly disposition with each staff member as they came. Agnes felt very proud of her husband that day.

The day also marked the beginning of Christmas and end-of-year break for the staff of the company each year. So, the occasion was also a time to wish each other a parting joyous Christmas celebration, at the end of the occasion, as they would be meeting again in January of the succeeding new-year. This, they did happily, as they dispersed at the end of the relishing occasion. For those who would be travelling out of the country, mostly the expatriate workers, it was also a time to say goodbye to as many colleagues as they could. 'See you in the new-year,' became the parting word for many, as the feverish Christmas season had already seized the air at this time.

Robert and his wife got home late that evening. The children had long been expecting them before their arrival, so they were very excited to see them emerging from their car all smiles. Ansco's van was used to bring the large-sized television to Robert's home. It was quite a surprise to the children when they saw two junior staff workers and the driver of the van bringing two big packages into their apartment. They became excitedly curious, wondering what were in them. Looking at their parents' smiling faces and the two packages, they felt that good surprise packages were coming to them. They just could not wait to see them: They all came close at once to have a look. Those carrying the two packages also began to smile as they understood the children's feeling. One of them whispered to Ovo who was very close, 'Guess what?'

But Ovo had no idea; he simply smiled.

The two packages were opened immediately they all came in. The children shouted with joy on seeing the contents and they started celebrating the luxury. A re-arrangement of the sitting room was effected at once. Under Robert's supervision the three men took the old television with its stand from its position and positioned the new large one in its place, connected it, and switched it on, to the admiration of everybody. Behold, it was so magnificent and lofty.

'Wow, this is a cinema!' exclaimed Agnes, and every one of them burst into laughter. The television looked imposing such that it had changed the entire ambience of the sitting room, making it much more splendid. All the members of the family were all lost in their excitement and admiration of this gift of splendour in their home, as they sat down to watch a popular soap opera on the television as if they were seeing something beyond their world, as the former one was an old fashioned small size television.

'Oga, we'd like to leave now,' announced one of the three junior workers, after some minutes of setting the television.

'Oh, my brothers, thank you very much,' returned Robert with a tone of apology of not being mindful of them, as soon as the new television was flipped on.

'Oh darling, we forgot to give them drinks,' reminded Agnes.

'Ma, still talking of drinks?' one of them said and the three young men laughed as they took their leave.

'There was really so much at the party,' admitted Agnes, smiling.

Everyone in the family remained glued to the television after supper that night. They eventually retired towards midnight, with the joy of the television still in their minds; they could not sleep until after sometime. Agnes was most excited that day. When she went to bed with her husband, they both talked animatedly about the party, about individuals that Agnes took particular note of, at the ceremony, as she wanted to know more about such persons, because they impressed her very much at the ceremony. While they were still talking, her husband was dozing off intermittently, though struggling to be awake to keep the conversation going, as he observed that Agnes was still very much interested in talking about the party, with no sign of sleep in her eyes. But sleep has overwhelming power of domination. When it wants to act, no one can resist it for long, so it was not long before Robert plunged into a deep sleep.

When Agnes noticed that her husband had slept off, she did not know what to do next. She wished to sleep but felt no sign of it, so she just lay vacant on the bed. Then, it occurred to her that the family did not pray that night before retiring. She immediately left the bed, picked her Bible and went back to the living room, where the family usually had their prayers. She wanted to do a prayer of thanksgiving for the honour done her husband and for the gift of the television. While she was reading Psalm 100 to prepare herself for the prayer, she dozed off. She saw her husband struggling to put out a raging fire. Her husband tried all he could to put out the raging fire but the more he tried the more the fire spread. It was so overwhelming that her husband lost all his strength in his effort to put out the fire, yet the fire was raging on in an all-consuming manner, beyond what he could cope with. All of a sudden, she found herself panting, out of sleep with so much fear. She realized that she had been dreaming. She looked around and observed that she was all alone in the living room. Fear gripped her completely and she was trembling. The dream was so frightful to her.

'My God, what kind of dream is this?' she said to herself in her anxiety. In that mood, she knelt down and began to pray against any misfortune coming towards her husband. She appealed to God to frustrate any evil against her husband and she retired to bed after the prayer. When she got to their bedroom, she examined her husband thoughtfully. She wanted to be sure that he was in a good condition of life. She looked at him so hard as if she could see his inside and his spirit world to truly ascertain whether he was in perfect peace. Robert was in a deep sleep, his innocent-looking face presented a man that always wanted to be at peace with the world, a man who wanted no harm for anyone. After Agnes had gazed at him for some time, she came to the conclusion that her husband was a man of peace and love, so no evil or trouble would come to him. With this feeling, she planted a kiss on his forehead, a kiss that signified, 'I love you, my good darling, sleep in peace.' She climbed to the other side of the bed and wrapped herself up. She closed her eyes and desired sleep by all means, as she did not want the memory of the dream to linger on in her mind. Five minutes later, she was breathing deeply, completely unaware of everything around her.

CHAPTER SIX

'Let me use this opportunity to thank everyone that attended the revival last week. There are testimonies of God's marvellous blessings in the lives of many who attended and many more will still manifest in due time. All our prayers in the revival will be answered. If you have not received yours, you shall surely testify! Beloved, it may tarry but it shall certainly come to pass, according to the word of the Lord. Just be firm in your belief and be expectant in your heart. Hallelujah, for the word of God never fails. The Lord says in the book of Isaiah that He will make a way in the wilderness and a river in the desert. Glory be to God, for He is not man that makes promises and fails. His words are yea and amen! hallelujah! Glory be to God. It is laid in my spirit that there shall be a bumper harvest of testimonies, showers of blessings to many that believe in their supplications during the revival. It was indeed a wonderful experience, and believers shall continue to experience miracles because the God we serve is a miracle worker. I am quite certain that more testimonies have manifested after the revival. The wonders of God in the revival are still being experienced. Beloved, if you have testimonies to share with us from the revival, raise your hands! Glory be to God.' declared Pastor Onokurhefe.

The pastor surveyed the congregation, and became more elated when he saw several hands up.

'Glory be to God' shouted he and the congregation applauded. 'I tell you, beloved, when we organize a revival session in the church, it is not for nothing. It is to renew, rekindle and strengthen the spirit of God in us. It is a spiritual exercise. As you exercise your body, so you exercise your spiritual relationship with the good Lord. That is why the church deems it necessary to organize such a revival from time to time. And in such a spiritual atmosphere, the presence of God is felt. God dwells richly in the gathering of His people because He savours the aroma of their worship and in His presence, there is anointing, breaking of spiritual yokes and bondages, giving out revelations, healings and miracles are experienced. Beloved, always make yourself available in such revivals. The next one can be where you will encounter your miracles. Always come, fully prepared, in fasting, to meet with the Lord.

'For those of you who raised your hands just now, we shall allow three among you to share their testimonies with the rest of us. Beloved, I am afraid those are the only ones we can take because of time limit,' explained Pastor Onokurhefe, though many indicated their interest in the congregation to share their testimonies. One of the ushers of the church called three worshippers out among those that raised their hands.

'Praise thy Lord,' began the first.

'Hallelujah!' chorused the congregation.

'My good people of God, God is wonderful and alive. On the second day of the revival, our guest preacher told us here that for God to answer our prayers we have to free our minds from all manner of grudges that we have against other people and resolve the differences we have with them. He says we must possess the spirit of the Almighty – the willing spirit of forgiveness. He said even if we were the ones that were offended and aggrieved, we should still go to settle with our offenders. So, in that prayer, I asked the Almighty God to give me the heart and courage, yes, the painful courage, to go to a colleague who lied against me and caused animosity between me and my boss, just because he wanted my position in the office and be my boss' favourite instead of me. He told my boss that I said without me he would not be able to perform his duties, that I said he was too incompetent and inept for his position. My boss was so angry on hearing the lie that he immediately transferred me from my strategic position. He went further to withhold my promotion and used every means at his disposal to make me very miserable in the office. I vowed never to have anything to do with the colleague in my life again. We were never on speaking terms since then. I was so vengeful towards him. But after the prayer that evening, the following day I went to him in the office. Before going to him, I prayed to God to equally touch his heart, so that the settlement would be possible. After greeting him that morning, I told him that I had decided to put the animosity between both of us away, as I did not intend to keep enmity with anybody in my life. I pleaded with him to also put away the animosity. He felt so happy. He told me he had also been very worried over our strained relationship, that he was indeed very sorry for whatever wrong he did me. And we became happy with each other. Just two days ago, I mean last Friday, my boss sent for me and told me that he heard everything about the settlement and had also discovered that I was wrongly accused. He thanked me for my understanding and said he regretted acting too hastily. I feel so happy now, praise thy Lord!' he shouted with joy.

'Hallelujah!' chorused the entire church.

'We bless the name of the Lord,' remarked Pastor Onokurhefe.

'Praise thy lord! Praise Master Jesus!' began the second worshipper in the testimony-sharing.

'Hallelujah,' returned the congregation with excitement.

'After the revival here on Wednesday last week, I got home some minutes to eight in the night. As at that time, my family had already taken their dinner, reserving only my meal. While I was eating an orange to break my fast, my wife was preparing to serve my food on the table. At that point, a neighbourhood "brother" who is unemployed walked in. He whispered to me that he had no food to break his fast and he was very hungry. I went to my wife in the kitchen and told her to set two plates of food on the table as we had an intimate caller who needed to join me at the table. But my wife told me regrettably that there was only one plate of food, which she reserved for me and had no other food ready. I went to the living room disappointed, not knowing what to do. At once, a strong thought came to me, a spirit of strength and determination, and said to me, "But, you can maintain your fasting till the next day." At that moment, I lost the appetite to eat that night and decided to continue my fast to the following day. When my wife had set the plate of rice on the table, I told our brother in the lord to go to the dining table, that his meal was ready. He thanked me and did so, not knowing that was the only meal in the home for breaking my fasting.

While he was eating, my wife came to the living room and was surprised that I left the food for the brother, knowing very well that, I had been on fasting throughout the day.

"What about you!" she whispered to me with great concern.

"Never mind, my dear, I have decided to keep my fasting till tomorrow," I whispered back to her. She was very worried for me, but I was so happy within me that I had made the sacrifice.

'My people, what I experienced the next day was unbelievable! I run a small shop in one of the business centres along Market Road. From morning to evening, it was selling all through, to the extent that, I had to go and get more from my neighbours' shops when I had exhausted some of my items. At the end of the day, I recorded five times what I used to sell in a day, it was wonderful.

'Praise thy lord!' interrupted a devoted member in the congregation, in her overwhelming excitement.

'Hallelujah!' returned the pastor and the testifier. 'As if that was not enough, when I got home that evening after the day's business, seven persons who refused to pay for the goods they bought from me for about three to four years now, brought those money to me. As a matter of fact, I had even written those debts off before. The revival has truly brought the full meaning of sacrificial giving to me. People of God praise thy lord!'

And a heavily charged hallelujah rent the air of the church, and was followed by a resounding applause, to the glory of God. The congregation became very excited.

'I am Johnson; my testimony is not really in connection with last week revival. But God Almighty did a miraculous and unbelievable thing in my life that also needs to be shared among God's people, to the glory of His holy name. People of God, p-r-a-i-s-e thy lord!' shouted Johnson, who came to share his testimony in a dramatized and sonorous voice.

'Hallelujah!' the church responded in the same fervent pitch.

'My good people of God, hold your faith strong. God is alive and good, especially to those who believe in Him and keep His commands.

A month ago, I was in the public hospital with a terminal disease. The doctor told me I needed to travel overseas, I mean to the advanced world, where I could get a better treatment as the facilities needed for my treatment are non-existent in the country. He told me when I was ready to travel, the hospital would give me a referral. According to the doctor, it would require eight to ten million naira, including my travelling expenses. My people, from where would I have got that kind of money? In fact, as at that time, I had exhausted all my money on the treatment – just living on my relatives and friends who had little to afford. After the doctor's report, they all lost hope in my recovery and abandoned me. I was just there in the hospital, waiting for my expiry in utter hopelessness. Oh, may God Almighty bless your church, this beautiful church! P-r-a-i-s-e thy lord!' he shouted with joy.

'H-a-l-l-e-l-u-j-a-h!' returned the entire church in a highly charged atmosphere.

'While I was just there waiting for my last breath, your people, yes, some members of this church, may the Almighty God bless them and their ministry. They came to the hospital where I was. I understood later that they go there from time to time, may God bless them for their good work. The word of their leader brought hope to me that particular day they came. He said, "Jesus is the ultimate healer who can heal all diseases." That, it only requires our trust in His healing power. He encouraged us in the male ward that day, to look up to Him, and once He saw that we were trusting in Him absolutely, we would receive our miraculous healing. My good people of God, after his message and prayer that day, a strong spirit of faith in my recovery through the Master Healer, Jesus Christ, took possession of my soul, and I was absolutely convinced that I would get my healing through Him. From that moment, my spirit was lifted and I was hopeful. As days went by, I discovered that my pain was disappearing. At a point, I noticed that I was no longer feeling any pain, as I kept reading the Bible, praying and believing in the salvation of the Lord Jesus Christ. I became excited on discovering that the salvation of Jesus Christ is real! The doctor came to the ward one day, gazing at me with surprise, as he noticed that I looked lively and appeared to be recovering. I smiled towards him with great joy, ready to share my testimony with him. "Doctor, I'm healed! I'm healed, doctor!" I shouted excitedly. He looked baffled. "I feel no pain anymore," I said to him. The doctor came closer to examine me. Most patients in the ward told the doctor that, they observed that I appeared to be getting better daily. The doctor was confused and perplexed; he decided to conduct another test on me some days later, which confirmed that, I have been healed of the terminal disease. Church, I'm healed, praise thy lord!' Johnson shouted with all his strength, with his two hands raised in worship.

'Hallelujah!' shouted the congregation as they stood up spontaneously, clapping their hands and jumping up with the shout of halleluiah repeatedly, to the glory of God.

The entire church was very happy for the testimonies that the three worshipers had just shared. Their faiths in the Almighty-Ever-living God of all, were renewed. Pastor Onokurhefe took advantage of the charged atmosphere by bursting into a familiar song at that moment:

He Is alive Amen (Repeated Twice)
Jesus Is Alive Forever, He Is alive, Amen.

The entire congregation took it over and the whole church began to render it in a refreshing mode of vigour, praising God for his goodness and mercy. While all the worshippers in the church were standing and clapping their hands in praise, some caught the flame of a more passionate worship. They fell on their knees and began to offer prayers of adoration to God. Some others fell on the floor to show their worthlessness before the Lord in their adoration of Him. There were yet, some others who took advantage of the fervent mood of worship to make passionate supplications to God over their own requests. Here, the barren, the jobless, the sick, etc., all in a fighting spirit, wrestling, so it seemed, to have their own testimonies of answered prayers. When the pastor saw the spirit of these worshippers, he burst into another song:

Do something new in my life
Something new in my life, something wonderful in my life today!

Which he repeated several times. The church became wild with supplicating pizzazz and they continued in this mood in their praise worship for about thirty minutes.

After this, the pastor thanked the three worshippers for their testimonies which he believed had strengthened the faiths of other worshippers who might be having challenges in their faiths in God Almighty. He assured every worshipper in the church that whatever prayers they had presented to God, during the adoration and supplication session would be answered, according to His purpose and will. He further said that he could feel the palpable God's presence during the supplication that followed the testimonies.

'I believe many of you felt the same too. If you know, you felt God's presence, may we see your hands up,' said the pastor, and all right hands were raised up.

'Glory be to God,' exulted the pastor. 'Now, how many of you enjoyed the joy of the lord during the adoration?' he enthused.

All right hands were raised up including his.

'Blessed be the name of the Lord. It is a confirmation that, in the presence of the lord, there is fullness of joy. Beloved, I decided to shelve my sermon today, because I wanted to demonstrate to you that sharing of testimonies is a faith-tonic to believers and a billowing aroma of appeal to God in heaven. It is also a huge embarrassment, shame and defeat to the devil. God Almighty welcomes it, so don't hesitate to share your testimonies of the presence of our awesome and heavenly God in your lives with others. Such testimonies please the Lord and reinforce the faiths of others, especially the faiths of those who are facing challenges of one trial or the other.

'Secondly, let me use this opportunity to quickly talk about the importance of offering praises to the lord always. As the word of God tells us in the book of Psalm: *Let everything that has breath praise the lord*. Praising the Lord is never gratuitous, do it as much as you can. God requires it always from us. God Almighty is the Creator and Sustainer of heaven, earth and all its resources. He is the owner of our lives and souls. We all are at His mercy and pleasure, and whatever we are, is by His grace and mercy. So when you are still counted among the living as God unveils each day, thank him, as there are many who wished to be alive that day and proposed something better for the day but they are no more. Not that you are more righteous, more important or more useful or more intelligent than such dead people. It is simply because of His grace upon your lives, that's why we must appreciate His goodness upon our lives each day. Moreover, we must recognize, lest any person should boast, that whatever we have: wealth, intelligence, talents, positions or authorities, etc., are all from Him. He gives them to whoever He pleases. We must appreciate Him in humility for the favours. More importantly, it is expected that such beneficiaries of His grace use such favours to serve humanity and to the praise of His holy name. Anything short of this, beloved, is unacceptable to the Holy of Holy. Let us read Ephesians 2:10 in the Bible, to confirm what I am saying: *For we are his workmanship created in Christ Jesus unto good works, which God hath before ordained that we should work in them.'*

For Pastor Onokurhefe, it was a matter of principle that he would always make a salvation call to end every worship service in the church, believing that there were still many social worshippers, who 'flowed' along in the faith without really belonging.

'Now, before the benediction and closing prayer, let me use this opportunity to ask: Do you really have a personal relationship with the Lord? Have you really encountered Him? Do you really believe in the gospel of our lord and saviour Jesus Christ? I have to ask these pertinent questions because Christianity is practical. When you have one-to-one relationship with the Master, you no longer need any strong sermons of a preacher before you obey God. If you know, beloved, that you are not truly born again, this is an opportunity. Tomorrow, may be too late for you, please come forward, come to the salvation of the Master and you shall be truly saved. The good Lord is here with open arms, ready to welcome you to His fold. It is a great privilege; don't allow the devil to deny you this chance. Come beloved! We are ready to pray with you, so come,' he demonstrated with his two hands. 'This is your moment of decision that will change your entire life. I bet you, your life shall never be the same again. Please come, I beseech you! We are waiting for you.'

He was anxiously looking everywhere in the congregation. Pastor Onokurhefe's entreaty pierced through every soul in the church. Every worshipper was anxiously silent, it was like the judgment day. Only that it was everyone that was judging his own life, weighing it in his heart, whether he truly belonged to the faith he professed. Many of them were now very uncomfortable with this moment of truth and decision, and the pastor's constant and prolonged urging, made it more tormenting, as many were not sure of their salvations. Among them were leading officers in the church. *How can I, a leader in the church come out? Will it not be embarrassing to me and even to the entire church?* Several of them reflected inside. Few unknown ones came out, totally overwhelmed with contrite spirit.

'Let us clap for Jesus,' said the pastor, and the entire congregation clapped their hands excitedly. But truly, many clapped for being released from the torment which the salvation call brought to them, with the mind of totally breaking away from the hold of the flesh on their own accord. One could almost hear many of them especially the affected leading church officials swearing under their breath; 'Never again!' But as soon as they stepped out of the church into the self-seeking world, full of temptations and trials, all that commitment was forgotten, until another of such occasion.

CHAPTER SEVEN

Lea had spent three years with Ansco Company in Otu. He was brought in as an expatriate worker on a two year contract with the specific purpose of supervising a bridge project, as Ansco had no expert in bridge construction in Otu. When they won the contract of building the bridge, the chief executive officer overseeing Ansco at Otu, made an urgent request to their general head office in Austria, for the immediate deployment of a good expert in bridge construction for the execution of the contract. He attached a photocopy of the approved contract. Unfortunately, the few experts in that area in the entire company were all engaged. The head office decided to recruit such an expert through a consultant firm, which placed the advertisement in two newspapers, stating the conditions and the location of the job. At the end of the interview, Lea was appointed for the job. He was excited to come to an African country, to experience a new life in a new environment, more so, when his salary with fabulous allowances was very attractive.

On getting to Otu, the capital of Langa, he was given a well-furnished bungalow, an official car with a driver and three domestic aides. Meanwhile, the company's security department always detailed a security man, day and night, to man his iron-gate residence. Lea was very pleased with these facilities attached to him personally. Though, they were all part of the conditions of his appointment, seeing and experiencing them heightened his excitement. Lea could not contain himself the first time he was enjoying these good conditions. He saw himself as one of the lords in the United Kingdom, and it was a huge boost to his morale on the job, so he embraced the bridge construction with great determination and zeal. The first day, the Area General Manager, Mr. Fisher, conducted him round the firm and called for an emergency meeting of all the unit heads in their conference room, where he introduced Lea to them and they in turn introduced themselves. When the meeting had ended, the Area General Manager took Lea to his office, where he had a private discussion with him, on how to conduct himself in the construction site and its immediate environment.

'Well, you don't have to worry any way your immediate assistant is a person you'll like to work with. He's Mr. Robert Onoyoma, I introduced him to you earlier. He's a man with a good sense of industry, very dependable too. Share your ideas with him whenever you are facing a challenge.'

The Area General Manager called Robert with the intercom at that moment.

'Robert good afternoon...where are you?...That's fine...Please can you see me immediately? It's very urgent...That's all right, thanks.' The Area General Manager turned to Lea with a smile, 'He'll be here directly.'

'Mr. Onoyoma, you're going to work closely with Mr. Lea Alan in his special assignment. That's why I consider it necessary to formally bring both of you together after the meeting. I've no doubt about your competence and high performance. But I do know that where there's no synergy between two experts working together, they can hardly achieve anything meaningful. That's why both of you must work together with understanding. Differences must arise, as you may not always have the same ideas in executing the project. But you must resolve such differences professionally, by submitting to superior argument, without bringing your egos into it. Personal ego brings brinkmanship and brinkmanship always spoils things in work place. It's all about understanding our purpose of working together and you know it, to complete the bridge project on time. We need to do that to attract more patronage from the government. Anything that'll delay the project must be put aside for the work to move on. Mr. Alan,' the Area General Manager turned particularly to Lea, 'there're several engineers — mechanical, civil, structural and surveyors, besides the technicians, artisans and labourers — you're going to be working with. Mr. Onoyoma will co-ordinate all their activities for you. Materials and equipment required shall be brought in, on your request, by our Material

Department. Mr. Onoyoma shall also take care of that for you. All you need to do is to direct him and he'll take care of the rest. Mr. Alan, we're relying on you for the know-how and thorough supervision. Please, ensure a good professional work in each aspect of the project, before progressing to the next stage. We have a track record of excellence in the country. We'll continue to protect and consolidate on our high professional reputation. So Mr. Alan,' a smiling Mr. Fisher, as he was about to round off, 'you're welcome, have a fulfilling stay with us.'

'Thanks,' returned Mr. Lea Alan with a smile.

When they began the bridge project, Lea and Robert worked together little understanding of each other. Gradually, they began to understand each other as they worked, and eventually became friends. But their friendship did not come easily. In their working together, sometimes differences in professional view were getting in the way. But as time went by, they were able to overcome them. Two persons can always unite for a purpose, no matter their differences if they are willing to work together in harmony and understanding. Lea's idea of work ethic was that the boss should direct the work, giving the fact that he had the professional expertise and he expected the rest workers to support his ideas, by carrying out his directives. Before the coming of Lea, Ansco's project workers were already used to Robert as their supervisor, though some of them often complained of his strong supervision. And the workers saw Lea as a foreigner who just came to handle the bridge project and would leave at the end of its completion, so they remained loyal to Robert who had been their boss, hitherto.

Mr. Fisher, the Area General Manager, might have understood the situation very well, when he counselled that Lea should rely on Robert for the organisation of the workers in the project execution. However, Lea was uncomfortable with this and he wanted to break through the ranks of the workers and be seen as being in charge. With this in his mind, Lea started ordering Robert around with a queer, haughty manner of deliberately trying to belittle him before his subordinates. Sometimes, he assigned Robert tasks meant for a technician. Robert carried out such orders without betraying any sign of disaffection. He remained unwavering in his loyalty to Lea. But the construction workers were not happy about this development. They saw Lea's overbearing attitude towards Robert as annoying and malicious, and Robert had all their sympathy. One day, Lea called the senior technician to mobilize the other junior workers to set rods on the mapped out lines for the construction of the bridge while Robert was away to their main office to arrange some needed materials from their warehouse to the project site.

'The new white man wants us to begin the bridge project work now,' Jonah announced to the gathering of the workers that morning.

'When has that new *oyibo* started giving us orders?' said one of them. 'I don't like the way the man is behaving, especially to Oga Robert,' chipped in another.

'He'd better learn from the other white men and stop behaving like a king here,' said another and the mood was set for a protest

'What's even wrong with that Lea? He'd better behave himself or we teach him how to respect others. Tell him, he's not to direct us,' answered one technician with great vehemence.

'You will go yourself to tell him so,' said Jonah, the senior technician, who felt worried over the remark.

'That's okay, I'm not afraid of him,' returned the worker who became more daring. 'Hay! all of you here, listen to me,' continued he with focused determination. 'We're not going anywhere. Let him come and tell us. We'll tell him that he's not our supervisor, so we won't take his order. Until Oga Robert comes to us, we won't leave here. Oga Robert is our supervisor, that white man should stop treating him with disrespect.'

Though no other person spoke after that, they all seemed to have yielded to the idea, so none of them left where they had gathered.

Lea waited impatiently for them for some time. When he could no longer bear it, he decided to walk to them at the make-shift shed in the site where they usually took shelter. Anxiety rose among the junior workers as they saw Lea coming. Lea knew their action was unusual and thought that something had gone wrong somewhere which he needed to find out. As he got closer, he became a bit nervous when he observed that the workers were all staring at him defiantly. His steps were unsteady now, betraying his unsettled mind. He tried to be composed and reinforce his confidence as he did not want to be seen as not being sure of himself by those local African junior workers whom he thought saw him as a special and impeccably polished breed, in an established comfort beyond their world. The workers became anxious when Lea came face to face with them. They did not know what would happen now. Some of them thought they were risking their jobs by their action, as Lea would not take their disobedience lightly.

'Were you not told that I sent for you?' queried Lea in a thunderous voice.

But none of them answered him.

'You don't want to talk, uh?

The workers remained silent, just looking at one another somehow in retreat.

'Nobody is talking?' continued the special project director angrily.

'Now, you follow me,' and Lea started walking back to the construction bridge, expecting them to follow him. But no one followed him. A whirl of discomfiture swept through him when he noticed that they did not follow him, and his castle air of superiority and importance fell to pieces. He painfully realized that he did not have any grip of authority on his project workers. He felt so stupid and regretful for being in this embarrassing situation. He sadly thought that he had lost his dignity and pride among the project workers.

When he got to the bridge project, he sat dejectedly in a shade of the bridge project, totally confused. He thought of reporting the matter to the Area General Manager, in order to have the workers disciplined. *After that what follows?* he thought. He was thinking of the impression such an action would create in the firm. He believed that would make him lose his respect the more among his project workers as he could not handle them himself.

'A unit head should be able to deal with his own challenges,' he said to himself. He regrettably realized then that he had not been acting properly. He was not expecting any support from Robert in the matter; rather he thought Robert would take advantage of the situation to make a fool of him, considering the fact that he had been unfair to him. Lea became more nervous over such a thought. He saw his huge world of comfort and pride crumbling before his very eyes.

'Mr. Alan, where are the workers?'

Lea turned and saw that it was Robert.

Robert observed that Lea was full of worry. He looked tense and angry.

'Why have the workers not resumed?' continued Robert when his first question was not answered, searching Lea's eyes for possible answer.

'They are there under the shed,' said Lea reluctantly. 'They refused to come over here when I directed them,' he added calmly, with a small voice of dejection and frustration which elicited Robert's sympathy, as he seemed to understand the frustration Lea was going through at that moment. Without further delay, he went to meet the workers at the shed.

Robert was very angry with them when he had learnt of what actually transpired in his absence.

'Mr. Lea Alan is our boss here. We must respect and obey him. I used to be your boss but now he is the boss, so you must give him your loyalty. He has far more experience on the job than I, so he deserves our respect and loyalty. There is no one here who has his expertise and skills that is why Ansco had to go overseas, in faraway Europe, to fetch him. He is an Australian but he had his education in Europe, so he has mixed with many more different kinds of people across the world. In all parameters, he is our superior and he deserves all our respect. Besides all these, we ought to treat foreigners in our midst as our guests so that they feel welcomed in our society. If not, what impression of us do you want Mr. Alan to take back to Europe when he is leaving? I'm his immediate sub-ordinate. Have you ever seen me disobeying him or being rude to him any day, let alone you junior workers? Do you know that if this act of insubordination is taken up, you might lose your jobs? It is against the rule of Ansco. But I want this matter settled here in the project site. Now, all of you must follow me to see the special project director. We must apologise to him, and earnestly entreat him to accept our apology before he takes the matter up.'

After Robert had upbraided the workers, they became sorry for their action, and they followed him to see Lea.

'Mr. Alan, our workers have grievously offended you and their act of insubordination is an offence that should attract a serious punishment. But here they are, with a strong sense of remorse, to beg for your forgiveness. They have earnestly beseeched me to beg for forgiveness on their behalf and to tell you that they are truly sorry for their regrettable action this morning. I therefore wish to plead on their behalf that they should be forgiven. They have promised to be of good conduct henceforth,' pleaded Robert. At that point, Robert turned to the workers who gathered behind him, 'Now, say you are sorry!' he commanded.

'We are sorry, sir,' they all said.

Lea breathed in great relief with a sudden upbeat mood. He did not know exactly what to say. He was struck dumb with unexpected joy. At that moment, he thought he saw a god in Robert. He looked at him with surprise, surprise of something beyond his understanding. 'This is truly divine,' he said to himself. He sprang up to his feet and threw his arms round Robert, pressed him to himself and patted his back with great savour. He turned to the workers smiling,

'Well, there's really nothing to forgive. I'm just happy that we all can work together again. I believe when something good or bad happens, there's always something to learn from it. I have learnt something from this incident. I believed you too have,' smiled Lea, turning to Robert, 'You're noble,' and shook Robert's hands with gratitude. 'No more time to waste. Everybody, back to work,' he smiled. And they all went to work in high spirit. This settlement turned out very well, as it brought about better understanding in their working together.

After some months the bridge project was proving tough. Lea and Robert observed that the project designs had some grey areas to be improved upon, as the work progressed. But as they put their heads together, trying to work things out, the pictorial aspect of the design began to form in a fresh perspective to their understanding. However, they continued to encounter some technical hitches at times as they moved on with the project. In such circumstance, Lea and Robert would go back to the drawing board, studied the project designs, and where they saw the need for improvement they would amend. From experience, Robert knew that there were always some areas to be amended in the designs during construction, so it required an experienced and creative engineer to actually bring the expected construction to perfection. As Lea and Robert faced the enormous task of constructing the bridge, they brainstormed from time to time, especially when they ran into a major difficulty. This had greatly improved their relationship. Sometimes, they celebrated together when they had overcome such a major challenge. They would retire to a quiet hotel to unwind and have some good time together in the evening, after such, a very hectic day at the project site. They knew their choices of drinks, Robert would have his soft drink while Lea took his favourite stout beer. At the end of such relaxation, they would part ways to their places of abode, hoping for another fulfilling and successful day after the night. At times it could also be very frustrating and distressing when they ran into a very difficult hitch and were not making any headway. And as they struggled together daily to construct the bridge their mutual relations eventually became very close.

CHAPTER EIGHT

The bridge was completed in record time despite the several challenges during its construction, especially constraints came from government, for not always providing funds when required. When Ansco Company saw that the bridge construction was satisfactory, the management appealed to Lea for one year extension of his contract, so that he could also take charge of their new dam contract which the company had just won. Hitherto, Lea had been looking forward to reuniting with his wife and two young daughters whom he left in Austria for the bridge project in Otu. Although he travelled back twice a year, and had always ensured that, during such vacations he took them to interesting places in the world and had a fun-filled vacation with them. Their last vacation was spent in Kenya and Botswana where they experienced a first-hand wildlife in a beautiful countryside, exploring natural life – a sublime and fabulous experience they fondly talked about back at home. Their two children were most fascinated, seeing different strange wild animals live. They had a stop-over in South Africa where they experienced boat-sailing for the first time. The two children kept reliving their experiences several months after. Lea had earlier taken them to Paris, as he had been made to believe by one of his former lecturers in the university that Paris was the acme of the world civilization. When Prof. Kent was in a good mood in the class, he sometimes shared with his students the places he had visited in the world, as he would like to impress on his students that going to places, was part of civilization and knowledge. In such instances, Prof. Kent would end his interesting story of his travels with, 'Go to Paris and die,' so when Lea got this fabulous contract of his, his first plan was to actualize his dream instilled in him by Prof. Kent – spending an holiday in Paris. Lea actually found Paris as beautiful as Prof. Kent described it, only that it was quite expensive for him. He spent all that he had saved on the travel.

When the offer of one-year extension of his contract was placed before him, he was caught between having to be with his family and getting more money to make them happy. He eventually chose the latter after much consideration.

He and Robert like before, worked so hard to construct the dam within the specified one year. Unfortunately, the government appeared constrained in funding the project, so Ansco Company was unable to complete the dam within that year.

'Mr. Lea Alan, I must thank you for your patience and for doing so well. Your work had been satisfactory. Unfortunately the government could not fulfil its own side, by way of funding. Now we cannot complete the work within the specified time, so you're not to blame. This is one of the major constraints we face in the developing world and I guess you won't like to stay any further,' Mr. Fisher looked at Lea to confirm his doubt. Lea shook his head in the negative. 'I understand, my special project director, after all, you have your family to look after. All the same, we thank you for your good work here. You're a very competent and skilful engineer and we'll definitely miss you, especially in the completion of the dam. If it is within our reach we'll have gladly retained you. All the same, I wish you success in your future engagements and a safe journey back to Austria. Please convey our very special and warmest greeting to your lovely family,' remarked the Area General Manager with some pain. 'I'll surely do that, I promise,' said Lea with a smile, while they both had a parting warm handshake. 'Thanks for all your assistance and kindness. They'll certainly remain green in my memory for a long time,' added Lea. This was Lea's last-day in Ansco Company. He had made all necessary arrangement to fly out of Otu the following day. That evening, Lea and Robert went to their favourite joint to spend their last time together before Lea's departure. They wanted to make the most of this last time together, enjoying themselves as they would wont, creating a more lasting impression of their togetherness at their parting.

'I don't really know how I'm going to cope after your departure,' said Robert calmly, after a sip of drink, trying not to betray his emotion, that evening in the bar.

'I'm quite convinced you'll cope very well on the job,' returned Lea.

'We've shared a lot professionally. We've worked so closely together that I feel there's nothing I can do now without you. Lea, I don't know, I don't really know...,' Robert shook his head. 'I feel like leaving Ansco and have a fresh start somewhere after you have left,' he added, looking downward and pretending to be searching for something on the floor, as his emotion was overwhelming him at that moment. Many things in the past were rushing back to his memory, especially those Lea's unexpected kind gestures.

'Please have your ₦60,000. Thanks for the bail-out,' said Robert as he was returning the money he borrowed from Lea when his brother Ovoke came from their village. He returned it after receiving his salary that month as he had earlier promised.

'Robert, I didn't lend it to you,' said Lea politely.

'What do you mean?' returned Robert in disbelief.

'Free cash! Robert, free cash! I didn't mean to take it back,' laughed Lea, shaking his head in the negative.

'Lea, this is too much to be free,' answered Robert with a confused look.

'Robert, don't worry yourself? We are friends. You came here the other day, looking visibly shaken over cash challenge as if the entire world were collapsing on you. I pitied you; I know you Africans carry the burdens of several of your extended family members on your shoulders. That's Africa's number one problem, ha-ha-ha,' laughed Lea.

'You think I don't know? I know. Even in Europe, you see your brothers eking out living, stinting themselves, for their larger family members back home. You guys can't grow that way. Africa can't grow that way! Every guy gets to be responsible for himself and his immediate family. Robert, giving is good but it shouldn't be a burden, really. That's one aspect of Africa's culture that I don't accept, you know,' continued Lea.

He noticed that Robert was not willing to say anything.

'Robert, you're my friend, my only friend here, so don't bother about that cash.'

'Lea you amaze me. It's huge! Not taking it back might make me reluctant to come to you for such assistance next time,' pleaded Robert.

'It shouldn't stop you. That's nothing to me,' smiled Lea. 'I'm a foreign expert, contract worker, not in the same pay category with you, don't you understand,' emphasized Lea.

Robert finally and reluctantly kept the money with much gratitude. It was a great relief for Robert who was left with almost nothing to support his family that month if Lea had taken his money back.

As they both sat together, enjoying themselves for the last time in the bar, Robert relived this unforgettable assistance from Lea and several others. He began to feel the pain and reality of Lea's leaving much stronger. He excused himself immediately and went straight to the bar convenience and the tears he had been struggling to suppress rushed out in a free flow at that moment. After five minutes, he returned to Lea, having wiped his eyes. But emotion is one thing that is difficult to hide. Lea noticed that Robert had been sobbing. It was hanging on his cloudy face like collections of water in several places on the ground after a heavy rainfall.

'Why are you doing this? Be a man!' Lea said to Robert in a firm voice.

'I can't help it...you've been so nice to me. I can hardly believe that you're white man, from another continent entirely. Lea you're my brother. I cannot afford to miss you, the bond is strong,' returned Robert and he began to sob.

'Robert, you think you're alone in this? We've been stuck to each other for three years and now I'm leaving. You think I don't feel it? I try not to think about it, right now, so that I can have a good evening with you. Really, l don't want to contemplate it...I mean your vacuum in my life. Please, let's not think about it now, before you make me cry too,' said Lea.

Lea's words seemed to present Robert as a weak person. At least, that was the impression Robert got from it. It made him to check his emotion and he became brighter. Lea ordered a plate of hot dog which was his favourite food at the restaurant while Robert took a roasted chicken and a soft drink. Lea was prepared to drink himself to stupor that night. He opened his fifth bottle of stout beer. Hitherto, he hardly exceeded two bottles.

'I was not expecting you to take more than two. Going on a binge?' asked Robert with surprise, as Lea opened the fifth bottle.

'I've told you repeatedly that I fancy your brand here. It's stronger than the ones you can get in Europe and today being my last time here, let me have enough of it,' answered Lea.

'You'll get out of your senses, soonest,' Robert cautioned.

'Don't worry about that, after all, my driver is here to drive me home. But I can assure you, Robert, I won't get drunk,' assured Lea.

'Are you settling down fully in Vienna with your family?'

'I don't know yet, I'll settle that with Nancy. You know she's an Irish. We met at the university and since then we'd spent all our lives together in Europe until this job. But my parents, particularly my father, want me back in Australia. I understand things are getting much better there. Your faith too is spreading rapidly there now and my parents and siblings, I understand, have caught the fever. They told me Australia is now second to the USA. That's quite feverish and I know it's good news to you,' smiled Lea.

'That's good news really and I believe you'll soon catch it too,' enthused Robert.

'That'll simply be madness,' laughed Lea.

'No Lea, don't say such a word,' cautioned Robert.

'I know. You just desire my going back to Australia and catch the bug, huh?'

'Of course, yes, I'll make a very big celebration of it,' returned Robert.

And they both began to laugh very loudly.

When they had spent a long time relaxing together in the bar, it suddenly dawned on them that it was getting late. Very few persons were in the bar then. The bar was just getting set to wind up the day's business.

'Lea, I think it's time to go,' announced Robert with the full consciousness of the fact that they had over indulged themselves that night, as it was not his practice to stay out late at night.

'Yeah, Robert, I think we've had a very good time together. I'm very happy spending my last evening with you like this in Otu. It'll make a very lasting impression on me,' Lea enthused.

'I'm happy too that we had such a very good time together before your leaving,' returned Robert.

'My most affectionate and kindest regard to Agnes. Oh Robert, I'll miss her dearly, especially her percipient comments during our conversations in my frequent visits to your family. Robert, you're blessed with such a wonderful lady. I've said so much about her to Nancy who'll be very pleased to meet her someday. She'll definitely welcome your family visit to us,' added Lea excitedly, as he was about to get into his official car.

'Please, a minute, I almost forgot,' Robert said darting towards his car. He ran back with a pack, 'Our souvenir!' announced Robert as he passed it to Lea. 'How would I have explained it to Agnes if I had forgotten? It was actually her idea to give you and Nancy something uniquely different, our local dressing.'

'Your native attire?'

'Yeah,' Robert nodded his head with a smile.

'Wow, that's fantastic! Nancy will surely like it. What a memento! I love that,' enthused Lea and embraced Robert. 'I'm so glad to know you and your family. You made my stay here a memorable and a happy one. My special thanks to Agnes. Once I get to Austria you'll definitely hear from me and Nancy. Many thanks Robert, good night.'

'Good night,' returned Robert as he walked to his car following Lea behind.

CHAPTER NINE

'Pastor, I'm very glad to see you in our home. Our Big Mama in the Lord, you're welcome,' enthused Agnes who was overjoyed to receive their church pastor and his wife in their home. It was a Saturday morning, Pastor Onokurhefe and his wife, Sarah, decided to pay an unscheduled visit to the Onoyomas.

'Please, have your seats,' curtseyed Agnes as she pointed to the sofa in the living room. 'Just give me a second please,' she pleaded and dashed to their bedroom. 'Honey, we've very special visitors! Pastor and his wife are here,' she announced as soon as she met her husband.

'Pastor and his wife? Oh, what a blessed day! Please be with them, I'll join you shortly,' said Robert and Agnes darted back to the sitting room as she had come. Robert quickly put on a presentable attire as his hand could find in the wardrobe.

'Please, my husband will soon be with you,' Agnes told her visitors who had relaxed in the living room comfortably, when she returned from her husband.

'Pastor, very pleased to see you in my home,' said Robert with a broad smile on his face as he appeared in the sitting room. He went straight to Pastor Onokurhefe and threw his arms around him. Then, he turned to Sarah their pastor's wife, to have a warm handshake.

'It's a great pleasure,' said Robert.

'Thank you sir,' curtseyed Sarah.

'Honey, I think we're really blessed to be visited by the pastor and his wife this morning,' Robert said to his wife.

'Indeed!' Agnes answered delightfully and they all burst into laughter.

Robert's children who were in the room were immediately attracted by the hilarious laughter in the living room.

'Oh, my blessed children,' smiled Pastor Onokurhefe as he stretched out his arms to receive them.

'*Miguo*,' said the children, one after the other as they came to the pastor and knelt down in greeting, as if they were at the church altar to receive a special blessing from the pastor. After each greeting, the pastor placed his right hand on each of their heads and said, 'bless you.' The children turned to his wife and repeated the same greeting.

'O dear, how do we attend to our august visitors?' Robert said to his wife after the greetings of the children. This was a way of telling Agnes to bring the best of whatever drinks that were available in their home.

'Please, let not our visit be a burden, bring whatever you have at home even if it is water, we'll gladly have it, it is the joy and love of being together which we're already enjoying that's most important, any other things are extra,' remarked Pastor Onokurhefe in a convivial spirit.

'You're absolutely right my pastor. We'll provide whatever that is available,' agreed Robert.

At that point, Agnes went into the room and came back with an imported expensive wine.

'Brother Robert, we can't have this, this morning,' protested Pastor Onokurhefe shaking his head. 'Are there no ordinary soft drinks in the home?' added he.

'Well, we'll get that for you if you prefer. But this wine will go with you,' returned Robert.

'I'll not go against your wish Brother Robert but you're making our visits too expensive for you,' said the pastor. You always offer us something special whenever we visit. I'm afraid, your over generosity is constraining us. You can see that for some time now we had not visited you,' noted Pastor Onokurhefe calmly.

'Please, do not see it in that light. It's just that your visit to us is always a great delight to this home, and we consider it a special honour upon us. Sir, we covet more of your visits, it's a blessing to us because it makes us stronger in the faith,' pursued Robert.

Agnes soon brought two canned soft drinks for Pastor Onokurhefe and his wife, and they both began to drink. The children had returned to their room, leaving their parents and their venerable guests to have an uninterrupted time, as they had been instructed by their parents to always make such allowance for adult visitors in the home except they were requested to be present.

Pastor Onokurhefe often paid visits to as many members of his church as he could, especially the active ones to encourage them. He saw it as part of his pulpit duty to maintain close relationship with his members, in order to rein them closer to God. He also believed that such close tie would bridge the yawning gap between the pulpit and the congregation beyond the atmosphere of piety in the church. Robert was one of his favourite members, with whom he wished to cultivate friendship, as a result, he and his wife had been paying frequent visits to the Onoyomas. Sometimes, they would include their two children. They often spent valued time with their hosts during their visit. But the pastor was not happy that the Onoyomas were not visiting him in return as expected. This had diminished the rate of his visits to them. Though, he still visited them but not as frequently as he wanted. There was something Pastor Onokurhefe had not understood about Robert. Although Robert seldom visited him, he had been very generous towards the pastor and his family. Robert made it a matter of obligation to always put the pastor on his monthly budget, beside his tithing and other sundry contributions to the church. He believed that members of a church should not allow the servant of the Most High to be in any material want, so that he was not distracted from his focus of nurturing his flock. Much as he liked giving to the pastor, he wanted to avoid any undue influence on him. He believed that such closeness could exact undue influence on the pastor's conduct of the church.

'Priests are God's representatives on earth and for them to really play this unique role, they must stand aloof from the activities of the world, and be fully dedicated to God's service, dwelling in prayer and on the spiritual word daily. In this way, they will surely hear from God rather than the flesh. This is what makes them different from the rest of us. That is why, we specially revere them and trust whatever they tell us.' This was part of Robert's short remark to the youth organization in one of their special sessions when he was invited to address them; it was a clear affirmation of his thought on the clergy.

'Sir, your sermon last Sunday was most inspiring,' said Agnes to Pastor Onokurhefe after a while.

'Thank you, my dear sister, it is by His grace, we're only His vessels through which He passes messages to His people,' returned the pastor, after a sip from his drink.

He had received commendations like this many times from his church members after his preaching on Sundays, which often encouraged him in the ministry. But he had realized that, not all such commendations were genuine, some of them were just complimentary - a way of showing courtesy to the pastor whenever such members came in contact with him. As a result, such accolades from members carried less appreciation from him these days. But he was certain that this one coming from Agnes was quite sincere, as he saw the Onoyomas as a family with the highest sense of responsibility; not given to such frivolities, so he particularly appreciated Agnes' remark.

'This kind of remark is necessary for the pulpit duty. I would be very glad if I hear comments on my sermon every Sunday. Not only when it is good, if it is not inspiring or falls short of expectation, please let me know, so that I can be improving on both my areas of strength and weakness. Pastors are human beings too, flesh and blood, they are not infallible. They have their own frailties. The only perfect one is our Saviour. So my dear sister, comments on my sermons even my conduct is most welcomed,' said Pastor Onokurhefe. 'Sometimes, we pastors may be wrong in our actions or conduct, it behoves on members to also advise the pastor where they observe some lapses. It's a case of "iron sharpeneth iron" if I may borrow Apostle Paul's words in the Bible, it is presumptuous of some pastors to think that everything they do or say is perfectly right. That is the ideal and it is possible by His grace, but we're still humans with limitations. That's why we pray for so much grace to carry out our sacred responsibility, for the work of salvation is a continuous striving, helping one another with encouragement, to get to the mark.'

Pastor Onokurhefe had bared his mind openly and sincerely because he believed Mr. and Mrs. Onoyoma were very well informed on the ways of the faith. He hardly spoke openly like this on issues of the pulpit. There was some silence after he had spoken.

'My sister, how about taking a leadership role in the Women's Group of the church? I'm seeing great potentials and capacity in you for the work of the good Shepherd,' said Sarah to Agnes with some encouraging smile.

Agnes laughed for a while. She never expected such invitation from Sarah as she was not prepared to take such responsibility now. She had always wanted to be seen as Brother Robert's wife with no ambition of any sorts in the church.

'What a great compliment from a great quarter!' Agnes exclaimed and laughed.

'I think you're under-estimating yourself, but the Good Lord is waiting to lift you high in the various women activities,' continued Sarah.

'My good sister, thanks for your encouragement but it can't be now,' said Agnes with a smile.

'Well, I leave it to you. But let us pray for God's will in our lives,' returned Sarah. 'I know someday the Lord will touch you,' she added.

'That'll be good,' answered Agnes jovially.

The pastor's wife had been wondering why Agnes had not been showing equal commitment like her husband in any of the various ministries in the church and had been thinking of how to draw Agnes into the Women's Group which Agnes rightly belonged. Sarah's disappointment was further heightened when she later discovered that Agnes was a university graduate with a second class upper division degree. Such highly educated female members were not many in the church and the ones that were active were being over-used. Every one of them was co-coordinating two or more activities in the church. As the wife of the pastor of the church, Sarah co-ordinated the women's activities and also oversaw the female teenagers' group of the church. She was also very active in the women literacy program. She thought Agnes could be a great relief in one of these areas in the church. The women's missionary effort was another area of great challenge. It was an area where they identified the various women's groups in the society and sought to speak with them in a talk-show on how to handle some of their domestic challenges besides evangelization. This was where their educated female professionals mattered most. Female nurses, educationalists, doctors, guidance-counsellors, nutritionists, among them were scheduled from time to time to lead such discussions. *All these were huge responsibilities that needed extra hands in the church,* thought Sarah as she spoke with Agnes. Though disappointed with Agnes response, especially her inability to appreciate the enormity of the responsibility, she did not want to press Agnes.

While the discussion between Sarah and Agnes was going on, Robert's mind went to one dream he had during the last revival of the church. He was not very sure of its meaning and he believed that the dream was a divine revelation. He therefore saw the pastor's visit offering him the opportunity of having a clear meaning of the dream.

'Sir, I want to appreciate your effort in reviving our Christian lives in the church, from time to time, and I believe that we'll always encounter the Lord in a new way each time we revive our spirits in Him,' Robert complimented.

'Absolutely,' returned Pastor Onokurhefe with great interest, expecting some good news as it were.

'I had a kind of celestial encounter in a dream in our last revival, which I'm still struggling to understand,' confided Robert.

'Can we hear it?' asked the pastor eagerly.

All of them in the sitting room became attentive, fixing their eyes on Robert as if he were the biblical Moses with a mirror face, just descending from Mount Sinai with the ten commandments, after many days of being with God.

'I saw myself lifted up in the atmosphere and was being carried away by a wind. Soon after, I found myself in a forest, I thought I was going to collide with the trees in the forest, but I did not. The force of air propelling me appeared to understand the direction – it was leading me to a definite place, a strange place, I know not. At a point, I found myself in a sloping swamp leading towards a river. I became afraid, wondering to where the whole adventure was leading. "Am I going to be dropped in the middle of the river and get drowned?" I asked myself. I was really scared. But the wind took me to a shallow place of the river, where people seemed to be fetching water, and dropped me into a place almost as deep as my height. As I rose up from the water, I saw about five extremely beautiful innocent little white children coming to me with pity from the bank of the river. When they reached where I was, they immersed me into the water with their hands, as if I were in another baptism, and as I tried to rise out of the water, I saw that they had changed into huge beautiful men with angelic appearance, having long beards. They stretched forth their hands upon my head, as I was rising out of the water and I heard them saying prayerfully, "Lord God, have mercy on him". At that point I saw myself being lifted upwards into the firmament with sounds of trumpets. I woke up at that moment, only to find out that it was a dream,' ended Robert finally.

Pastor Onokurhefe thought for some time, as the rest of them were waiting patiently for his interpretation.

'Well, I think your dream is a confirmation of heaven's endorsement of you – just being listed into the book of life I suppose, so congratulations, Brother Robert. Those "beautiful" men you talked about should be angels, my congratulations, once more,' added Pastor Onokurhefe.

'Sir, does that mean that if my husband backslides tomorrow he shall still inherit eternity by this acceptance?' asked Agnes.

Pastor Onokurhefe gazed at her for some seconds. He knew that the issue raised by Agnes was one that had generated debate in the faith, and he had always tried to avoid it. But he saw now that his interpretation had brought him some trouble he did not really anticipate. He was just thinking of how best to handle the question without really boxing himself into an unpleasant corner of unnecessary argument, which he thought must be avoided by all means, in the interpretation of the Scriptures. He prayed in his mind for the spirit of God to do the interpretation for him. There was a strain on his look which tingled with severe pangs of hard contemplation; a manifest sign of the hassle the issue had put him.

'I know you are referring to the doctrine of "Once saved is saved forever", began he. 'Well, the Scripture is not categorical on this doctrine, but a believer who is saved or accepted by Heaven will certainly be guided by the Holy Spirit to gain eternity. As humans we may slip at one point or the other but the spirit of God in us will not allow us to stay in our straying, as the spirit has made us, Christians, very uncomfortable with sin, so, a believer is very, very averse to sin – he does not enjoy it at all. As fish is uncomfortable out of water, so a believer is with sin. There is even a more controversial doctrine in the faith – Antinomianism – which says that good deeds are of relatively little consequence, since salvation comes from God's grace. The doctrine draws its strength from Ephesians 2:8-9 in the Bible; *"For by grace are ye saved through faith, and that not of ourselves, it is the gift of God, not of works lest any man should boast.* Juxtapose this with Apostle Paul saying, "Should we therefore continue in sin because grace abides? God forbids". True, the Holy Spirit which is the spirit of God in us, is there in our inner thoughts to rein the saved onto salvation. But from the saying of Apostle Paul as quoted from the Bible, it means for us to be truly saved we must yield to the promptings of the Holy Spirit and abide by the Scripture, if not, there will be no salvation,' ended the pastor.

When Pastor Onokurhefe and his wife got back home that day, they saw an envelope in the polythene bag which Robert put the wine he gave them. On opening the envelope, they found ten thousand naira to their surprise.

'You mean Brother Robert added this money to the wine?' said Sarah.

'Look at it and count it yourself,' answered her husband with surprise. 'He's fond of doing this. I've told him several times that we are okay and shouldn't be stressing himself for us, but he won't listen. I'll return the money to him, my dear.'

'Oh no, that won't be courteous, what we should do is to pray for abundance upon his life,' counselled Sarah, and they both knelt down at once, holding each other hands and began to pray to God to open heaven and pour abundance upon Robert and his family. After Pastor Onokurhefe had finished praying, his wife continued as she was so touched, and was prepared to empty her soul for the Onoyomas, at that particular moment. She was praying with passion and tears as she thought, a man like Robert deserved all the blessings heaven could offer upon someone on earth here.

CHAPTER TEN

Before Lea left Ansco Company at Otu, he was able to convince the management that the dam construction could be handled by Robert, arguing that it would be economically wasteful to request for another expert from their headquarters overseas, when they already had one who had the expertise to supervise the project successfully. He told them that the three years he had work closely with Robert, he observed that, Robert had no need for a supervisor.

'I found myself relying on him to get through some very knotty technical hitches in some cases. Administratively, he is a cracker in handling workers, I cannot see a better person. I completely relied on him in that area,' he told the Area General Manager.

The management of Ansco Company at Otu in Langa, consisted of the Area General Manager, Assistant General Manager (operations), Manager (utilities and procurements), Personnel Manager, and the Accountant. Besides the personnel manager and the accountant who were blacks and had little say in the decision making of the company, the other three were whites determined what happened in Ansco Company. So when Mr. Lea Alan who was the Assistant General Manager (operation), but was dubbed 'Director of Special Project' because of his contract status, passionately averred and canvassed this opinion to make Robert the Assistant General Manager (operations) in their last management meeting before leaving for Austria, he was only being objective and that would automatically put Robert in a very strategic position of the company – one who was in charge of the core operation with plum conditions of service. Predictably, the whites in the management were not favourably disposed to the idea, for that was what it seemed at first. No black man had been upgraded to such a strategic position in Ansco firm in Otu. Besides getting to know the company's strategic business interests, it would also prove wrong their presumption that the indigenous people had no high technical manpower, which had always made the government to rely on foreign companies to handle their infrastructural development. They feared that such development might convince the government to set up their own indigenous agency to handle their infrastructural projects.

Somehow, the management allowed Robert to supervise the dam project immediately Lea left without formal elevation. He remained in his old position without even additional income. The impression created by the management was one of interim measure. Robert was a stop-gap, handling the construction while expecting a new substantive project director from their overseas headquarters. The dam project went on smoothly under Robert for some time. One day, while Robert was in his make-shift office at the site of the dam construction which was about a hundred and twenty kilometres away from Otu, where Ansco office was, examining the dam design and the extent of work they had done so far with a critical study of the aspect of the design that was to be executed at that moment, some dispatches from the main office were brought in, among them was a letter from Lea. It was just three weeks after he had left. Robert was so excited to see his letter because he had been expecting to hear from him. He immediately ripped the letter open and gave it all his attention:

Dearest Robert,

How're you and your family? Hope you all are fine and well as usual. I arrived Vienna late the day I left. There was a little delay, in my departure in Langa. I flew to London first, as I told you earlier, since there's no direct flight from Otu to Vienna. The flight from London to Vienna appeared longer than I expected, probably because I was too anxious to see my family. All the same, the journey was smooth; I was very excited to fall into the warm embrace of Nancy and my two little daughters, Cathy and Rose, at Vienna airport – they had been expecting me all day. What struck me immediately I arrived was the change of weather. I realized at once that I was already adjusted to the warm weather in Langa.

We drove home instantly and had a good dinner which Nancy had earlier prepared- my favourite rice and chicken – my two kids were over-excited to see me back home. They never left me right *from the airport. They were either telling me several things that happened in my absence or asking me too many questions about Africa and my whole experience than I could answer. Do you blame them? Poor little children, they missed me so much.*

The next day when Nancy and I unwrapped your souvenirs, wow! they're so splendid. Nancy particularly loves the embroidery on them, truly African I must say! When we put them on for the first time, we looked like living master pieces of an extraordinary artist. How come the measurements are so accurate? I remember just before I left, your lovely Agnes requested me to give a vivid description of Nancy. I didn't know what she meant then. I thought she was just being curious. But now I understand. As for my measurement, there was no speculation about it. You both played a trick on me. We thank you both for the mementoes. We really do appreciate them.

After all the challenging and stressful work in Langa, I'm taking a career break to have some good time with my family. They need to have a full feel of me, after such a long period of being away from them. We hope to visit Sydney one month after. Nancy and I have agreed to go in our spectacular African designs to give my parents and younger siblings a surprise.

How's Ansco now? The other day Mr. Fisher phoned me to know if I had arrived Vienna safely. He told me that management had agreed to make you the supervisor of the dam project as I had earlier recommended, and I told him, that was the right thing to do. I hope they did, my congratulations. But you must be very careful of the AGM (utilities and procurements). I think that guy has some stuff of racism. Be mindful of him, I just hope he won't give you any trouble.

I don't know how to thank you and your lovely family. You fellows are very wonderful people – my very special greetings and thanks to Agnes. As I wrote, Nancy was beside me, reading every sentence of this letter. She's saying many thanks to you all, as well, while hoping that we 'll be able to come someday as a family for a visit – our warmest regard!

Sincerely

Lea.

When Robert had read Lea's letter, his suspicion of Jove, the assistant general manager (utilities and procurements), festering some evil against him was heightened. Robert was always seeing that forbidding expression on his face, whenever he went to him for tools and materials to work with, and Jove's nonchalance towards his requisitions had been a source of concern to him ever since he became the supervisor of the dam project. This had impeded the pace of work at the dam, as the materials needed were always delayed at the company's warehouse. Robert was just thinking of what to do, so that Jove would not be able to frustrate him in the execution of the dam project. The more he thought of Lea's words: 'I think that guy has some stuff of racism. Be mindful of him,' the more he felt Jove's intent to undo him, which hitherto had not been so clear. His fear of what Jove could do to frustrate him began to unnerve and overwhelm him at that moment.

After further reflection, he thought of bringing Jove's effort to make him fail to the notice of the Area General Manager. He hoped to do so at the right occasion. Fear makes one hypersensitive to one's environment. Soon, Robert's disposition in dealing with his workers albeit with strict supervision began to change. He was now over-reacting to matters of little significance, in the course of his supervision, making him to become overbearing to the workers. Unknown to him, he was gradually estranging himself from the workers who had been loyal to him over the years. Many of them became disenchanted with him and the spirit of working with their supervisor for the success of the dam project began to droop. The workers started seeing Robert as a bad-tempered boss who had become insensitive towards them and they disliked him for it.

Some days later, Robert applied for some materials. He needed the materials urgently. When Jove received Robert's requisition memo the following day, he looked at the memo for some time after reading it and flicked it back into the rack on his table. There was a flicker of anger in his eyes.

'African native instructing me?' he hissed.

After that day, Jove never looked at Robert's memo again. When the requested materials were not delivered on the fourth day of applying, Robert wrote a reminder to Jove, noting the urgency of the materials at the dam site. They had no materials to work with the next day. The dispatch rider took the reminder to the head office that early morning with an express order to ensure that the memo reached Jove immediately he arrived the head office. Their radio had been malfunctioning for some time now and the company had not been able to effect a repair on it which had made communication difficult between the dam site and their main office at this time.

Work stopped at the dam site the next day because of lack of materials. Robert had to drive to the base that early morning. Although he was given the official car Lea was using before he left, the driver attached to the car was redeployed to another unit. Surprisingly, Robert found out that there was no arrangement to convey any materials to the dam site when he arrived.

He went straight to see Jove in his office, right away. Then, Jove was in his office laughing with the store manager. But immediately he saw Robert walking in, a forbidding countenance appeared on his face at once.

'Good morning gentlemen,' greeted Robert with a smile while he shook hands with them, I am here in respect of the requisitions I applied for, five days ago. We need the materials very urgently. Are they ready now?' said Robert with all sense of urgency.

'Is that the reason why you barged into my office like that? Can't you see that I am discussing with the store manager!' retorted Jove. 'Have some manners Mr. Onoyoma. You are now a manager,' Jove added disdainfully.

'I didn't barge in. Your secretary allowed me in. Anyway, I am not here for such irrelevance, Mr. Jove. Can I have those materials and get going? Workers are waiting at the site,' Robert said.

'You consider an issue of acceptable social behaviour in the office irrelevant? That's the problem with you natives, I said it! Giving someone like you top position in a reputable international company is a great mistake which I know will be regretted in no distant time,' reacted Jove in a more angry tone.

There was uneasy calm in the office for some time. Robert flushed with angry but he tried to control himself.

'Any arrangement for the materials?' said he in a decisive manner.

'I think you'll have to come again after you have learnt some manners,' remarked Jove calmly without looking at Robert.

'You mean I should apologise to you for insulting me and my people?' retorted Robert.

'You must apologise in writing,' returned Jove angrily.

'Apologise to you Jove for insulting and embarrassing me in your office without cause?' answered Robert.

'I've said,' added Jove brashly in a definite manner.

Robert left the office at once and headed straight to see Mr. Fisher, the Area General Manager. But before he reached there, Jove had already related his own version to him through the intercom and Robert met a brick wall in the area general manger, as he related the matter to him. After Mr. Fisher had listened to Robert, he directed him to go to his secretary's office and wait.

'I shall address the issue directly,' he said.

Robert thought. Mr. Fisher was talking about addressing his requisitions at once, believing that the Area General Manager had taken the responsibility of providing the needed materials at the dam site upon himself, considering their urgency. Ten minutes later, Mr. Fisher's handed Robert a memo where he was sitting, it was a query:

MISCONDUCT IN OFFICE ETIQUETTE

The Area General Manager's attention has been drawn to your impudent conduct at the office of the AGM (utilities and procurements) this morning 2nd March. And when you were politely asked to apologize for your faux pas, you shouted abuse at the Assistant General Manager (utilities and procurements) and walked out on him. This was most unexpected of you, in your capacity as the Ag AGM (operations) of our company — a company with a reputable history of excellence.

You are hereby given forty eight hours to explain why you should not be disciplined for the above misconduct. Thank you.

Steve Fisher

Area Gen. Manager

When Robert had read the query, he froze with shock at once in his seat. He thought he was dreaming. The query paper fell out of his hands at that moment. He suddenly felt a terrible splitting headache, and was completely dazed. After about three minutes, he attempted to read the query again, as if he did not get the idea clearly in his first reading. But he could not make any meaning out of it, as he was too confused and distracted. When he had recovered a bit, he put the query in his breast pocket.

'What's happening?' he said unconsciously.

He thought for some time and wanted to see the Area General Manager but Mr. Fisher's secretary would not allow him without the permission of the overall boss.

'Well, the GM said it is needless if it has to do with the query. He says you should include whatever you have to tell him now in your response to the query,' the secretary told Robert after consulting with Mr. Fisher.

Robert was so shocked by the query that he could not even talk about it when he got home. His family were not expecting him at home that day as they knew he was working outside his base. He usually came home at weekends, so when he walked in that evening very ruffled, Agnes thought that it was fatigue and stress of work, giving his new challenging position. She felt he needed some rest and good sleep, so she did not engage him in much talk. She served his food at once after he had taken his bath.

'My love, I've prepared the bed, I think you need a good sleep, I know you must be very tired,' she said to him after Robert had eaten and he retired to bed willy nilly. Agnes observed later that Robert ate very little of the food she served him, which was very unusual of him. That gave her cause for concern. But she soon dismissed her worry, thinking that her husband might have taken some food that evening in an eatery when he could not bear to wait till he got home.

At night, she noticed that Robert was not sleeping as he kept turning on the bed from time to time. He later left the bedroom to the sitting room and sat there alone. Agnes thought at first that he had gone to the convenience, but after waiting for thirty minutes for his return she got up to see him.

'My love, what's going on? You are here all alone, when you are supposed to be sleeping. Is anything the matter?' asked Agnes as she went close and put her arm around him. She looked at Robert appealingly, her eyes were begging him to let her into what was troubling him, Robert thought for a second.

'My GM gave me a query today over what I can't really understand and I fear they're out to sack me. I can sense it in my spirit.'

'My dear, God is in control. He won't allow them,' encouraged Agnes with some concern. 'I know it is not God's will. But you know God allows us, humans, to exercise our freewill, good or bad, the consequences may come later if He doesn't overlook it, and you know He is ever merciful too,' returned Robert.

'Are you saying that He allows the evil ones to prevail over the righteous?' asked Agnes like a child who was very inquisitive.

'Not at all!' answered Robert, 'but he allows individuals to exercise their free wills. He has put in our inner minds a spirit to tell us what is good or evil, however, he will not force us to do good or his will. But most people ignore the good and do evil which is more agreeable to our natural tendency. And if the evil is directed at a righteous person it may happen. Ultimately, God is more interested in the eternal salvation of the righteous while his condemnation awaits the evil-doers. But on earth here, God wants us to imbibe the fruit of the Spirit as expressed in Galatians 5:22-23 in the Scripture; because that is the only way to survive the vile nature of the world. All the same, let us pray to God to intervene,' he said.

And they both knelt down and prayed. Agnes led the prayer.

The next day, Robert prepared his explanation to the query, debunking the allegation of his official misconduct. He also included in his explanation how Jove had been undermining his efforts in the dam project. He gave several instances, saying that he was surprised that he got a query for making all effort to see the dam project progressing.

Mr. Fisher went through Robert's explanation to the query that day and realized that the query was unnecessary in the first place, as it was evident that Robert was only striving to see the dam project going. He later invited Jove to his office to explain to him why disciplinary action should not be taken against Robert.

'With all due respect Mr. Fisher, who do you now believe, Mr. Onoyoma or myself? It is my word against his. I'm very surprised that you choose to believe his against mine. It's okay, I'm the one lying against him, you can as well tell me to apologize to him,' charged Jove.

'That is not what I mean. You are taking the matter too far. I'm only telling you that we should not discipline him on the matter, period,' asserted Mr. Fisher.

'Well, it's up to you, you are the boss here. But I'm so surprised that you believe a native more than myself. It's a great pain to me.' With those words, Jove left the office of the Area General Manager. Mr. Fisher knew that Jove was angry with him over the matter. Though he was the Area General Manager in Otu, Jove wielded a greater influence than he in Ansco Company. He was close to some of the directors, especially the current managing director in Vienna.

After that day, Robert was allowed to continue with his work, as the supervisor of the dam project and the issue of his query gradually faded away. But he tried to be very careful not to have any trouble with Jove again.

Robert got the materials he requested for, after he had answered the query and the dam project continued. Three weeks later, it was discovered that thirty out of the seventy rods recently supplied from the company's warehouse were missing, an incident that had never occurred in the company before. Robert instantly summoned the three security men on guard to explain how such a large number of rods could disappear under their close watch. But they had no explanation – they could only express shock and were speechless. Robert wanted their explanation in writing as a proof that he took necessary action when he found out that there were missing rods at the dam site. The three security men knelt down and begged Robert not to give them query yet, that they needed some time to find out what happened. He dismissed their plea, warning that if they failed to answer the queries within two days, they would be suspended and eventually dismissed from their work. The other workers in the site seemed to be in sympathy with the three security men. Although they appeared indifferent in the matter, they had their reservations over the way Robert was handling the issue. They believed that Robert ought to have carried out preliminary investigation before issuing them query, as they thought the three men could not have been held culpable altogether. Some of them who were quick at pointing out Robert's cold attitude towards the workers lately, saw this as a clear instance of his rashness in dealing with the workers.

While Robert was still doing everything to see how the matter could be handled at the site, the information got to Jove who later brought it to the attention of the Area General Manager and Mr. Fisher summoned Robert immediately to the base for explanation.

CHAPTER ELEVEN

The management of Ansco Company had an extra-ordinary meeting the following week to look into the circumstances of the disappearance of the thirty rods from the dam project site, which appeared to be a major concern to the management. They thought the matter should be handled with utmost seriousness, in order to send the right signal to every worker in the company, that the management would not entertain any incidence of negligence and theft in the firm, especially one that would cause a major setback to its operation like the current one.

The extra-ordinary management meeting began in the Area General Manager's office at ten in the morning, two days after Robert had received a summon to the meeting. Before then, there had been some underhand references to the matter among key management members at several informal meetings and the opinion canvassed at such occasions were most likely to shape the direction of decision-making at the extra-ordinary meeting.

Robert on his part thought that he had a water tight defence that could hardly be faulted, so when he walked in that morning, he was confident that the matter would go in the way of the first query.

'Now gentlemen, this meeting was called to look into the circumstances involving the disappearance of thirty rods from the dam project site under the supervision of Mr. Onoyoma, yes Mr. Onoyoma, let's hear from you on the matter,' began Mr. Fisher in a very determined voice, after some introductory remark.

'Thank you for the opportunity, Mr. Chairman. Gentlemen, we all know that the supervision of the dam project began with Mr. Lea Alan. One of the major steps we took then was to employ three ad-hoc security men, who were ex-service men to guard the site and all its materials for the period of operation there, which was understandingly approved by the management and since then they had carried out their jobs at the site satisfactorily until last week when we noticed that thirty rods out of the seventy rods our company recently supplied to the site had disappeared. I immediately demanded an explanation from the three security men. I issued them formal query to that effect. The essence of the query was for me to truly identify the real security guard responsible for guarding the site during the period when the theft occurred. But I discovered from their interrogation and in their answers to their queries that the three guards could not have been able to guard the entire site adequately both day and night every time. What they were doing was for one of them to guard in the day and the other two at night every day, and at the end of every week they would rotate positions until the three had done equal numbers of nights and days. It goes on like that and if you look at it clearly, the three guards were involved in securing the site at night for the two weeks' period those rods had stayed at the site, so there is no way of knowing which of the days or weeks those rods were taken from the site. What I was about doing, before the summon was to write my report on the incident with the mind of recommending that the cost of the stolen rods be deducted from their emoluments equally for a period of six months, after which, they should be relieved of their jobs, as I believe it was either they were not there when the rods were stolen or two of them that guarded that night of the theft which we cannot ascertain, were involved in stealing the rods. Either way, they cannot be trusted anymore; this is my submission, gentlemen, thank you.

'Now, your reactions,' Mr. Fisher urged the other members, after Robert had given his explanation.

There was some silence for a few seconds.

'With all due respect Mr. Chairman, I rather see our hearing the matter now as premature. I think Mr. Onoyoma should be allowed to write his report on the incident as he has stated in his oral presentation. Then we study it individually, so that we can come here with some preparation in looking at the issue. In that way, we will have some facts to rely on or refer to,' reacted Mr. Ojo, the accountant.

'What do you mean? Are you implying that we should stop this meeting, Mr. Ojo? A meeting Mr. Onoyoma drove one hundred and twenty kilometres to attend, abandoning the whole operation at the dam project site! The GM and the rest of us left all our various and important duties for this meeting and you are saying that we should stop it right away?' bellowed Jove.

'Must you shout to be heard?' returned Mr. Ojo,

'Why shouldn't I shout? Your statement is very provocative and insulting. You are questioning the wisdom of our respected GM in summoning this meeting. That's insulting and provocative! Mr. Chairman,' exploded Jove, looking at the Area General Manager.

'Please, please, don't read meaning into what I said. I was only expressing my opinion,' argued Mr. Ojo.

'Well, gentlemen, that's alright. We are not here to quarrel. Mr. Ojo, I quite appreciate your opinion but as Mr. Jove has said we are already here to consider the matter, it will be wasteful and senseless to cancel the meeting right now. Besides, Mr. Onoyoma has presented his oral report which is as good as a written one, so gentlemen, let's do with that,' calmed Mr. Fisher, the Area General Manager.

'Mr. Onoyoma, in your oral presentation, you alluded to the fact that the security men are not adequate for the job, how come you never drew management attention to such a serious lapse,' inquired Jove after the Area General Manager's remark.

'As you all know, the issue of security rests squarely on the shoulders of the security unit. At the point of recruiting the three ad-hoc security men, Mr. Alan and I recommended six security men, knowing full well that they would operate shift between day and night, three each for both day and night, you know. The chief security officer, Mr. Akpan endorsed our recommendation. It was at management level the figure was reduced to three,' answered Robert.

'Oh yes, we observed that the cost of six security men was too much for us to bear at that time, after all, we are here to maximize profit,' the Area General Manager chipped in. 'Be that as it may, I believe that if the three men were dutiful and credible there wouldn't have been any problem, so the issue isn't about the number actually but the calibre of persons employed. This is where blames go to you,' the Area General

Manager pointed at Robert, emphatically. 'If you were a vigilant supervisor, which you ought to, you would have observed after some good period of working with them that those three security men have some disapproving traits that cannot be tolerated, and we won't be in this mess, Mr. Onoyoma,' charged Mr. Fisher.

'Besides that chairman,' began Jove, 'why did it take a summon from the management for the dam project supervisor to inform the management of such a ruinous plundering at the dam project site? It is now one week plus since the theft incident was noticed at the site,' said Jove. 'If we had not got wind of it, it is most probable that we wouldn't have heard anything of it. It could have been covered up! I suppose. Who knows if any other unpleasant happenings have taken place at that site without our knowledge? I hope we won't wake up one day to find out that we are in a much greater mess due to this kind of negligence or incompetence. Mr. Chairman, I'm afraid to say that Mr. Onoyoma can no longer be trusted with the supervision of the dam project,' affirmed Jove.

'Mr. Chairman, I will not agree with Mr. Jove. One week or so is not enough to accuse Mr. Onoyoma of not passing such information to the management. Mr. Onoyoma is the supervisor of the dam project – the manager on the spot – he should have some discretion and initiative to take decisions that he considers necessary in his supervision. It is when he thinks he can no longer manage the situation, only then, he should have recourse to management. However, situation and progress report is expected of him to keep the management abreast of what's going on at the site from time to time, which of course, he has been doing. I listened very well to him. He said he was already preparing a report on the matter, suggesting how to recoup the loss through direct deductions from the security men's salaries, after which, they should be relieved of their jobs. Which other decisions can be better than that?' argued Mr. Okotete, the personnel manager.

'Well, that is alright, we have heard Mr. Onoyoma and all our reactions to his oral report on the matter. Mr. Onoyoma, you can take your leave and go back to site. You will certainly hear from us on this matter soon,' declared Mr. Fisher and Robert bowed his head before the rest members and left.

When those at the top conspire together and are determined to checkmate one of their members in an organization, any spurious accusation is legitimate enough to kick him out. Two weeks later, Robert was suspended from work indefinitely. A week after, Mr. Fisher detailed a memo to the managing director of Ansco Company at their headquarters in Vienna, requesting for an experienced supervisor for their operation, stating that the one they had, had left, following the expiration of his contract for three years, while there were major projects to be executed in their operations. After a month of his memo, Vienna sent them a new supervisor, Mr. Murphy and Robert was finally relieved of his job.

Though it came to him as a rude shock, Robert believed that Ansco Company had made a mistake in sacking him and he thought that they would recall him soon. This made him not to worry so much.

However, the reality of life without income began gradually to dawn on Robert, more so when he was the breadwinner of his family. In truth, Agnes was far more worried about their precarious condition. She was always thinking of how they could cope if the situation subsisted. She was so confused. She did not know now whether to blame her husband for not allowing her to work since their marriage – it was Robert's idea that Agnes should concentrate on raising the children and take care of all the domestic responsibilities which he thought were enough challenge for a woman, let alone of adding more, by way of working for additional income for the family. He also believed that, for children to have proper upbringing, their mother should fully be with them, as he believed that only a committed parent could truly bear the enduring pain of raising a child properly. And as for him as a father, his main responsibility was to provide for his family while also lending his support as much as he could in raising the children. He believed that once the children were well bred, they would be able to take care of themselves when they became adults. By so doing, their lives as parents would be fulfilled, making their old age a blessed one.

At first, Agnes strongly opposed the idea of dedicating herself to domestic responsibilities after her university. She wanted to make a successful and fulfilling career in the teaching profession, which she had always wanted to be as she believed, that was her true vocation. It took both of them three good months to settle this issue before their marriage, with the assurance from Robert that as soon as their last child started college, she would begin her professional career.

But the course of life, sometimes, does not agree with individuals' plans, herein lies the vagaries and the vicissitudes of life and those who keep their courses going in life where there is a misadventure along the way, are those who see the adversity as a temporary setback, so they see beyond their present misfortunes and that reinvigorates their will to confront their situations and brave their way out of the quagmire. But the weak hardly see beyond their misfortunes, so they lose their will and wallow in endless hopelessness.

After six months without income, the Onoyomas' situation became very precarious. By then, Robert's retirement benefits alongside some savings left in his bank account had been spent, and now, a new academic session had just begun. The children's school fees had to be paid if they were to remain in private schools. Unfortunately, the public schools which were tuition-free, were no alternative, as they were overcrowded without effective supervision and support facilities. Feeding in their home had become an uphill task for Agnes, and Robert was so harassed by his inability to provide for his family that he had become too dejected and confused to think of anything. These days, Robert and Agnes hardly talked to each other. Their lively and happy home was fast becoming a desolate place of frustration and sadness with a haunting consciousness of how to survive daily. Their regular morning worship lacked spirit. They carried it out daily because they were already accustomed to it – not with joy, hope and faith anymore.

Their children were worst hit. They watched helplessly how their condition was turning worse, day by day. It was a frightening situation for them. They quite understood that their breadwinner, their loving father, had lost his job and they also knew that his inability to meet their needs had brought so much sorrow and pain to him, as they could observe it clearly in his look. As a result, they hardly complained or asked when they needed one thing or the other in the home, even when their school uniforms were getting worn out, they did not complain.

One morning when the children had prepared to go to school, Oro began to sob, the other two children were by her, trying to comfort her, as they all seemed to share in her grief.

'Why are you crying? What is the matter?' said their mother anxiously, as she walked into the children's bedroom when she heard the cry.

Oro did not answer her mother.

Agnes looked at her intensely, trying to construe the cause of her distress.

'What is wrong with her?' frantic Agnes asked the other two children, who appeared to understand the cause of Oro's agony, but they both kept quiet. 'Am I not talking to you or are you all deaf?' she exploded.

Her outburst attracted Robert who was in the sitting room then.

'What's happening?' said Robert when he dashed in.

'Her teacher said she should not come to school today,' answered Oke, their last daughter.

'Why?' asked both father and mother almost together at once with great concern.

Oke pointed at Oro's sandals and both parents understood straightaway. Oro's teacher had told her, the previous day at school not to come to school until she replaced her worn-out school sandals, which had cut in several places and was too decrepit to wear to school. Oro's class teacher had repeatedly told her to replace the sandals from a month ago, yet she had not been able to tell her parents. But now that her teacher had threatened to refuse her entry into the class, she did not know what to do, so that morning when they were about going to school, she began to cry because she knew her father had no money to buy her a new pair of sandals neither had her mother. She knew very well like the rest two children that they even found it difficult to eat in their home. At that moment, both parents felt sharply how the living standard of their family had sunk in the home, and they almost wept.

Robert left the scene immediately to where he was sitting in the living room. He was thrown into a deep distress at once. Agnes stood there helplessly, not knowing what to do. She was completely lost in thought, tears were about dropping from her eyes at that moment but she told herself to be strong, lest she opened a flood gate of weeping in the home.

'That's alright, my daughter,' said Agnes to Oro and she immediately put her hand round Oro shoulders. 'We shall buy you new sandals very soon by His grace, but I will take you to your teacher now and explain why she should allow you stay in school till we do so.'

She wiped away the tears in Oro's face and took her to school that morning. At school the headmistress was quite sympathetic, after Agnes' explanation of their condition and she allowed Oro to continue with her worn-out sandals for that term.

When Agnes reached home, she explained to her husband how Oro was allowed to continue her school with her old sandals for the term. But Robert did not say anything and Agnes did not bother about his silence, as she was getting used to his taciturnity lately. However, within Robert, he was full of gratitude and admiration for his wife who seemed to be weathering the difficult financial storm in the family.

There was a particular evening, when they had nothing to prepare for supper and Robert did not know what to do. He was confused and felt useless. He wished very much that manna could fall from heaven, like the days of biblical Moses in the wilderness, while wondering throughout that evening what the children particularly would eat. Their last child was already crying for food when it was some minutes past seven. Robert could not bear the cry, so he went to his bedroom and flung himself on the bed like a lifeless being, allowing his worry to fully absorb him there. About an hour later, Oke, his last child came to him.

'Daddy, your food is ready,' she said.

'Food? What food?' queried Robert.

'Mummy has prepared *eba* and vegetable soup and we have all eaten. She says I should call you to have yours,' explained his little daughter.

Robert could not believe Oke but he went to see. Truly, his food was on the table. After eating, he asked his wife, 'How did you manage?' Agnes laughed, a sort of victorious laugh.

'I realised that we still had some garri and I later saw some pepper and onions. I cut some vegetables and okra from my garden I started three months ago. They've grown so well. I added the pepper and onions to the vegetables and okra. Got some smoked fish from Mrs. Ogba, my friend next door, and that's the supper we have just had,' narrated Agnes to the delight and admiration of her husband.

'Darling, you're a genius,' smiled Robert.

This and other similar hopeless situations that arose now and then in the home, which Agnes was able to handle by her sheer ability to manage things, made her the focal figure of the home, at this critical time.

Before Robert became jobless, he never knew his wife had such capability. Sometimes, he was confounded by Agnes' sheer ingenuity of surmounting such difficult situations in the home. The children began to look up to her for their daily needs as Robert began to slide to the side-line in the home. As his incapacity in the family was becoming obvious daily, Robert became more withdrawn and taciturn, making the crisis in the home more severe for his family. He knew that this attitude of his was compounding the situation in the home but he could not help it and it worried him very much.

CHAPTER TWELVE

When Robert's church members heard the news that he was sacked from his job, they were shocked. Robert was the least member expected to lose his job in the manner it happened. When he won the 'overall best worker' of the year in his workplace in the previous year, he gave an open thanks-giving in the church, by way of testifying to the goodness of the Lord in his life. Besides, he had always lived an exemplary Christian life both within and outside the church. More often than not, he was quickly and obviously pointed at as a model among members and worshippers of the church, hence the news of his termination was received with shock and embarrassment in the church. For two weeks after the unfortunate incident, his church members kept pouring into his home to sympathize and comfort him.

Pastor Onokurhefe and his wife were prompt in coming. They went to see Robert immediately the news of his removal from Ansco Company reached them. That was the next day after Robert was sacked. They were truly saddened by the unfortunate news. First, they could not believe it. But when it became clear and confirmed, they were both bemused. They found it difficult to place the incident in a context in their minds. Pastor Onokurhefe saw the tragic incident beyond Robert. He feared that the incident might weaken the faith of worshippers in the church, as Robert was seen as an epitome of true worship among members. When he and his wife visited Robert, Pastor Onokurhefe quoted the word of the Lord to him.

'My brother, be of good cheer,' he said as he looked at Robert, with affection and sympathy: *Lo, I am with you always, even unto the end of the world (Matthew 27.20b).* 'Please Brother Robert always have this good word of the Lord in your mind at this particular time. He's not abandoned you, and he'll never abandon you. This is the work of Satan to deceive you; to make you fall as a Christian and weaken your faith in our Almighty God who never fails, never sleep – He is the omnipotent, omnipresent and Omniscient God. My dear brother, it could be a test of faith for you. Please use the situation to prove to our good Lord that your faith in Him is not conditional and you will experience a greater elevation in your life to His glory. Please, don't fail the test. Damn this trial of the devil and be celebrated in heaven. And I am quite confident that you will pass this test excellently. And after the test, what will you gain?' prodded the pastor with a beaming smile.

Robert merely expressed a knowing smile and nodded his head with the indication that there were several things to gain without uttering a word. Pastor Onokurhefe wanted to be very certain of what he meant.

'One, satan will be put to shame to the glory of God. Two, by so doing, you will cause heaven to celebrate your victory over satan. Three, you shall be rewarded with greater blessings of elevation and life fulfilment. Four, your Christian faith is further strengthened by your victory, I mean, after you shall have experienced the faithfulness of our good Lord, which you will use as a testimony to encourage and strengthen upcoming Christians, especially those facing trials and temptations. This trial of the devil is for a short while and he shall fail,' concluded the pastor, and all the people with Robert in his living room concurred and chorused, 'Amen.' They all acknowledged that the cleric was truly professional even in counselling.

Robert felt relieved with the good word of Pastor Onokurhefe. His face became brightened by the good word of the pastor and he believed that the job-loss was a temporary test of God as enunciated by his pastor. He and Agnes became confident that they would overcome it. This brought a lot of hope to the entire Onoyomas, and all the gloom and despair in the family disappeared that day.

Pastor Onokurhefe was very pleased too that his word made an impact on Robert and his family, including all those that came to comfort Robert that day. After prayer, he and his wife left. As Robert and his wife saw them off to where their car was parked, the pastor whispered, 'Please focus on Job in the Bible. Let him be your inspiration in this trial. May the good Lord be with you,' he said prayerfully and Robert nodded his head.

As the pastor was driving home that day, the idea that Robert was among the few persons the church members looked up to, for inspiration, and the news of his job-loss might weaken their faith plagued in his mind. He decided immediately that his next Sunday sermon would be 'Why Bad Things Happen to Good People' to allay members' fear and remained unwavered in their faith.

That Sunday the church auditorium was full to its capacity as usual. After 'Sunday School,' praise worship, collection of tithes and offerings, the sermon began. In attendance also, were Robert and his family.

'Good morning my beloved, today, I am going to speak on one area of our Christian life that many have pondered on several times without answer, while they reflect on promises of God in the Scripture,' began the pastor. 'Yes, why do bad things happen to good people of God? In Psalm 91 which is a popular psalm in the Scripture, God promises his people absolute protection from evils and dooms. Yet, righteous people come across great misfortunes from time to time, why?' he questioned, looking at the entire congregation. 'I know we, sometimes, ask this question when we are experiencing unpleasant times in our lives. I presume that if it is possible to challenge God physically on this subject, some of us will do so several times. Today, we shall know why such bad things happen to God's people. The Scripture provides the answers to this poser. First let us look at Acts 14:22: *Confirming the souls of the disciplines, and exhorting them to continue in the faith, and that we must through much tribulation enter into the kingdom of God.* It has to be so, because the world we live in is evil, it belongs to satan, so the way of the world is of the devil. That is why the Scripture admonishes that though we are in the world we should not conform to it (Rom. 12:2). So brethren, if our ways as children of God are contrary to the way of the world, it is expected that we shall face confrontation, oppression, persecution and injustice in the world as long as we follow the way of God. But with the fruit of the Spirit as recorded in Gal. 5:22-23, we will be able to overcome the wickedness of the world. And where it is not possible, the mighty hand of God will deliver us from such trouble. God assures us that in all such afflictions he would deliver us. This is an assurance, and that's why the good Lord says he will not allow us the temptation that's beyond us. Remember His word: "I will be with you always" So brethren, whatever we are going through, our good Lord is aware. He keeps His watch over us, so we should not be afraid; he's our keeper, protector and sustainer in this evil world of satan.

'Secondly, bad things sometimes happen to God's children to grow their maturity in the faith. Beloved, what does James 1:2 tells us? It says *Count it all joy when ye fall into divers temptations.* It is very true because as we face challenges of trials and overcome them, one after the other, our faith and knowledge of the Lord becomes deepened, which eventually makes us a rock that can never be shaken by any storm of life. In this way, we come to the point where we see every other trial and temptation like a wind that blows for a while; we are no longer moved by them. At that level, we are now matured in the faith and we now use our past experiences to build and strengthen our upcoming brothers and sisters who are still struggling to grow up in the faith. This is another good reason why the righteous suffer some unpleasant circumstances of life. Beloved, wealth of experience is not cheap!

'Besides, for there to be crown there must be a cross. There cannot be victory without a battle. For the crop to reproduce itself in a bigger quantity, it must first decay in the soil. Beloved, these are natural principles of life we must understand. Go through the scripture and look at the heroes and heroines of the Bible including the Saviour Himself. They all lived a life of extreme sacrifice and pain before their crowns of glory. Check it out. Is it Abraham, the father of many nations, or Joseph who was sold into slavery? Moses? David? David at a time even desired to reject the kingship of Israel because of his travails. Check out the women _ Ruth? Hannah? Esther? Now, let us talk about great men of the world because some people will say these were people in the Scripture. How about Nelson Mandela of South Africa? Read his autobiography: *Long Walk to Freedom. Let's look at* our own dear nationalist leaders here! Have you read *My Odyssey* by Dr Nnamdi Azikiwe where he says at a time he wanted to commit suicide on the railway because of his travail? Or our sage Chief Obafemi Awolowo, an orphan, his life was a terrible long suffering before he saw the light at the end of the tunnel.   Also, check out the life of one of the great America's presidents, Abraham Lincoln.   His life was a great struggle. Beloved, those whom the Lord wants to use mightily, He makes their ways rough first for them to have the capacity, the toughness and the extraordinary courage to cope with the high demands of the great responsibilities He has earmarked for them. Do you now see the other reasons why James says in the Scripture that you should count it all joy to have diverse challenges and trials!   Know that, for gold to be that precious jewellery of high value, it must spend enduring time in the furnace. The Scripture makes us to understand that whatever happens to a righteous man is for his own good.

'In all these that I have said, one thing stands out – we must be ready to accept the perfect will of the Almighty God, our maker, in our lives, until we have come to that place which He wants us to be ultimately, in His perfect plan for us. It is by doing so, we reach our heights in His perfect will. Beloved, it requires our total yielding onto Him for use. It is my prayer that we will not fail or fall short of His glory in our lives according to His perfect will.' 'Amen!' chorused the congregation. 'May God be with you, keep you and strengthen you through His Holy Spirit against the virulence and whirlwind of the devil,' prayed the pastor, and the church chorused 'Amen!' again. This was followed by the benediction and closing prayer.

In this sermon, Pastor Onokurhefe was able to impress it on members and worshippers that Christianity was full of trials and tribulations. But the Almighty God would see believers through all of them and help them to reach their fulfilled ends. The sermon was particularly very encouraging to Robert giving his present travail. One encouraging lesson he particularly took from the sermon was that, trials were temporary and would be overcome – all it required was to hold on to one's faith in God, so the sermon gave him hope and renewed his absolute trust in God Almighty. His wife was quite happy to see him in good spirit after the church service that day. He appeared to have got his spirit back and was quite lively in the home again. This was contagious, as the children too were happy to see their father in this mood and they were readily around him, laughing and joking like before.

Regular visits of church members at this time also encouraged Robert. Some even came with food items and financial support. Robert was really amazed by their kind gestures and was very grateful to every one of them. But the human capacity to respond to the distress conditions of others is often short-lived; it hardly endures beyond the initial impulse of wanting to help, so as time went by, the visits and supports began to thin out and the number kept declining until it finally fizzled out. Also Pastor Onokurhefe's regular visits to Robert took a downward curve. After sometime, he stopped coming, too. And Robert's jobless condition was gradually forgotten in the church. Not long, Robert became constrained by his condition in his position as the head of the ministry, attending to the sick and the prisoners in the hospitals and prisons respectively. As a result, he was replaced by someone.

This made him much less visible in the church and he eventually fell into the remotest background in the church. Consequently, Robert regressed to deeper slough when his pastor and members of his church stopped visiting him; however, he was still trying as much as he could to attend Sunday church service. He could not contemplate missing Sunday service to the Lord, as it had become part of his life. Most times, he had no money for fare, he had to trek down the four kilometres to the church. He would wake up early, take his bath and put on any of his clothes that he could find and leave without his breakfast. These days, he neither asked for food nor cared whether his family had something to eat. Every time, he was told by one of his children that his food was on the dining table, he would go over to the table, have his food and return to where ever he was before. These days, he hardly showed any concerns for what was happening in the home. In fact, he never bothered about anything anymore. He had become so apathetic about everything in the family that sometimes his family forgot that he was present in the home. But Sunday service to the Lord was different and all important. It appeared that was the only thing Robert seemed to be living for. He clung to it as if his entire life depended upon it. He usually waited upon it all through the week, dreaming and expecting his early rise to be in the service every Sunday. There appeared to be something that he drew strength from in the church service, a kind of tonic that was keeping him alive in his sea of gloom and depression. So, for Robert, the Sunday service was an abiding passion that could never be compromised as long as he was alive.

Oftentimes, he was the first to be in the church, usually much earlier before the service began, patiently meditating through the word of God in the Bible in his preparation for a true worship of the day. The church officials had come to know him more for his unusual punctuality, and they thought this was another way Robert was expressing his avowed devotion to the faith. However, when they saw him now, they felt deeply sad and full of pity for him and were quite uncomfortable with his threadbare appearance and sunken eyes. They realised Robert was no longer that 'brother' full of vitality and strength in the ministry of charity of the church, but now the ashes of his former fire, and they thought there was nothing they could do about his predicament. If there was nothing else, one basic thing Robert needed from them now was affection and the feeling that he was wanted. But this seemed not to be the case; rather the church appeared to be far from him with their attitude. Their general uninterested attitude towards him made him more miserable with a forlorn feeling, even the members of his former ministry who used to be very close to him often treated him as if they had never been close to him before.

But he seemed not to bother about their attitude. He did not betray any signs of disaffection towards the church members, even though, he was deeply hurt by it – Robert hardly expressed any feeling these days. Agnes was unhappy that the church abandoned her husband in his adversity, in spite of his huge sacrificial service to the church before he lost his job. But she did not express her feeling to anybody, either. She just wanted to believe that God Almighty would do something to show that He had not forgotten her husband - that was what she was just looking forward to seeing, as the condition of the family was becoming too precarious. Sometimes, when she thought of how everything had changed in their home and the fact that there seemed to be no ray of hope in sight, she would feel like crying. But she wanted to be strong for her husband and her children as she realized that she was now the pillar of strength and hope in the family. Anytime she was about to crumble with emotion under the weight of the challenge, rather than cry, she would exclaim, 'The devil is a liar!' That seemed to revive her on such occasions. But she was really getting tired of the situation and just wanted to see their bad fortune turn around at once. This was what she prayed and hoped for every day.

CHAPTER THIRTEEN

One day, Robert had a sudden longing to go out. He was tired of staying indoors day in, day out. He just wanted to go out. There was no real purpose in his mind. 'Just going wandering?' he asked himself. That's insane. Instead, let me check some work places where I've submitted applications,' he said to himself. This made his desire to go out more reasonable. It was in the morning, the children had all gone to school. Agnes had also gone to her nearby garden where she planted vegetables, okra and tomatoes for both domestic use and sale. She had redoubled the size lately to make it more commercial, as it was gradually becoming the obvious support of the family. The work of the garden had kept Agnes very busy recently. The children often joined her at the garden sometimes after school, and were almost always there with her on Saturdays. Besides becoming a dependable source of living, it had given Agnes a kind of engagement which relieved her from the sickening boredom their home had become. The children too had found a new life in the garden. They always wanted to be there with their mother, even when Agnes preferred them staying at home.

'Pastor! pastor! pastor!' a young man called, beckoning from a distance. 'Someone is calling you, sir,' said a passer-by to Robert who was at a bus stop and Robert turned backwards to see. He saw a young man of about thirty years of age, running down with all excitement towards him. Robert looked at the young man. He was not familiar to him at all, so he did not show any interest towards him, contrary to the young man's expectation, as he was running down with all enthusiasm, waving his hand as he ran to Robert.

'Pastor, it's me, one of the convicts you often preached to, at the prison. I'm out! I've served my term and had been trying to see you since I came out. I'm born again, pastor. Your message touched me. I regret living a life of crime in the past. Now I'm different. Pastor, I'm born again 'cos of you!' and knelt down in appreciation. 'Sir, I really want to thank you for making me to see the light and know the truth. I'd been longing to see you. Glory be to God, I've found you today. Pastor, you changed me! You led me from crimes. I thought I was brave, strong, seeing my victims crying and begging me. I felt being on top of the world seeing men submitting their cherished possessions to me, entreating me not to take their lives in addition. I felt great seeing beautiful ladies submitting to me sheepishly, ladies I could never even dreamt of touching, all b'cos of the power of drugs and weapons. But pastor you led me out of all that evil!' He broke down and began to cry. 'Pastor, I want to be like you,' he cried.

'Be like me!' returned Robert, and the young man nodded his head as he was getting up.

'Pastor, I want to be close to you and just be the way you are,' he repeated as he stood.

Robert shook his head.

'Taking my place is something you may not wish for, if you know it,' replied Robert reluctantly. 'All the same, I'm so glad to hear that my effort at the prison had changed you. May the good Lord keep you in His salvation till the last day, in Jesus' name.'

'Amen,' answered Michael.

'Where do you worship now?' asked Robert.

'For now, I'm worshipping with a church near my place, New Jerusalem Church,' answered Michael.

'Are you sure you experience God's presence there? 'Cos there are many churches today that perform miracles only, and people flock to them to get their miracles. Hope that church is not one of those miracle centres. Real born-again Christians don't look for miracles. The miracles are within them – that's the presence of the living God in their lives – that makes the difference, Michael. Are you led by the spirit of God? The word of God says in Roms 8:14 in the Bible that those who are led by the spirit of God are truly the children of God. Do you understand that Michael?' asked Robert, staring at his convert for a true conversion.

His emphatic questions with so much authority made Michael to feel that he was being cross-examined by a divine authority and he saw Robert an angel of God questioning his sincerity. He did not know what to say now, as he was a bit confused, neither did he know whether he was truly a born-again Christian. But he believed that the message of salvation that was preached to him by Robert while he was in prison, led him to church and he had stopped his old way of living. This was what he thought Christianity was all about. He was no longer moving with his former gang members. But the question his mentor was confronting him with now, made him doubt whether he was actually a Christian; a question to which he had no answer.

'Sir, that's why I've been longing to see you. I want to be close to you and worship in your church. Sir, I want to follow your footsteps,' answered Michael meekly.

Robert wrote the name of his church and its address on a small piece of paper and handed it to Michael.

'Meet me there, next Sunday!' said Robert while passing the paper to Michael.

'Thank you, sir. I am so grateful. I'll surely meet you there, on Sunday,' he said.

And they both exchanged greetings and parted ways.

As Michael walked away, he kept looking back to see Robert again, wondering why the 'man of God' had become so emaciated lately. *He looks so different now. May be he has been on the mountain fasting and praying.* His mind immediately went to Moses' appearance when he was returning from Mount Sinai in the Scripture and thought that he might have encountered a man who had been with God lately.

'If he says a true Christian must have God's spirit, it means I've encountered God in that man,' Michael said to himself. *I'll like to be with him again*, he thought.

When Michael had disappeared from the scene at the bus stop, a car drove up and parked. A middle-aged woman emerged from the car. Though Robert could not recognize the lady, the car was very familiar to him. It was Pastor Onokurhefe's. He quickly looked towards the driver's seat. Expectedly, it was him, Pastor Onokurhefe. Robert was very glad to see him at that moment. Pastor Onokurhefe had just come to drop his cousin who came to visit him at the weekend, at that bus stop where she could get a bus back to where she lived. Robert believed that seeing Pastor Onokurhefe at that material time was providential, as he was just thinking of leaving the bus stop to see the pastor and relate his encounter with Michael, an ex-prisoner, who was now a convert and wished to be a member of their church. There was a procedure of becoming a member of the church which was through baptism after the convert had undergone some weeks' teaching on the basic tenets of the faith. Robert believed that it would be a piece of cheering news to his pastor who had always been encouraging evangelism in the church.

But as soon as the pastor's cousin alighted from the car, Pastor Onokurhefe was in a hurry to leave the spot at once, and he wasted no time in driving away. Robert was calling and waving him to a stop, but Pastor Onokurhefe seemed to be too much in a hurry to pull out of the place. As he was driving away, he looked back through the side mirror, to be sure of what he saw. Just then, Robert observed that his pastor was looking back through the side mirror and his focus was on him, as he was still running towards the car. Instinctively, he stopped running at once, flung his hand down in frustration and shook his head in utter disappointment.

'Oh, avoiding me?' he muttered unconsciously and a great pain of betrayal and rejection struck him suddenly like a thunderbolt in his consternation at that moment. The whole world appeared to be turning upside down in his imagination, even the Christian faith. He had always believed hitherto that Pastor Onokurhefe was the bearer of the salvation light in the church. *Is it possible for light to need light again?* Robert panted with thought. There was something happening to him now that he could not understand.

'What's happening to Christianity?' he asked unconsciously. He was confused and filled with indignation 'Pastor Onokurhefe? Pastor Onokurhefe? I can't believe this!' exploded Robert in a soliloquy and he shook his head repeatedly several times as he reflected deeply upon the ostrich show of the pastor at the bus stop. He became too agitated as he plodded along the road absent-mindedly and was almost knocked down by a vehicle as he was crossing the road to the other side. The driver of the vehicle swerved quickly to the opposite direction, narrowly missing him. It was very close. The driver was furious.

'If you want to die, go and hang yourself, don't put it on me, idiot!'

Robert did not answer him. He was rather shocked by the level of his absent-mindedness.

'The man looks like a walking corpse,' remarked one of the passengers as they were leaving Robert behind and everyone in the vehicle laughed at both the remark and the stupidity of the pedestrian.

When Agnes returned from her garden late in afternoon that day, she observed that her husband appeared almost lifeless in his bed that everything seemed to be meaningless to him. He could not even greet her as usual when she returned from the garden. He kept mumbling something quite unclear with morbid look in his face. Agnes attempted to interact with him but he seemed not to be aware of her presence. She placed her hand on his cheek to feel him. It was all pale and numbness. She became very worried. She could not imagine how Robert just slumped into this adverse condition suddenly. He looked hale and hearty when she left in the morning for her garden, after the children had gone to school. She feared his look and was really scared of his condition.

'How was your father when you returned from school?' Agnes asked the children.

'We've not been to his room. I think he's been there all day,' answered Ovo.

Agnes searched their eyes one after the other as if she could locate what was wrong with her husband in their faces but all she could get was a blank look of surprise, fear and confusion, indicating only worry just like hers. Their father had oftentimes kept to himself in his room, so the children had little to say about his state of being. As Agnes looked at the children one after the other, she could feel the anguish and uncertainty the condition of their father had thrown them, and they were all afraid of what might happen. At that moment, Agnes' eyes began to fill with tears.

'Why are you crying mum,' said Oke who was about to break into her own tears also.

'I don't know. Oh – I'm not crying,' murmured Agnes as she kept rubbing Oke's eyes of tears while struggling to control her own feeling.

Without wasting further time, Robert was rushed to the public health centre with the assistance of some good neighbours. Getting money to foot the treatment was making Agnes' mind run riot with great agony while they were heading to the hospital. Fortunately, the neighbours provided the initial deposit amount without her asking. They quite understood the financial difficulty in Robert's family. It was a great relief to poor Agnes, she knelt down, thanking them. All through that night, Agnes could hardly sleep. She was worried sick over her husband. She prayed furiously and cried at different times in her bed.

'How's he now, doctor?' asked Agnes anxiously the following morning when she went back to the hospital.

'A bit better,' returned the doctor who was attending to Robert, calmly.

'Oh, thank God!' Agnes fell down on her kneels.

'But what really happened to him yesterday? Did he receive any shocking news or have a serious disputation with anybody?' Doctor Enoch asked Agnes.

'Shocking news or serious disputation with anybody?' repeated Agnes, reflecting. 'I don't think so,' replied Agnes, but she quickly realized that she was away to her garden almost the whole day as Dr. Enoch considered her reply with some doubt in his look. *As for shocking news, I don't know of any. With whom would he have had a disputation? I was away. The children were in school and he was always in his room – he hardly stepped out*, thought Agnes. 'Well, doctor, I cannot really say with absolute certainty. I was not with him for most part of yesterday,' Agnes added.

'I asked that question because, from all medical examination, your husband has a high blood pressure, probably recently, and his condition triggered sharply yesterday, which has caused him to suffer some impairment,' said the doctor, trying to avoid the word 'partial paralysis.'

'What is happening?' cried Agnes. 'Please doctor, just tell me he'll be alright,' pleaded Agnes with much concern.

'I hope so,' answered the doctor, seeing that Agnes was becoming very nervous.

Agnes had been pacing to and fro in front of the male ward frantically in great agitation, while she stepped aside during Robert's treatment. In her agitation, she had been crying to God to have pity on her and her children as she could not contemplate the prospect of losing Robert in the sickness.

Somehow, Robert's condition appeared to have improved the third day after he was taken to the hospital. Agnes came with the children that morning, to see her husband. She was very pleased to find that his look had improved. Robert managed to smile at her and the children. He felt them one after the other on his bedside. This gave Agnes and the children a lot of relief and hope. They now believed that Robert would definitely get well again. They left him after one hour when the superintendent nurse reminded them that their visit time had expired. They were really sad to leave him. As they were leaving, Robert gestured towards his son, Ovo, to come close and he did. Robert patted him on the back and bent his head closer to his.

'The word of the Scripture nourishes the soul, feed on it. If you don't, your soul shall perish. Are you listening?' whispered he to Ovo.

He looked at the boy's eyes to be sure, and Ovo nodded his head in the affirmative.

'Pass my word to your siblings. And you must love one another, too. Do you understand?'

'Yes, dad,' answered Ovo and he allowed Ovo to go.

'Why did your dad call you back?' asked Agnes when they came out of the hospital.

'He says we should feed on the Bible because if we don't, our souls shall perish, and we should love ourselves, too,' narrated Ovo.

Agnes was silent for some time after she had listened to Ovo. She was just wandering why Robert would speak in that way to Ovo. After a little walk, they got a taxi that took them home. They reached their home when it was just some minutes to twelve noon that day. When they got home, they saw a letter hung on their main door. Agnes became very curious. She looked at the envelope and the stamp. They were both foreign. That increased her curiosity. The letter was addressed to her husband with his former company's address. She guessed that one of the Ansco Company staff who knew their residence must have brought the letter. Agnes immediately ripped the envelope open. It was from Lea:

Dearest Robert,

How're you and your family? Hope you are all fine. Nancy and our two lovely daughters – Cathy and Rose – and myself are quite fine except that we're still struggling to settle down in Canada, our new place of settlement. I know that'll be a surprise to you. Yes, the other time I told you, I'd not really made up my mind where to settle – that I wanted to have some time with my family whom I had left for three good years, albeit with some intermittent visits while I was working with Ansco in Otu. The next plan was to visit my parents and siblings who were becoming too anxious for my long absence from home, in Australia, since my university days in Europe. We did make the journey to Australia. It was a big celebration for my extended family – almost like that of the prodigal son in your Bible, only that I went back home a big time boy – an experienced engineer with a lovely family, and never a prodigal son! Our African dresses you and Agnes gave us provoked great laughter among my relatives and friends in Australia – we were amazing objects of entertainment in those dresses to our people. We're now called 'African Ambassadors' in Australia. We spent a jolly one month with them – but that really wasn't my plan – my plan was to spend two weeks, but those guys wouldn't let me go so quickly – they forgot that I'm grown up now. Sometimes, you allow them have their way, you know. While there, a friend called me from Canada, urging me to apply for a particular job in Canada and I did. A month later, I received their letter of interview which I attended and I was immediately offered the job. 'Wow, it's a real plum – better than Ansco., Lucky me!' I screamed when I saw the salary package. All these were what delayed my writing to you.

So how's Ansco? Hope you're just okay with those guys at the top, especially that imperious Jove – hope he's not a hell of a problem. In any case, if you won't mind, I'll want you to join me in my new workplace. I can guarantee you a place here. It'll just be lovely – oh, how I miss working with you – but I fear you'll turn down my offer 'cos of your family and your local church activities. May be, I'll have to speak to Agnes directly. It will really be nice having you two around. Nancy will indeed be very happy to see Agnes and you. My very warmest greeting to you all.

Cheers!

Lea

When Agnes had gone through the letter, she was very happy. She believed the good news would comfort her husband and quicken his healing in the hospital. She was so full of excitement to give Robert the letter the following morning. 'What a Mighty God we serve!' She exclaimed at once after reading the letter, and the children became curious about the content of the letter. When Agnes told them, they were all very happy. They became more excited when they saw the prospect of travelling with their father overseas, and the entire gloom and despair that had blighted their home since their father lost his job would disappear, and their life would turn around again.

Life can play a trick on one at times: when it seems to be raising hope at a point, it suddenly turns the opposite direction to plummet one into unmitigated disaster. That is part of its mystery. That was why Agnes' eyes were out on stalks, when she went to the hospital the following day to see Robert, only to find that he was not there in his sick bed.

'Where's my husband?' she screamed with great concern. 'Nurse, where is he? Tell me nurse, to where have you taken my husband?' cried she.

But the nurse on duty and all the patients in the unit remained silent, looking at her with great pity. Agnes was running out of patience.

'Please, tell me, where is my husband? my darling husband!' she screamed tearfully. 'To where have you taken him? Can't somebody answer me?' she cried with great anxiety. 'I want to see my husband!' she held the nurse's arm tight in her outburst. 'Please madam, where is he? I left him here yesterday smiling to me. I came to see that smile again. Please ma, where is he?' she expressed herself in a much lower tone, suggestive of a woman, losing all her energy in an overwhelming emotion.

'My dear sister, take it easy,' pleaded the nurse.

Agnes raised a shrieking cry at that moment, which pierced through the hospital, as the suggestive word of the nurse confirmed her fear. Some other nurses and medical personnel came and took Agnes to the consulting office where she was calmed down and was told what happened.

'Your husband slept permanently last night and he is fully resting. Death is a hard and painful reality and the earlier we accept the hard reality of its existence in life the better prepared we are, when we are faced with it. We cannot prevent it. It'll certainly come to everyone. Accept my sympathy,' calmed the consulting doctor.

For once, Agnes looked calm and distracted as if she did not even hear what the doctor was telling her. But suddenly she raised a loud cry and fell on the floor and began to throw herself everywhere in the office. More health officials came in to calm her down. Agnes was in surreal state and did not know what she was doing. The hospital officials eventually succeeded in holding her down to one place before she did something terrible to herself, and she began to wail there.

'O Robert, why, why did you do this to us? You didn't pity me and our children! You always showed that you loved us. Where is the love now if you can abandon and condemn us to a life of widow and orphans. O Robert, where are you now? I came to tell you how we felt last night at home, only to see that you are gone.'

She started talking in distraction like this, for some time, before she broke down again in tears. At a point, she relaxed and stared at the ceiling as if she was trying to look at something that seemed difficult to see clearly as she lay down on the floor of the consulting office, completely devastated by the crushing blow of her husband's death.

By late afternoon of that day, the news of Robert's death had travelled to many places. The residence of late Robert was swarmed with numerous people especially members of his church. Pastor Onokurhefe and other leading members of their church were inside his apartment, all in great mourning. They all had been crying. Many of them actually wept tearfully like a baby over the sudden demise of one of their beloved members. Pastor Onokurhefe was seen dabbing his eyes with his handkerchief from time to time while his wife, Sarah, was crying together with Agnes in one of the inner rooms. Everyone in and around the apartment was stricken with sorrow and shock.

CHAPTER FOURTEEN

There was a massive turn out for Robert's funeral service in his church. The church had to hire some canopies for people who could not find seats inside the church. Accolades and tributes continued to pour in for him amidst tears for a long time, during the service. Almost all the staff members of Ansco Company including all the managerial staff were at the funeral church service – all with handkerchiefs to wipe away their tears. Black was the dressing colour and it was indeed a black day for the church – the tears of church members could not stop flowing.

The officiating minister summed up the general feeling when he began by saying, 'Good and enjoyable thing does not last long, so it is with our late brother, Robert. He was an absolute gem.' His voice was solemn as he caught the grim air of deep mourning in the church. 'Well, I am not here to sing his praise but to tell us all who gather here now to emulate his lifestyle. That's the best way to pay him our last respects. We don't need to mourn Brother Robert. He has played his part in this our journey of life on earth here and I think he has played it very well. Beloved, it is not how far but how well. In his departure, if our good Robert is well embraced by the Lord in heaven as we all believe, then, glory be to God. Beloved, that is the challenge for each and every body here on this earth. It is great gain to transmute into eternal glory, and if we believe indeed that our brother, Robert, lived a worthy life of Christ with us here on earth, why do we then mourn him? We have no reason to mourn him rather we should be rejoicing that he is presently with our Lord forever. What a great gain! in the word of Apostle Paul. Beloved, let me remind you of the word of God in the Scripture at this moment:

> *Blessed are the dead which die in the Lord... that they may rest from Their labours, and their works do follow them (Rev. 14 verse 13).*

So we have no cause to mourn our brother, Robert, but to rejoice with him in his transmutation at this hour,' he affirmed. 'Yet I do appreciate that things of deep emotion like this are much easier to talk about than to control. Robert, our brother has played his part and indeed his good works will certainly judge him aright. He'll certainly have his reward in heaven. A time like this gives us the opportunity for introspection,' he continued after wiping his face with his handkerchief for a second. 'We need to look inward and ask ourselves individually. If the bell sounds for me now as it has done for our brother, Robert, where will I be? In hell or in paradise? Beloved, we need to self-examine ourselves and mend the areas of our lives we know that are not right with our God, our maker, so that when the final bell tolls for you and me, we have all the reasons to give God glory,' he stated.

'A time of a departed soul, always reminds us about life – that the world is not a permanent place for us, yet we stake all our lives on it in our efforts to make it very comfortable for living. Beloved, it is a short sojourn. Our permanent resting place is with the Lord,' he emphasized before commencing his prayer. After the short message of the officiating minister, almost all of them in the church were prepared to mend their ways and lived the way of the Lord, in their sober reflections. But the way of the flesh which works with the devil, always comes like a thief to steal away that spirit from them immediately after such occasions, replacing it with their former warped spirit that only understands the rhythm of the world.'

After the burial church service, the body of Robert was immediately taken to his birth place for final rites and interment. The church hired buses for this purpose, as majority of the members were prepared to see Robert's corpse finally being lowered into the grave. Ansco Company also arranged to convey their delegates down to Robert's final burial rite at Okah. They all felt very sad that Robert died. Two members of management staff were to lead the delegates to pay their last respects. The management knew that Robert was a distinguished and dedicated management staff member who was unjustly discharged from his work to serve some interest. At his death, they all thought they owed him so much. Management directed the company's workers to close work by noon that day, as a mark of honour and respect for one of their former devoted senior staff member. The management also made a substantial contribution towards Robert's burial ceremony at Okah to make it more befitting.

The news of Robert's death came to his extended family at Okah like a thunderbolt. They were not even aware of his recent joblessness and sudden illness before his death. It was after his death, they got the whole story. Robert was a high profile figure in the family, the only person with a university degree in the family. The rest of them could not even attend college. They were peasant farmers in Okah except Onose who managed to obtain his GCE O/L, through self-study and extra-mural lessons, while working as an assistant clerk in Yare, and had been rising through the ranks in his workplace. He had risen to a senior executive officer. Robert was their source of pride in Okah, and had been doing all he could to encourage his nephews and nieces to continue their education to university level, as he was not happy that he was the only graduate in the family. Before his death, Robert had promised to sponsor two of his nephews who were in their final class in the college to university if they gained admission. This was when he was still with Ansco Company. His immediate elder brother, Ovoke, had taken it for granted that Robert would take the full responsibility of all his children's education to whatever level they wished to attain. He thought Robert was well off to do that. He presumed that working with a university degree was an automatic right to wealth and high social status. He was always boasting to his many children that his young brother, Robert, was a great engineer in the city.

'He's next to the overall white man in a large white man's company,' he would tell them with great pride. 'Several white men answer him "Sir" in the company. I want you to be like him. He has promised me he is going to sponsor the education of everyone in the family. So if you cannot attend university, the fault is yours. He has the money! Go to his house in the city and see where he lives. He lives better than many white people in their own great cities. My brother, Robert, is a great man!' he would tell his children and his three wives, especially when he wanted them to believe that they were important people in Okah because they were related to a great educated man. He often brayed at people at meetings or any social gatherings in the village to accord him respect, on account of having a great brother in the city. He used this to intimidate and obtain respect from people in the village and equally wanted his wives and children to do the same, as very few families in the village could boast of a university graduate with high profile position in a reputable transnational company. He was quick at picking quarrels with people, boasting that he would put them in jail if they dared him, readily using Robert's name to threaten them. Most times, such persons whom Ovoke was intimidating would either walk away or remain silent without talking back. Ovoke knew that they did so because of his brother, Robert, and Ovoke never ceased to remind them of him in his quarrel. Any time younger persons walked passed him in the streets, he expected them to greet him with much expressed reverence, if not, he would insult them especially the teenagers and children, for lacking in manners. And when he was well greeted as he expected, he would be greatly pleased and answered such greetings with great pleasure. He would feel that such persons knew that he had a great brother in the city. Because he often prided himself with Robert in Okah like this, the people believed that his brother, Robert, was extra-ordinarily great and rich in the city.

Ovoke collapsed on the chair he sat when the news of Robert's death reached Okah. The entire family of Onoyoma was thrown into wailing at once. Immediately, the entire village gathered at their family compound to mourn with them. It took about some minutes before the people were able to revive Ovoke from the shock of the news. And when he had recovered, he was wailing uncontrollably, blaming the people for reviving him.

'What am I living for? Is death not better than this torment?' he lamented in his wailing. 'Oh my brother Robert, my pride, my honour, where are you? Don't leave me alone! I'm going with you. We must go together,' he cried.

After a while, he became calm and the people stopped holding him, thinking that he had finally heeded their entreaties. Not knowing that Ovoke's momentary relaxation was only a ploy to have a chance to wreak havoc upon himself. At once, he hit his head against the wall and fell. It was so hard that the people with him feared that he must have passed out again. They gripped him firmly while he struggled with them to be left alone to do whatever he liked with himself. Ovoke then intensified his wailing. He cried and wailed uncontrollably in agony. After about two hours of continuous wailing, he became exhausted and tired; his voice also became dry and hoarse yet he could not stop. All the people around him began to entreat with him.

'Please leave me alone, let me die,' he answered. After sometime he stopped crying. But the people were wiser now. They all sat round him, holding his hands, believing that he could spring a surprise any time like before. 'Oh Robert, you have stripped me naked before everybody. I'm so naked! Robert, why have you done this to me. You have removed my clothes of pride and dignity and I'm now naked before the public. I have no clothes any more,' he lamented and resumed his wailing, and for a long time he remained impassioned until he became too weak and stupefied to cry.

The day of the final burial rite and interment was uncontrollable. The entire Okah village witnessed overwhelming presence of cars, buses and humanity far more than the village could cope with. Almost all the people were wearing black clothes. Among them were some white men. Buses of various descriptions conveyed a great number of people down to Okah. There was a huge traffic jam in the village that day. Okah village had never before witnessed such a long queue of vehicles. At a point in the jam, many people left the vehicles they were in. They became too impatient and did not want to miss any aspects of Robert's final burial rite, and there was an endless outflow of people, walking down to the burial ceremony.

The burial programme as planned by his church was carried out without delay. The Okah people crowded the ceremony to watch in sympathy. They had never witnessed a large burial ceremony like this before. It had always been their own affair. At best, their people who lived in cities and their friends used to be the special and important people at such burials. In this burial, Robert's family and the entire people of Okah appeared to be the strangers in their midst, although special permission was sought from the Onoyoma's family to give Robert a pure Christian burial rite, which they granted willy nilly, after they had been given reasonable amount of money, to appease them, to set aside their traditional rite for Robert's burial.

During the burial, almost every person was sobbing from time to time as the officiating minister continued the programme of the ceremony. The special choir used for the burial, rendered various hymns with subdued tone of sorrow. Their last hymn of benediction and farewell, which was to accompany the interment, immediately after Robert was laid in state for people to pay their last respects, turned out to be an outpouring of grief. The choristers started it. It appeared they had been waiting for this moment. And other people picked it up and a general atmosphere of wailing and weeping followed instantaneously. It was so infectious that the entire village of Okah was thrown into weeping include those who had never seen Robert while he was alive. Indeed, it was a day of wailing in Okah. Many of the people could not wait any more to witness the interment. They were all crying back to the vehicles that brought them.

One person that was seriously shaken at the burial was Pastor Onokurhefe, Robert's pastor. He threw caution entirely away, and wept like a baby by the side of his wife. This was after he had seen Robert lowered into his grave. He watched the body intensely as it was going down after the officiating minister had said the last word: 'Dust, you came, dust shall you return.' At that moment, Pastor Onokurhefe could no longer hold his emotion, it overwhelmed him. He broke down at once tearfully and wailed uncontrollably. The church driver that drove him and his wife to Okah was amazed to see the pastor in such uncontrollable outburst of emotion. He never believed that the pastor could be devastated to that level – a man he considered as one of the impeccable finest gentlemen of the clergy through whom the Almighty God loved to pass His message to His people. And Brother Stephen, the driver, was getting confused with the word of God.

In the sermon of the officiating minister, members were enjoined not to mourn, but to be happy that 'Brother Robert' had ascended into the glory of the Great Saviour. The driver thought that if mere members like him who were still struggling with their salvation cried as they all did in the burial ceremony, it was understandable. But for an anointed oracle of the Almighty God who had been completely possessed by the Holy Spirit, having all his fresh crushed out of his mortal body to do the same was what he could not comprehend. Sarah, the wife of Pastor Onokurhefe, was becoming worried over her husband's continued weeping in the car as they were returning home.

'Dear, that's alright. It's a great pain indeed to see that Brother Robert is gone. But we shall see him again on resurrection day. That's our consolation, my dear,' she patted him on his shoulder.

'That's true, darling. You didn't need to remind me of that. But I'm so affected by his sudden death. It's hitting me beyond what I can control. My dear, I don't know. I don't know...,' he shook his head repeatedly in the negative and resumed his outburst afresh.

Sarah was now at a loss over how to console her husband as they drove back home.

Pastor Onokurhefe managed to pull himself together by the time they got back home. But he was not entirely free from the grip of Robert's death. He bore it daily on his face. There seemed to be something his wife, Sarah, could not understand in his grief. She knew that Robert was a very devoted and active member of the church until he lost his job. Notwithstanding, she was just beginning to have the feeling that her husband telling grief had a deeper meaning. After the fourth week of Robert's death, Sarah still observed that her husband had still not recovered from his grief. Besides wearing him off physically, his moody disposition was getting worse. There seemed to be a new dimension to his grief.

One morning, Sarah took a good look at her husband and she believed that there must be a more serious matter rocking him inside.

'This can't just be the pain of Robert's death,' she said to herself. She went to him at that moment where he was sitting, held his hand and looked straight into his eyes. 'Dear, is all this for Robert?'

Pastor Onokurhefe could not answer. She dragged him to the wall mirror in the bathroom.

'Please take a look at yourself and see what you have become,' said Sarah.

'My love, my look is better, if only you can see the hell inside. I'm going through an unending crucifixion,' he lamented in tears.

Sarah became very curious and much more concerned. She turned closer to her husband with great worry on her face.

'What do you mean?' she said anxiously.

'Something tells me that I'm responsible for Robert's death!' he said tearfully in agonizing sorrow and began to wail. 'How do I answer this?' he cried.

'How?' returned Sarah with great surprise. 'Why did you feel so?' added she almost unconsciously.

He then narrated how he avoided seeing him at the bus stop and two days later he died. He later understood that Robert was taken to the hospital that day as a result of a sudden shock he experienced, which triggered off his blood pressure.

'I think my behaviour at the bus stop caused the shock,' said the pastor and he broke down completely in tears.

'Why did you do that?' shouted Sarah in painful surprise.

'I don't know what came over me then, my dear. I really don't know.'

And they both began to cry together.

CHAPTER FIFTEEN

When the dust of Robert's burial had settled, the Onoyoma family at Okah fixed a date on how to handle whatever Robert had left behind, as their tradition required. This was after the observance of the three months of mourning in keeping with their tradition. Agnes was told to come with her children to the meeting. Hitherto, the Onoyoma family had sent a delegate from the family to take inventory of all that Robert had left behind in his apartment at Otu.

Agnes received the invitation with utter resignation. She had gone through so much turmoil recently that she was no longer anxious about anything. Most times, when one has passed through too much trying time that has strained one's endurance to its limit, nothing seems to matter to one anymore – one just allows things to happen as they will. Agnes already knew what to expect from her in-law family.

'Coming to take the belongings of Robert? Let them come and have everything,' she said to herself.

But there were areas she would resist with all her strength – marrying her to any of Robert's siblings or taking the custody of her children from her. A woman should always pray that she and her husband attain old age together. For a woman to lose her husband in his prime can precipitate some very precarious hair-raising condition that is most trying for her. In the first instance, the death of a husband in his prime often results in mutual distrust and suspicion between the widow and her late husband's family at the point of death, especially as it concerns the burial and the handling of the deceased property. Agnes was lucky with the first hurdle. The church and her husband's former company voluntarily took the responsibility of the burial arrangement and expenses, so the idea of tasking her children, no matter how little they were, to perform the burial rite of their late father as tradition required was out of it. But handling the belongings of late Robert would not be as easy as his burial.

Already Robert's family had earlier summoned Agnes immediately they received the news of Robert's death to a full family meeting at Okah, where she was asked to explain how Robert, their brother, died without their knowledge. At the end of that meeting, tongues were wagging with great anger, why the family was not notified when their brother was in a critical health condition. They presumed that their brother would not have died if they were informed in time and concluded that Robert died due to negligence, as he had no assistance from anywhere. In their anger, the women in the Onoyoma family taunted and glowered at Agnes and almost beat her up, as she was leaving the compound that day. They clapped their hands over her head and hooted at her, for being a bad wife. This was after the remark of the head of their extended family at the end of the meeting: Our brother died in neglect as if he had nobody in this world, in a family of very large number of people, it's so painful' said Okome with obvious bitterness as he shook his head in great sorrow and pain and all the family members in the meeting expressed great sense of outrage in direct response to Okome's remark that day.

On the day of the meeting in which Robert's belongings were to be decided, Agnes went to Okah with her three children and her two elder brothers to the meeting. Though looking wretched, she was prepared for anything, as she was not expecting any favourable outcome from the meeting. By 2.00 p.m. that day, the house of Okome, the eldest man of the Onoyome's extended family was already filled with their male relatives. Agnes arrived there about that time. She was surprised to see that many people were interested in the matter. She sat together with her children and her two brothers in the house. And the business of the day began.

'Our good wife, we thank you for coming, especially with the children,' said Okome, and the attention of the entire house was focused on Agnes and her children.

They looked much different. Their urban air gave them amiable look in the midst of countrified peasant farmers, their mournful frustrating circumstance notwithstanding.

'I believe these are your relatives,' continued Okome, pointing to Agnes' two elder brothers who came with her, and Agnes nodded her head in the affirmative.. 'My in-laws, you're welcome. It's quite fitting that you came with her,' and the other members of the family nodded their heads in agreement. 'It is most unfortunate that we're all in a sorrowful situation which does not favour the befitting reception you truly deserve in our midst,' added Okome.

'It's understood,' returned one of the two Agnes' brothers.

'I think we all know the reason why we gather here this afternoon,' continued Okome, while surveying the entire house with his eyes to ascertain whether everyone understood him. 'Well, to be certain, we are all gathered here to decide how our late brother's possessions should be handled and taken care of. I'm sure we all know how it is done. None of us is a stranger to it, besides these little ones,' he pointed to late Robert's three children. 'It is a tradition we all came to meet. I have to say this from the beginning, so that nobody will feel he or she is being treated unfairly in the matter. I'm particularly happy that our brothers-in-law are here. I believe they are very well aware of how this arrangement is done.'

And the two Agnes' brothers nodded their heads in agreement.

This was what Okome wanted to see when he looked particularly towards them, to be sure of their positive response and he was very much delighted to see that they both responded accordingly. The only person he was not sure of supporting what they would decide in the meeting was Agnes, and the reason was well understood. The modern women of nowadays, especially the educated ones were averse to the traditional practice of giving their late husbands' belongings, to their husbands' relatives following the death of their spouses, in a situation where their children were still young and tender. They thought it was unfair to them and they had been contesting it in their own individual ways.

In those days, the women saw nothing wrong with the practice. But modern-day women with good education had become aware of their rights as guaranteed in the legal system. These educated women now considered traditional marriage alone as shibboleth. They now insisted on registering their marriages with the local council or had a wedding in the church or mosque to have their marriages registered, immediately after the traditional marriage, to give the marriage official recognition, in order to safeguard their family property against any interloper in the guise of tradition in such eventuality. There had been many cases of women dragging their late husbands' relatives to court over property rights. All these had generated so much awareness among women that the tendency to resist the tradition had become very strong among them.

Incidentally, Robert had very few belongings of interest before he died. Besides his car and his inherited parcel of land in the village, all others were household items and clothes.

In the meeting, the first issue to be tabled was the most contentious one – the wife of the deceased - Agnes. As expected, Oshevire, Robert's immediate younger brother was to inherit Agnes as a wife. It was the belief among their people that a wife of a deceased should be given to a member of the family to inherit in place of her late husband. The implication of that was for the inheritor to take full responsibility of raising the deceased's children and for continuity. This could be a way of stabilizing the home of the deceased within the extended family.

After Okome announced that Oshevire would inherit Agnes as a wife, the older of the two Agnes' brothers signalled to speak, and Okome gave his approval.

'Well, my brothers-in-law, I greet you all. We are not here to dispute whatever decisions you are going to take over the belongings of late Robert, as we understand the practice and it is entirely your affair. But in making your decisions on your late brother's wife, you must know that the world is changing and we must adjust our steps to that reality, if not, our dancing will be out of tune with the rhythm of our time. And that will cause trouble for us and the upcoming children of Robert. Your late brother, Robert, was highly educated, so his wife. They both went to the highest school in the world – university. No school is higher than that. They also had their marriage in the church after their traditional marriage. They were Christians and Christianity does not follow the tradition of our people, so they have chosen another way of life. Good enough, Robert's burial followed his Christian way. We were all here during his burial. It was his church that buried him according to their rite. Your family did not object to it or his marriage in the church. I understand he was not also participating in many of your traditional activities that were against his faith. I know that if Robert were to be present in this meeting, he would not allow tradition to dictate how his belongings should be shared. Please take note, Agnes was never a property of Robert to be assigned to someone else after his death. She was Robert's helpmate. That's what the Bible says. And I believe she played that role very well when Robert, your late brother was alive. The decision you have just taken is not recognised by Christian faith, so it is unacceptable to us,' he stated emphatically.

Agnes was very pleased with her brother's presentation as he did not mince his words at all. He said it as she had wanted it. As a woman, she was not expected to speak in a family forum except she was asked to. She had to speak through a male person and she knew this, that was why she came with her two brothers to speak for her, and she was quite happy that her brother had represented her very well.

Somehow, the argument of Obere seemed to have thrown the meeting into some confusion, probably because the Onoyoma family did not expect it so straight and direct the way Obere had put it. They started putting their heads across to each other before responding to the issue Obere had raised. Okome, the eldest man of Robert's family became worried and thought for a while, after conferring with some of his relatives. It took some good minutes before he could respond to Obere's.

'Well, my brother-in-law, I thank you very much for baring your mind which I believe is the mind of our wife, Agnes. We quite appreciate the fact that our late brother was a Christian and a very devoted one for that matter. We also allowed his burial ceremony to follow his faith as pleaded by his church. We allowed it for one good reason. Robert's children as we can see are still little. They have no means yet of playing their role as children of the deceased, so when the church took away that responsibility from the children, you will agree with me, it was a welcome relief. I do not think any reasonable person would have objected to that. Before Robert joined the white man's religion, he came from a family, a family that nurtured him to that level where he joined the church. You can't take all that away from him,' he shook his head in the negative. 'We remain his people and Robert recognized that while he was alive. He was still part of the family till death snatched him away from us.'

He paused for a second before continuing.

'Well, as it is now, it appears we all are not having one mind on the matter. But there is a way out of it. We, as a family of your late husband, has bequest you, Agnes, to Ovire, Robert immediate younger brother as our custom demands. It is now left for you and Ovire to formally accept the marriage. If either or both of you object to the family's decision, we know what to do next. First, let me ask you, Ovire. Do you accept to inherit Agnes as a wife from your late brother Robert?'

Okome became very business-like with tough and decisive posture.

Ovire who was already married with children looked at Agnes and the entire members of the family in the meeting. He took a deep breath in his thought. His delay in response was creating some suspense in the house. He would gladly welcome the idea of marrying Agnes, an urban-bred beautiful lady who was very polished and elegant in the way of highly educated ladies. But he knew Agnes was not going to marry a peasant farmer like him and he felt he really did not deserve a lady like Agnes. He also believed that his family knew that, but they did not want to break the tradition. He further thought that it would be shameful for him to disappoint the family at that critical moment.

'I really do not have any decision to make in the matter. Whatever the family decides, I'll wholeheartedly accept,' he finally said.

'Well, that's good,' said Okome and he immediately turned to Agnes.

'I think we have made our position known,' answered Obere.

'Please answer yes or no, I am not here to belabour the issue!' barracked Okome, as he was becoming very impatient with the matter.

'No!' answered Obere emphatically.

There was silence, some of tension.

'Now, the matter is clear. Since Agnes is not prepared to marry Ovire, we have decided she must return our bride-price and all the expenses, we incurred in her marriage ceremony, within one month. Then, she ceases to be our wife,' declared Okome.

'Give us a figure,' returned Obere.

'One hundred thousand naira,' answered Okome

'That's outrageous. We know the bride-price was only one hundred and twenty naira. How did it get to One hundred thousand naira?'

'That includes all the expenses of the marriage ceremony.'

'Is it supposed to be so?'

'For a woman seeking a divorce, yes. She pays everything *in toto*.'

'We will return ten thousand naira.'

'No haggling, please.'

'But haggling is part of it!'

'Not when a woman is seeking the divorce.'

'What about the children? Who takes care of them?'

'Leave them out of this! They're our own children. We know what to do with them,' answered Okome angrily as he looked at Obere balefully.

Okome was a chip off the old block. Though, modernity was gradually making incursion into many aspects of the traditional life of the people, there were still some people who were so rooted in the past that they were not prepared to recognize and accept it. Hitherto, women were not expected to seek divorce. It was a man's preserve. It was considered improper for a woman to attempt it, and in such event, she should be ready to pay through the nose, all the imaginable amount of money spent in the process of her marriage.

The meeting eventually bogged down in this disagreement and Agnes and her two brothers left in annoyance, as they saw that Okome was not prepared to listen to their point of view.

'Return the one hundred thousand naira by next month, if not, be ready for battle,' warned Okome to Agnes and her two brothers, while they were walking out of the meeting.

Agnes got home late that day. She managed to dish some meal for her children and retired to her bedroom. She was too upset and disconcerted for anything. All she fancied at the moment was a deep sleep at least to calm down all the turmoil inside her, before it shattered her to pieces. She thought she needed some good dose of sleep by every means possible. But for a long time she could not sleep. She left the bedroom and came to the sitting room where she threw herself on the sofa. She lay there for a while batting her eyelids for some kind of fantasy that could take her away from all the sickening trouble that had besieged her world. She lay there vacantly in her entire world of confusion for a very long time before she managed to doze off after midnight.

A week later, Okome summoned some young men of their family, nine of them, to his house. He gave them enough money to go to Otu.

'Go to Otu, clear all Robert's belongings from that devil woman. We need them here. And remind her of the one hundred thousand naira she needs to return by next month or be prepared to be bundled down here to marry Oshevire,' he instructed them.

Agnes met the boys at the entrance to her apartment when she was about to close the main door and put the curtain behind it, as the weather was getting draughty. It was rainy season and there had been frequent rainfalls that week. She recognized three of them and quickly deduced that they were from her late husband's family, and made way for them to come in. As soon as they entered the apartment, they started packing things as they could find. They started from the master bedroom where they thought Robert must have had his most valuable personal effects. They collected all his shoes and clothes including his suits and ties. They forced all the boxes and suitcases open and took all they contained, including several bed sheets and pillow cases that had not been used. They gathered all of them in the sitting room. When they saw that they had gathered so much, they packed them into a waiting bus they had hired for this purpose.

At first, Agnes was bemused with the manner with which they were going about the packing, without the slightest courtesy of informing her of what they came to do. Her three children watched helplessly, as they gathered around their mother, with an overwhelming feeling of having been invaded. The boys came back, after arranging the things in the bus and began to move the television in the sitting room and the refrigerator in the dining section. Agnes' first two children ran towards them to resist the moving of the two most important valuable belongings in their lives. But the boys pushed them aside and continued the packing, as though they were never distracted by the two children. Agnes called back both children, held them tight to herself, and began to caress them fondly, by way of comforting them and herself, as holding to them became a source of having something to cherish after all. She told them not to worry. The boys were not yet satisfied – there was much rapacity and a great sense of urgency in them. They moved into the kitchen and began to collect cooking utensils: jugs, containers of all sorts, spoons, bowls, breakable and expensive plates. It appeared they were prepared to empty the entire apartment. When they eventually stopped packing and were arranging what seemed to be the last items in the already filled bus, it occurred to Agnes to check her own personal effects in the bedroom. She ran in swiftly, to her dismay, she discovered that the boys had collected all her jewellery from her own box. She ran to them at once. But they refused to give them to her. She wanted to go into the bus to search for them but they would not allow her. They resisted her with all their strength until the bus sped away.

Agnes came back to see how her own apartment had been ransacked and turned upside down. She looked towards the children who were perplexed and embarrassed with a strong sense of having no protection and material support any more, following this unwarranted dispossession of their belongings. Agnes felt like crying but she quickly realized that she had to be strong and be seen by her children, of having the ability to look after them, despite the death of their father. However, at night when the children had slept, she came to the sitting room and began to weep. She felt the situation was too much for her to bear. Her spirit could no longer resist all the pent-up bitterness in her and her emotion overwhelmed her. She cried for a long time where she sat until she became tired.

CHAPTER SIXTEEN

When life becomes unbearable, without any hope, only faith in God can sustain. After six months of her husband's death, Agnes had turned cadaverous, almost beyond recognition, with little or no will, as she had become so weary of life. Her three children were the only thing that gave her the spirit to live. She saw no other reason to justify her existence. That feeling that if she died what would become of her children was always there in her mind, as she thought there would be nobody to look after them. She struggled daily to provide some food at home. She had two more gardens to grow vegetables and okra for sale. Every morning she would rise to tend her gardens, moving from one to another, tilling and weeding all day, without any sense of fatigue. Very early in the morning on Friday, she would cut some of them that were matured for sale. The family presently subsisted on the proceeds from her vegetables and okra. From time to time, she would plant new vegetables and okra to replace the ones that were no longer productive. In this way, she kept the three gardens. The children always joined her on Saturdays to grow the gardens.

One Monday morning, Agnes was just getting set to go to her gardens after she had prepared her children for school. These days, her routine life was between the gardens and her home. Her friends and companions were her children. Just then, she heard several taps at the entrance of her apartment. She was surprised to see that her three children were there waiting.

'What happened? Why are you back from school so early?' She asked with palpitation, as her mind ran to their dreadful school fees which had not been paid for the term.

The children were silent but the sulky mortifying expression which they bore on their faces said it all.

'It's school fees?' Agnes asked with alarm and they nodded their heads listlessly. An unexpected spirit of a widow determined to play the role of a father to her children overwhelmed her at that moment.

'We're going back to the school,' she told the children firmly with confidence in her voice. She quickly dressed up and took the children back to school. She entreated the school head passionately to allow her children for some time, saying that she would definitely pay their fees. The school headmistress was deeply touched by her predicament but she equally realized that Agnes was incapable of sustaining her children in the school. She was at a loss of what to do when she could not resist Agnes' entreaty.

'Madam, why don't you take the children to public school where tuition is free and save yourself all this stress you're going through? The children can still develop their potentials there. All you need to do is to give them the solid home support of a good mother,' the headmistress advised.

'I understand ma and I thank you for your advice. But let's see what the Lord can do in the next two weeks,' she pleaded. 'Two weeks is two weeks, no more! Agree madam?'

'Agree,' returned Agnes firmly, and the headmistress allowed the children to go back to their classes.

They were the only ones who had not paid their fees in the school. The headmistress had been allowing them on sympathy grounds as she knew their situation. She was not the owner of the private school and had been doing all she could to make the school proprietor bear with Agnes' children. But the proprietor was running out of his patience hence the headmistress was sounding very tough to Agnes this time.

Agnes forgot to go to her garden that day after returning the children to school. She lay on the sofa in her sitting room with her pale face lined with thought. She was weighed down with the thought of paying her children's fees, as she believed that if her children were to realize their full potentials, she must struggle to keep them in private school until they completed their secondary school. She had a low estimation of public schools. She saw them as ineffectual, having overcrowded classrooms, without proper co-ordination and supervision. She painfully realized that her gardens could not do beyond keeping body and soul together. She felt she had to think of a much better income if her children must remain in their present school. She was just exploring other possible options in her mind when she heard a tap at her entrance. She got up with much reluctance and walked to the main door. Pastor Onokurhefe and his wife were there waiting. They had come to see Agnes for the first time since Robert's burial, a period of six months. Agnes was surprised to see them.

When Pastor Onokurhefe and his wife saw the surprise in Agnes' face with some forbidding expression and her scrawny appearance, almost beyond recognition, they felt very sorry for not visiting her for a long period. A renewed sense of compunction overwhelmed them at once. Agnes allowed them in without a word. For some time they both sat in the living room in silence, not knowing what to say.

'We're sorry, we've not been able to visit you after the burial,' prompted Sarah apologetically at last.

'There's nothing to be sorry about, I understand,' answered Agnes calmly, maintaining her cold disposition. 'I guess the church received my letter of appreciation on behalf of my family,' added Agnes after some interval of silence.

'Yes, we did and it was read to the entire congregation,' returned Pastor Onokurhefe heartily and Agnes nodded her head with some satisfaction.

And the silence continued.

'Well, my sister, we appreciate what you're passing through – it's really a trial and a difficult moment for you. We can feel it. But you must draw strength from the word of God. I believe our brother, Robert, is with the Lord. God says He's the husband of the widow and the father of the orphan. His words stand sure,' counselled Pastor Onokurhefe.

'My sister, the Holy Spirit is your strength,' added Sarah.

At that moment, Agnes' eyes softened and she whimpered, looking wholly mournful. Sometimes, words like these reminded her afresh of her bereavement and her state of helplessness. She wished she could just chase the situation away with a wave of the hand. Pastor

Onokurhefe and his wife became perplexed and confounded. They did not know what to say any more. Deep emotion of sorrow can make the condition of the bereaved so delicate that one does not know what to say to encourage the person affected. Sometimes, the reverse might be the case in an attempt to console the bereaved. Pastor Onokurhefe and Sarah allowed Agnes' tears to flow without hindrance. After ten minutes, the pastor noticed that his wife was equally in deep emotion. Tears had started dripping down her cheeks. Pastor Onokurhefe tried not to look at the faces of the two ladies. He focused his gaze on the floor and reflected deeply on the calamity that had hit the home of Agnes, and silently prayed to God to heal their broken hearts and give them the ability to carry on with life again. When he raised his head up again, he noticed that the luxurious television late Robert received as a prize of excellent service from Ansco was not in the sitting room. He became curious.

'Where is your telly?' he said with much concern.

'Television? Go into the apartment and see how empty it is. My husband's people came and cleared almost everything including my kitchen utensils. Do you see the fridge there?' Agnes pointed to where their refrigerator used to stand in the dining section.

Pastor Onokurhefe and Sarah shook their heads in total disbelief. 'They vow to bundle me to Okah to marry my late husband's immediate younger brother, one wretched peasant farmer in the village, unless I pay them one hundred thousand naira which they claim is the refund of my bride-price. I wonder why they have not even come. They gave me two months to do so.'

'What?' exclaimed the pastor and his wife in disbelief.

Though the story of the rapacity of late Robert's relatives on his family had further depressed Pastor Onokurhefe and Sarah, they were quite relieved that it became the ice-breaker of the frigidity that had existed between them and Agnes. Agnes conducted the pastor and his wife round the apartment to see things for themselves.

'They even took away all my jewellery' said Agnes sadly as they were taking their seats again in the living room.

For a while the cleric and his wife bemoaned the action of late Robert's relatives. Sarah was particularly furious.

'It is expected of them to give you and your children the fullest support at this critical time. Now, look at what they have done! Shameless and heartless people! Some people are just being wicked in the name of tradition. A tradition that supports this nonsense should be cleared from the society and heaped into the dump of history,' argued she.

'Exactly!' concurred her husband. 'In this modern and civilized world people should have a rethink and spare us those barbaric shibboleths for goodness sake!' continued Sarah who became vociferous in her annoyance.

'When I think of all the troubles and pains I've gone through, following the death of my husband, I sometimes ask myself – is it not better to die? Anyway, I try to avoid such a thought. But how can I imagine a life without Robert? Just imagine the huge responsibility ahead. How am I going to fill this vale? It is beyond me!' and Agnes began to sob. 'I don't like thinking of it,' she added bitterly in her tears.

'My sister, where is your faith?' returned Sarah with an encouraging voice.

'Well, I don't like thinking of it – I have the faith, God's in charge!' Agnes wiped away her tears and stopped crying at that moment.

'That's the spirit!' said Sarah.

Their conversation was now getting warmer as it used to be in the past.

'How is the church? You know since the burial I've not been able to come. Transport alone is a huge hindrance,' said Agnes regretfully.

'What about the car?' asked Sarah.

'Car? That was the first thing my husband's people took away. It was even before the burial. I'm sure they must have sold it by now,' narrated Agnes.

'My sister, it is well,' said Sarah with sympathy. 'Yes, it'll definitely be well in Jesus' name,' returned Agnes. Sarah and her husband answered 'Amen!' in unison amid laughter.

'Now, talking about the church, the church has a little parcel for you,' smiled Pastor Onokurhefe with an air of pleasant surprise.

'Parcel?' returned Agnes with some curiosity. One of the main items in the last council meeting of the church was to raise some money to support Agnes and her children following the death of her husband, whose active role in the church, the church truly appreciated after his death. And it was approved immediately. Pastor Onokurhefe earnestly appealed to members and worshippers the previous Sunday, to contribute generously towards it, and many members and worshippers responded accordingly. When the contributions were counted at the close of worship that Sunday, Pastor Onokurhefe and the rest council members could not believe their eyes. The entire collection quadrupled their expected target, and they were very happy for what the Lord had used the church to do for late Robert's family. At that moment, Pastor Onokurhefe gestured Sarah to bring out the parcel from her handbag. It was a filled large brown envelope.

Agnes looked at it hastily and dropped it on the centre table before her, without really trying to know what it was as she was making a point to Sarah at that moment. After that, the cleric felt it was time to leave. They prayed fervently together, earnestly requesting the good Lord to visit the bereaved home and healed their broken hearts according to His word which He vows will never fail. Agnes saw them to where they parked their car and bade them goodbye. She was very happy for their visit. She believed the good Lord had used them to bring respite to her that day, as their coming had rekindled her spirit with joy, which she had never known for a long time. She felt a great sense of relief inside. Her face radiated with smile as she walked back to her apartment.

As soon as she saw the big envelope on the table where she left it, her curiosity rose. She ripped it open at once.

'My God, this is huge!' exclaimed she.

Agnes locked the main door and drew the window curtains close. She took the parcel to her bedroom and began to count. When she counted to a point, she became too excited to count. She fell on the floor and was rolling over repeatedly in jubilation. She burst into tears at once and began to praise God. She was in this outburst of gratitude to God. When she had satisfied her soul and had become less excited, she went back to the parcel and counted the money carefully. Agnes realized it was enough to settle all her immediate financial challenges.

Sparing no time, Agnes took the children's school fees out of the envelope and headed straight to the bank where her children's school had its account. The headmistress was surprised to see her again in her office later that day.

'Madam, you're here again,' she exclaimed.

'Yes, I am here with my children's bank tellers,' she smiled.

'Really?' replied the headmistress.

'Yes,' answered Agnes while handing her the tellers.

'Wow, this is marvellous,' smiled the headmistress surprisingly.

'My sister, God's wonderful,' enthused Agnes. 'He never fails,' she added with great smile on her face and the headmistress nodded her head while she was issuing Agnes the receipts of the tuition fees for her three children.

That evening, Agnes prepared the children's favourite delicacy, fried rice and chicken – a meal that had not been on their table for a long time. The children were amazed to see their mother preparing such a very rich favourite diet that evening. They could not wait to see it being served on the table. Oke was the first to know. She came to the kitchen to wash the dishes, her assigned duty in the home, after her school homework. When she saw her mother preparing the food, she could not believe it. She thought she was dreaming.

'Fried rice and chicken in this apartment!' she exclaimed with her eyes wide open.

'Ssh!' her mother cautioned. Agnes wanted to make it a surprise to the children. She had been wishing that they remained in their room doing their school home work until she had prepared the meal. She told Oke to keep the secret. Oke readily agreed with her. But as soon as she left the kitchen, she could not help it.

'Guess what mum is preparing in the kitchen?' she burst out as she went back to meet her siblings.

'What's it?' Ovo asked excitedly.

'Fried rice and chicken!' announced Oke.

'Is not true!' said Ovo and Oro together, could not contain themselves and ran straight to the kitchen. To their it was true, and they danced back with great joy. They quickly completed their homework and came to their mother in the kitchen. Agnes chased them back to their room, blaming Oke for letting the cat out of the bag.

'Now, if I see any of you here again, that person won't have this meal again,' she threatened, and they quickly disappeared, never to be seen in the kitchen arena. But that did not stop their excitement of having their favourite delicacy that evening. They jumped about in their room falling on one another in the excitement of the food. They just could not wait to have the spicy food ready for eating.

When Agnes had prepared the meal, she dished it into three plates according to their number and finally called them for dinner. And the children came running. When they saw the meals, their joy knew no bound – it was lavish with appetizing aroma.

'Mum, *miguo*,' they began to greet their mother as each took his or her meal to the dining table. Agnes could not hide her joy, seeing the children so overwhelmed with the excitement of the food – she was full of smile as she found herself sucked into their delight.

After eating, they were all luxuriating in the seats of their living room, still relishing the tasty sumptuous dinner when Agnes drew their attention to something she had been expecting from them.

'I'm surprised that none of you has asked me the source of this evening food. You know it has not been easy with us, and you shouldn't have expected me to give you that luxury food when you knew I had not been able to pay your tuition fees.'

The children were somewhat regretful of this negligence. Though, Agnes knew that, by their nature, children hardly reason deeply, she wanted to use the opportunity to inculcate an attribute she considered very critical to their joyful living.

'Our church members contributed a huge amount of money – to be precise N300,000 – for us. You can see that it's huge. Pastor and his wife were here this morning to hand me the money when you'd gone to school. I immediately went to pay your tuition fees.'

'Mummy, you've paid?' Ovo cut in.

'Yes, I have.'

'Thank God!' exclaimed Ovo.

'The church members saw that we were facing hardship and they contributed money to help us. You know how tough it has been,' she said.

They all nodded their heads.

'But this evening we are all smiling – we're happy. They made it possible. Many of them might barely have had enough, yet they contributed – they did it out of great concern for us – that's how it should be,' she pointed to each of them with emphasis. 'Do you understand?'

The children nodded their heads.

'Help others when they need help, okay?' she emphasized and the children nodded their heads again. 'Everyone needs assistance from others at a particular time. That's how it is,' she added.

'Mum, I think we can have a new telly and a new fridge now,' said Oke and the two older children nodded their heads in support.

'T.V. and fridge are very important in the home but let's think of how we can live without much stress again,' answered Agnes.

The children could not understand exactly what their mother meant by that, for they earnestly wished they had a new television in the home, as the apartment was becoming too boring without one and a refrigerator for preserving their fruits and food and for having their usual cold water.

CHAPTER SEVENTEEN

Pastor Onokurhefe and his wife, Sarah, were glad that the church was able to raise the huge amount of money for Agnes and her children. They both believed that the lifeline would go a long way in bringing relief and comfort to them. The joy of the pastor and his wife became boundless when they went to hand the money to Agnes. The condition they found Agnes made them believe that the money the church raised came to her at a very critical moment of her life. While they were on their way home from Agnes' place that day, they were both full of praises to God whom they believed was behind the fund-raising as the response from members was unprecedentedly unimaginable.

As they were in this mood, Sarah burst into a known song: 'Lord never fails' and her husband was so glad that she raised that song at that moment and became more excited and joined her in singing it.

'Were you waiting for me before?' teased Sarah and they both burst into laughter.

'I think we're flowing together in the same spirit,' laughed her husband.

And they sang the song dramatically together, swinging their heads along until they got home.

They both had great relief after returning from Agnes. The next thing they planned to do was to cultivate their relationship with Agnes, and see how they could pull her from her misery and sorrow to the level where she could be happy with life again, so that, she would be active in the church and appreciate the goodness of the good Lord in her life. From what they could feel at their parting with Agnes, she was no longer holding any grudge against them and the money she would see after they had gone would further remove any ill-will that might still be harbouring. They hoped to be very close to her. Hitherto, they had felt very guilty from being far from her after the burial of Robert and what actually accounted for this, was the scruple they both bore following

Pastor Onokurhefe's confession to his wife, as he felt his conduct contributed to his death.

Sarah's shock over her husband's confession and the consequent coldness it brought into their home prolonged their visit to Agnes. After the confession, they both searched the Scripture together to find out what the word of God says concerning the situation, and after reading several passages in the Bible concerning it, they fasted and prayed to God for forgiveness. The next action is to confess it before Agnes. But they feared the way Agnes might react to it especially when she is still devastated by the death of her husband. So they thought they must tread carefully on that idea to avoid any negative reaction from Agnes that even might work against their intention to build a stronger intimacy with that family, helping them to pull out of their misfortune.

As time went by, Pastor Onokurhefe and his wife believed that they had the leading of the Holy Spirit, not to be disturbed over the matter, as God Almighty had already forgiven Pastor Onokurhefe. At the end of worship the following Sunday, Pastor Onokurhefe remarked, 'Beloved, I bring you greeting and special thanks from Sister Agnes and her children – our late Brother Robert's family – they were very happy and grateful for your wonderful contributions to lift them from their terrible conditions. My wife and I took your contributions to them last Monday and she received it with all gladness. On Friday, that's two days ago, I received her letter of appreciation to you all. Sister Agnes specially requests that the letter should be read in the church to all members and worshippers and I read:

Dear Beloved Brethen,

APPRECIATION

With a heart full of joy, I wish to express our warmest gratitude and thanks to you all, for your generous contributions to assist me and my family. Your contributions came to us in the nick of time. I believe it was God's own intervention through you, at our most trying moment. I thank you all for allowing our good Lord to use you to bless us. I pray from the depth of my heart that the good and ever merciful Father in Heaven will never forget you at the point of your need likewise. May the good Lord bless you and keep you from troubles in Jesus' name, Amen! Once again we say we are most grateful. Thank you.

Sincerely yours,
Sister Agnes Onoyoma

'Let me also join the Onoyomas to thank you for your contributions. May God richly bless you for it,' added Pastor Onokurhefe and the church chorused 'Amen!'

'Brethren, we still need to do more if we really want to get Sister Agnes and her children out of their deplorable conditions. When my wife and I got there, what we saw and heard concerning the primitive and barbaric treatments the relatives of late Brother Robert meted out to Sister Agnes and her children were most unthinkable. They had taken all their household items, including TV., fridge, clothes, jewellery, even cooking utensils. Brethren, it's unbelievable. This is not hearsay, we saw it with our naked eyes,' he demonstrated by pointing to his two eyes with his two fingers. 'Ask my wife,' he continued. 'Their entire apartment is now almost empty. Besides, there is another unreasonable demand by late Brother Robert's relatives, for Sister Agnes to return the bride-price paid by her late husband for refusing to marry one illiterate peasant relative of late Robert in their village. Ask me how much are they demanding for? One hundred thousand naira!' stressed Pastor Onokurhefe and the congregation shouted in disbelief. 'So brethren, we'll take it as a challenge to bail Sister Agnes and her children out of their predicament. You will agree with me that this is too much for her to bear. She will certainly buckle under the strain of these distressing circumstances, if we don't come to her rescue. So next week, let us prepare to raise another special offering for the family. Please be prepared! Do we all agree on this?' Pastor Onokurhefe said and the church chorused in the affirmative. 'God bless you,' said the pastor happily and the benediction and closing prayer were taken.

Meanwhile, Agnes had already used part of the earlier contribution from the church to pay off the one hundred thousand naira demanded by her late husband's relatives as the return of her bride-price, to set herself free from their harassment which was sure to come, on account of that demand. The following month, their yearly house rents would expire. The electricity bills had not been settled for two months and it was certain that the local electric power office would disconnect them in the third month. She had been worried over these daunting necessities for days. The money left with her could hardly settle the rent. She was also thinking beyond their immediate situation. She was thinking of what she could do to stabilize their living condition without much hiccup. Her mind was focused on using the money left to start something new, something to augment the little income from their vegetable gardens. Unfortunately, the money left with her could hardly rent a small shop, let alone stocking it. Yet, there was a strong spirit driving her to foray into a small petty venture no matter what was on hand. She remembered the story of the mustard seed of faith in the Bible. *But what venture?* She could not lay her finger on it. Her mind was turning here and there with intensity of purpose as she lay on her bed one night.

The next day, Agnes went into the town, looking for any place she could start a make-shift eatery. First, she searched round her neighbourhood, as she wanted to minimize cost by avoiding transport fare. But when she walked several distances without success, she boarded a public bus to the city centre. She looked around, walked down several lanes, especially commercial and industrial ones but she realized that the area was crowded with well- established eateries. She was getting discouraged and thought of returning to her abode, and probably concentrated and expanded her vegetable farms, when the idea of exploring some of the public schools that were thickly populated, for a space, crossed her mind. Again she tried three but they were already having some collection of sheds outside for ice-creams, snacks, biscuits which the students picked at break time. She was now very tired and discouraged, and thought of returning home. While she was waiting for a bus to come back home, an idea crossed her mind. *If you think of a virgin place to sell, you'll never get one. Business is all about risk. Why don't you try one of the public schools with something different from what others are selling?* She began to consider it seriously. The more she thought about it, the more her instinct was urging her on. While she was in the bus on her way back home, she was still thinking about it. By a flash of insight, the idea of preparing jollof rice hit her at once. 'Jollof rice! What about a shed?' she said to herself. *One of the sellers may accommodate you in her shed so long as you're not selling her kind of wares,* her 'sixth sense' said to her. Immediately Agnes accepted the idea, a strong sense of ardour in that direction suddenly gripped her. When she got home, she went to her kitchen to survey all that she had for preparation. She also took note of other items she needed for the business and wrote them all down. She collected the remaining part of the church contribution money with her and dashed to market.

That evening, she braised her meat and raw tomatoes half-way, got all the necessary ingredients ready in different bowls in the kitchen. After dinner when she had done all that was necessary for the next day's preparation, Agnes and her children were relaxing in the sitting room after the children had done their school homework. They were laughing and talking about the jollof rice business.

'Mum, I'll be assisting you in the preparation,' announced Oro, her first daughter who was in her final class in the primary school.

'Not now, focus your mind on your passing your certificate exam. You can assist me during your holidays,' answered Agnes.

The children always desired to be involved in whatever their mother was doing. Besides the basic routine chores assigned to each of them in the home, Agnes wanted them to focus more on their studies. When she was done with her cooking, she always looked at each of their note books to find out their performances at school, after dinner every day, no matter how tired she was. Where their performance was poor, she would explain to them. She had been doing that before her husband died. After his death, she found it more compelling to make them focus on their studies. Oke, the youngest child in the family, had a great appetite for rice. When she heard that her mother would be cooking rice every day to sell, she welcomed the idea very much, as she thought that would mean having rice for her breakfast daily.

'Mum, I'll follow you to sell tomorrow,' said she excitedly.

'Won't you go to school?' chipped in Ovo, the boy next to Oro.

Oke did not answer. She was thinking of the rice.

Her mother understood her feeling.

'My dear, I'll always give you yours before leaving, okay?' she smiled at Oke and Oke became happy.

'Is it only Oke? What about two of us?' said Oro.

'Do you both want to finish the rice here? What'll mum sell then to bring in money for our needs?' questioned Ovo.

'Thank you, my son, ask them very well. After we have all finished the rice, we should be prepared to starve afterwards,' their mother said, and they became quiet.

At 4.30 in the morning, Agnes was already up in the kitchen. She hardly slept in the night. She was so full of the jollof rice vending, she was just thinking and praying over it. *God, let everything work out fine, tomorrow,* was her constant wish and request. Because the whole idea about the jollof rice business was a leap in the dark, she was so anxious. She woke up from time to time to look at the clock in the sitting room. The night seemed so long in her anxiety. Sometimes, she felt like going to urinate, but she hardly passed out any urine in the toilet. Back to her bed, she became tired and bored as the night seemed to be crawling like a snail, if not really standing on one place.

By 6.30 a.m. the cooking was over. Agnes served the food into two large crispers. She arranged twenty-five plastic spoons and plates in a basket. Besides the basket was a container of sachet water. She then prepared the children for school as usual. In each of the children's food containers was jollof rice for their lunch. She saw the children to school by 7.30 a.m. At 8.30 a.m., Agnes was on her way to the school she prepared to sell her food.

Having a place to sell did not pose any problem for Agnes as she had earlier feared. A kind young woman among the vendors with a large shed accommodated Agnes as her good nature and respectful manner recommended her to the lady. She was quite happy to have Agnes as a companion in her shed and they immediately took to each other. She assisted Agnes to arrange her things in her shed.

'It's good you brought rice. I'm sure the students will like it,' said Stephanie, the shed owner, when Agnes tried to find out from her the prospect of having her food sold in the place. 'Just be patient. They will crowd in here at break time,' Stephanie assured her. But as first-timer who was just testing the water, she remained agitated until she saw it happened. Agnes noticed that besides the school children who were the target customers of the articles in front of the school, some artisans having their workshops across the road and other residents in the area often came to pick one item or the other from these sheds. As a newcomer to the place, Agnes was observing the place with some curiosity, although her companion was engaging her in a warm conversation in the shed.

When it was 11.30 a.m., a bell was heard within the school. It rang repeatedly for some seconds. Loud cheers of students coming out of their classes immediately followed. They were running towards the main gate of the school; they were mostly the junior students, as the senior students usually strolled down. The gate was flung open by one of the gatekeepers, and in a matter of seconds, the students came out like bees and swarmed the entire sheds, asking for snacks, ice-creams, biscuits, cheese and other manner of fast foods. Stephanie sold snacks and mineral waters. The students had known what individual sheds were selling. Many of the school boys and girls were there buying from her. None of them knew that Agnes was there to sell jollof rice, so they were not asking for her rice.

Stephanie, her kind companion and owner of the shed was so busy attending to the students who were crowding her impatiently, shoving one another and shouting for her attention. Agnes did not know how to introduce her jollof rice at that moment. She felt that it was improper to announce her item of trade at that critical moment, being at the mercy of a co-vendor, who might see such an action as taking away her customers. Her heartbeats increased rapidly and her face creased with anxiety and frustration, as she was watching every other seller making quick sales. Agnes was freezing with great concern in her tension. She could not contemplate the prospect of taking her entire food back home unsold. It was when the break was almost over and the majority of the students had bought whatever they wanted at the sheds that it occurred to Stephanie that Agnes had not been selling. At that time, she had almost exhausted all that she had brought to the shed that day, so also the others. The break time was the boom. Once it was over, very few sales were expected. A few minutes later, many of the traders had started moving away – they had very little or nothing left.

'Why have you not been selling?' said Stephanie with surprise.

'They have not been asking for my jollof rice,' returned Agnes calmly.

'They're not aware you have rice to sell!' Stephanie agreed.

'We have very good jollof rice here,' announced Stephanie with all her strength to the remaining few students still hanging around the sheds.

'Jollof rice?' one of the students said with great curiosity.

'Yes, jollof rice! Look at it here,' Stephanie opened one of the deep food containers, and all the students present raced down to her shed. What a great relief for Agnes! Without further prompting, she opened the basket of plates and spoons and began business. The rice was steaming with appetizing aroma. The first student to have his, smiled to a corner to eat. Others looked at him with envy. The students had begun to rush for their individuals' turns. Agnes could not be as fast as she wanted. She was like a starved dog whose master had long been away, only to throw lavish dish at it on his return. At that moment, the school bell rang to end the long break. But it appeared those students that had not taken their turns were determined not to leave until they had their jollof rice, while those who had got theirs were much in a hurry to finish up and leave. As the students were running into their classes, the teacher on routine duty that week realized that there were still some students out there. She quickly went in the direction of the sheds. She was surprised to see some of the students eating jollof rice.

'Have you not heard the bell?' she bellowed with anger at the students and all of them dropped their foods and were running back to their classes. It occurred to Mrs. Ojo at that moment that propriety required her to allow the students have their foods for which they had already paid, lateness notwithstanding. She called them back to finish up before going to their classes. 'But you mustn't delay next time!' she warned and came closer. 'By the way, how come this rice that you're eating?' said she, believing that nobody was selling rice in the sheds. The students pointed to Agnes.

'Good afternoon ma,' Mrs. Ojo turned to Agnes, 'are you the one selling jollof rice here?' she asked with some conciliatory air.

Agnes nodded her head in the affirmative.

'Do you still have to sell?'

'Yes mistress,' returned Agnes. Mrs. Ojo bought a plateful which one of the students took to her table in the general staff room in the school. That was enough advert of Agnes' jollof rice. Hitherto, the staff of the school had been desirous of a place where they could have a good lunch near the school, especially as many of them hardly had a good meal in the morning before resuming their work. Most times, they bought snacks and soft drinks from the sheds in front of their school in the absence of any eateries in the place. They were very glad to learn that day that jollof rice was now sold in one of the sheds. Many of them immediately ordered a student to get a plate for each of them while others especially the male teachers strolled to Agnes's shed to have their lunch. A delighted Agnes could not believe her eyes that she sold all the jollof rice immediately after the school break period. Some teachers were not so lucky. They came later to find that the much-sought after jollof rice had been exhausted and they went back to their staff room disappointed.

CHAPTER EIGHTEEN

Agnes and her children's conditions began to improve as a result of her food vending at Kuta College. Both teachers and students preferred her rice to those fast foods around. The artisans and other petty traders in the area also patronized her. It did not take long before she erected her own large shed in front of the college. She was now the envy of all the petty traders by the school. She had tripled her initial output to meet the increasing demand and had just employed a sales girl to assist her in the service. She had also bought a good number of plastic chairs and tables for her numerous customers to make her shed more comfortable for them, and soon, the shed became boisterous with customers. The remaining plastic chairs and tables were spread behind her shed when the shed could no longer accommodate her customers. By 1.00 p.m., she had already finished selling and she would return home to prepare for the next day. Though the food vending was a hard task, it had become the mainstay of supporting her family.

Agnes did not abandon her vegetable farming. She still found time to attend to her gardens and realized her usual income from them, as she was able to juggle the two sources of income. But for her these days, time was short and too fast. It was work all day, no time for leisure. Women do often enjoy swanning around friends and do a lot of private gossips among themselves. Agnes had no time for this luxury. This explained why she had no intimate relationship with the women in her neighbourhood. With the jollof rice vending in addition to her vegetable gardens, Agnes had been able to stabilize the home financially. They could feed well nowadays without any stress, and the children were happy that their mother had been able to provide for them. Agnes had bought each of the children several clothes and shoes. Hitherto, all their clothes were already worn out. She had also bought them new school uniforms, new school bags and sandals within three months of her jollof rice business and life was gradually returning to normal in their home. She had been able to replenish her kitchen with new cooking utensils which late Robert's relatives had almost emptied. Fortunately, the church had bought them a new television set and a big refrigerator, following the second offering collected for them. Agnes and her children had become active again in the church. Pastor Onokurhefe and his wife, Sarah, were very happy to see them in the church again. Members were not also left out. Many of them came to embrace Agnes and her children the first Sunday they came back to church. Since that day, they were always coming on Sunday. In spite of Agnes tight schedule, she still found time to attend weekly church activities like 'prayer meeting,' 'Bible study' and had always been very active in them – making very useful contributions.

When Agnes was about to resume worship after some period of absence, following the death of her husband, she made up her mind to play a leading role in the church. She had thought that was the only way to honour her late husband who despite his hard and frustrating condition after he lost his job, remained steadfast in his devotion to the worship of God. Besides this resolution, *In what other way will I express my gratitude to God and to the church for all the succour?* she cogitated. Sarah was very happy with Agnes' new attitude and she was doing all she could to encourage her. And they both became closer.

The women's regional association was made up of several women's groups, each representing its local church within the denomination in the area. The association planned for a camp-meeting for their female teenagers annually, during the long vacation. This year's camp-meeting was to be hosted by Pastor Onokurhefe's church. Expectedly, the local church that would host the camp-meeting also had the responsibility of organizing the camp-meeting with the support and co-ordination of the zonal women's leader, and this enormous responsibility rested squarely on the shoulders of Sarah and the other women's leaders of their church. Though, Pastor Onokurhefe had absolute confidence in his wife, Sarah, and the other women's leaders of the church, he still found out from Sarah from time to time about their preparation and planning; where necessary, he made one suggestion or the other to his wife, as he knew that if their church women's group failed, he would also take the blame. Both of them, Sarah and her husband, had agreed to give Agnes the responsibility of being the chairperson of the local organizing committee for the female teenagers' camp-meeting that year. The committee was to draw up the programmes and arranged the resource persons for the camp-meeting, besides planning the entire session.

The female teenagers' camp-meeting was all about preparing their teenagers for their future challenges and making them dutiful daughters of the good Lord. The theme of this year's camp-meeting was, 'Becoming a Good Christian wife.' The choice of Agnes as the chairperson of the local organizing committee by the pastor and his wife was seen as quite apt. Besides being seen as an exemplary Christian woman, they thought she had a lot to draw from her profound marriage experiences and challenges. She was also a mother raising her children alone at the time; an educationist by training. For the same reasons, the pastor also insisted that Agnes would be the one to handle one of the vital topics in the programme of activities.

This was a great and huge challenge for Agnes, giving her tight domestic and business schedule. But she also saw it as a momentous opportunity to serve in the church. Her topic was, 'Making the Right Marriage Choice.' The only time to prepare for this great task was during the night. Agnes was thinking and studying most of the time at night and was jotting down words. She was putting all her effort into the whole preparation. The opening ceremony of the camp-meeting was quite grand. Very important clerics in the denomination were invited. On the eve of the opening ceremony, Agnes made contacts with all the special invitees to be sure of their presence at the opening ceremony. All preparations were thoroughly checked by both Sarah and Agnes on that same day to ensure that everything was in place. Dress rehearsals of special presentations of songs and play-lets by the female teenagers' of their church were also conducted and supervised by both Agnes and Sarah before the opening ceremony. The two women had been working very hard, putting things together, while Pastor Onokurhefe was keenly monitoring their efforts. A special song ministration orchestra selected from several churches' choirs was also included in the package for the opening ceremony. All these arrangements were done to make it a huge spectacular occasion. Agnes believed that for the annual camp-meeting to be more attractive to their upcoming young-girls, entertaining and active participating activities should be included in its programme. So the year's camp-meeting was enriched with more special activities in such a way that every participant would be engaged and active all through the period.

It was the second day of the camp-meeting that Agnes presented her topic 'Making the Right Marriage Choice.' Agnes gleaned ideas from some books for several days before finally putting her ideas together. In her presentation, she categorized 'Making the Right Marriage Choice' into three stages. First, having a mutual attraction; two, testing the mutual attraction to ascertain whether it was truly agreeable and lastly, ascertaining whether it could produce a happy union. She wanted to be very practical on the subject. In the first stage, she told her female teenagers categorically that marriage must be founded on genuine love, which she termed 'mutual attraction,' as she considered the word 'love' a platitude that had been abused and misused. 'Generally speaking, at your teenage age to twenty-four years, that is the period when your body shines like diamond, particularly between ages eighteen to twenty-three. That is the period you magnet every young man. You see men all around you. Incidentally, that's the time you're naturally consumed in your consciousness to look very attractive, too. What a good prey to the libertine!'

And all the young women exploded in laughter.

'My daughters, that's the time you really need to be on the alert and be careful. There are many wolves out there, ready to devour you and turn this your glorious period – this your prime beauty to shame and nightmare for you, for the rest of your life – watch it!' Agnes cautioned. 'You know what?' she smiled, 'We, women, are easily moved by sweet words and enticing gifts and the men understand these our underbellies. I want you to know this – one of the greatest weapons of controlling people is to do them favour – so favour can be slavery and a real trap. Tell the next person by you, "watch it".'

Automatically, an exciting sound of 'watch it' rent the air of the church in the most hilarious amusement.

'There is more to love than sweet words and enticing gifts,' Agnes said calmly when the auditorium was quiet again. There are several criteria of knowing a man who has genuine mutual attraction with you. You must have passion for each other to the point where you're ready to tolerate each other's weaknesses, and that means having a good knowledge of each other, too. The emphasis here is having a good knowledge of his intrinsic nature before marriage. Most marriages have failed because the couple did not know whom they actually married until they are in the marriage – too late then! The question now is: How do you know your prospective husband before marriage? I know that's what is on your minds, right now,' smiled Agnes, and her audience smiled back understandingly. 'It means having an intimate relationship with him during courtship. It involves some practical steps. Relationship often begins with casual notices accompanied by greeting and observing each other from time to time. From that stage, reasonable interest is generated and when the young man is showing more than a passing interest in you, you know it; every woman knows it. And if he's attractive to you, you should also begin to show interest in him to encourage him. From there, friendship will germinate. And the stage is set. Both of you are now friends – the friendship should develop gradually. First, it could just be at the point of talking about things around or about life generally and about both of you sometimes. And as you journey in the friendship both of you will begin to reveal yourself to each other through actions and words. As the friendship continues, it will come to a point where you take a walk together holding hands. As you move on, you begin to attend occasions together. By then, much has been revealed to each of you about the other person, and if the interest is sustained, you'll now move to the next stage – visiting each other home and get acquainted with relatives from both sides. At this stage, the friendship is getting intense and more intimate. This is where you get closer and begin to see how your intending spouse really is. And that is when both of you know each other's aspirations, abilities and character – his likes and dislikes. Once you reach this level where you know each other quite well, it is only then you can accept his proposal to be his life partner - when you're sure you can get on well with him and you are convinced that he is ready to accept you the way you are. Once you reach this stage of courtship before you walk the aisle to exchange marriage vows, it is very likely the marriage is going to succeed. I also want to advise here that your intending spouse should be a believer and follower of our Saviour so that it will be well with you. But in most cases what do you find? Couples rush into their marriages in the excitement of that early state of romance and before they know it, they're crashing out of it, just as it began. In most cases, it is due to some irreconcilable differences that exist between them. But if they have known each other well enough, such differences will not arise.' Agnes went further to tell the teenage girls the place of God in the preparation. 'No matter how prepared we are, how intimate we have been with our intending spouses, don't neglect the place of God, through his Holy Spirit. The Holy Spirit is our teacher (John 14:26). He teaches us all things. We must place our courtships or marriages in the hands of God in our prayers. He alone can guarantee the right choice in our marriage. At times, the devil can be a spoilsport in our lives if we are not strong in the Lord. It is my prayer that every one of you will have a successful marriage in Jesus' name!' declared Agnes by way of conclusion, and all her listeners chorused 'Amen!' amidst laughter and excitement.

An overwhelming round of applause greeted Agnes at the end of her presentation. The upcoming ladies of different churches of her denomination in the area that gathered together, in her local church, to listen to Agnes' tips, were quite pleased for having her presentation. They really felt they had a good insight into courtship. However, Agnes' presentation threw up several questions for clarification on some of the grey areas which had become somewhat controversial in recent times among young ladies. The first question during the question time was.

'Ma, I want to thank you very much for your presentation. I've learnt so much from it. But there's an issue I would like you to clarify here,' the young lady began. 'There's this notion that many of my peers believe in, even those of us in the faith, that these days, a young lady needs to touch up her look and appearance without necessarily being a coquette. They say, that simply makes her divine and up-to-date. That, if you don't do that, you should not be surprise when coarse and undusted men are the only ones showing interest in you – that real good guys like pretty girls for wives. Ma, I would like you to enlighten us on this.'

When the young lady had sat down, the rest of the girls were very happy that the issue was raised. One could see their excitement over the matter in their faces. Agnes thought for a while and smiled.

'Well, having a good appeal is not wrong. But looking enticing is putting yourself unnecessarily in men's way – that makes you cheap, indecent and desperate – just like whores out there,' she demonstrated with her hand. 'My dear, just be in the most good-natured and respectful manner and be hard working – you'll be the most desirable woman under heavens,' she stated.

'Ma, your talk centres on having a strong relationship with our intending life partner, in order to know him quite well before we plight our troth,' said another girl who wanted to ask a question.

'Yes,' returned Agnes encouragingly.

'Could that not tempt some of us into the sin of fornication especially when the young man is pressing for it, as men would like to, or is love-making part of the intimacy?' added the young lady and all of them burst into laughter.

Agnes did not really anticipate this sensitive part of the relationship. She reflected for some time. She knew that having pre-marital affair was fashionable among youths including those in the faith nowadays.

'Well, the Bible remains our guide. What does the Scripture says concerning this?' she asked in a strong tone, and the expected answer was categorically in the negative. 'No matter what the world thinks of it today, chastity remains the abiding rule for the unmarried members of the Christian faith. Please don't follow the trend. Jeremiah 6:16 warns us. *Thus saith the Lord, stand ye in the ways, and see, and ask for old paths, where is good way, and walk therein, and ye shall find rest for your souls.* Agnes read it out to them, and the issue was laid to rest.

Another girl was interested in knowing Agnes' reaction in a situation where a girl had accepted to marry a young man who loved her likewise, but her parents refused to accept her intending husband.

'My advice is that, you take a hard look at your parents' reasons for refusing, if in your own judgment, they will not pose any threat to your good marriage, then try all you can to persuade and entreat them to accept your intending spouse, while you're in prayer. I believe if it is the will of God, your parents will eventually accept him. However, I'll insist that you need your parents' approval of your marriage before you go into it. It's very necessary they give their blessing,' emphasized Agnes.

The last question was on the duration of courtship. To this, Agnes had no definite time. She only stressed the need to have a good knowledge of the intending husband before marriage and be sure that he was a man they could be happy with for the rest of their lives.

The female teenage camp-meeting came to an end on the fourth day successfully. At the end, every participant acknowledged that the camp-meeting was very insightful and interesting. Every resource person invited to handle a topic did so with great interest. The organisers handled each of the activity for the female teenagers in such a way that each participant was encouraged to explore and use her imaginative intellect to perform her task. The result was unimaginable – many of the teenage girls never believed they could carry out such tasks; they had never had the privilege and opportunity of doing before. One of such tasks was to cook and serve their meals themselves throughout the camp-meeting – only ingredients and the facilities for the cooking were provided for them. They also organized and arranged each of the items of the programme themselves. Some of them were assigned to prepare talk on some specific areas like handling domestic chores at home, making the home a home for your spouse and children, managing difficult times at home, and so on. They also prepared two series of personality interviews for two Christian women leaders who were invited for interviews on their various aspects of their lives with specific focus on managing a home and a career successfully. Quiz on the knowledge of the Bible and a scriptural debate session were all part of the activities. The camp-meeting was so filled with very rich and exciting activities that so much was gained and learned, by each participant, especially those activities that involved 'Do-it-yourself.' The camp-meeting was rounded off by a sermon delivered by the host pastor, Pastor Onokurhefe, which he titled: 'Ruth: A Role-Model for Every Christian Woman' from which he drew several virtues of a good woman.

The four-day camp-meeting was also a period of spiritual renewal. The third day was set aside for fasting and prayers while the fourth night was an all-night of praise worship. At the closing ceremony of the camp-meeting, all the participants had a refreshing experience in the Lord, besides practical life knowledge, as they went back happily to their various homes.

Pastor Onokurhefe and his wife, Sarah, were particularly grateful to Agnes for the huge success of the camp-meeting. They credited her with the success, being the one who co-ordinated the whole programme, besides being one of the resource persons during the camp-meeting. They both agreed that Agnes was a very ingenious and imaginative person whose enormous potentials could be properly harnessed for the growth of the church.

For Agnes, her major role in the camp-meeting was an eye-opener to what she could do for the good Lord. She realized she could even do more in the church if she had more opportunity. Her earlier fear of not being able to manage her business and her family with church activities, suddenly disappeared with her huge effort in the camp-meeting, as she did not have difficulty in handling all the interests, which she attributed to divine grace. After the assistance of the church in pulling her from her financial difficulty following the death of her husband, a powerful spirit of gratitude had overwhelmed her to the extent that she believed she owed the church and God so much. This unmatchable sense of gratitude so energized her during the camp-meeting that she performed the task which knew neither fatigue nor exhaustion excellently well.

CHAPTER NINETEEN

Agnes had become one of the most committed members of the church. She was always present in every weekly activity and participated actively in all. Pastor Onokurhefe and his wife were very happy with her new development, especially the leading role she was playing in the church lately. They both saw an all-consuming passion for God in Agnes and were prepared to encourage her to put in her best and optimal service in the church. Sarah had become very close to her. She paid her regular visits besides regular phone calls. This had cemented their relationship so much that hardly a day passed without one calling the other. They both worked together in piloting the women activities in the church. Many dormant activities of the women had been reinvigorated and reinvented. New ideas had also been introduced to encourage active participation of women in the church, and their efforts had hugely impacted on the church - women began to dominate the activities of the church

Majority of church members were very happy to see Agnes radiating warmth and joy in a most affectionate disposition in her leading role. They observed that she had regained her ebullient spirit after the agonizing and depressing demise of her husband whom many knew was inseparable from Agnes while he was alive – both of them were always hand-in-hand in the church – and they all thought that the devastating death of Robert would certainly wreck her life. When the news of Robert's death hit the church like a bomb, their first concern was Agnes. Hitherto, many believed that she would not be able to survive the shock and trauma. But when they saw her nowadays beaming with smile and happiness in the church, they felt equally happy that she was able to overcome it. It was incredible in their imagination. Whenever they saw such effusive spirit of joy in her, they always thought Agnes must be a super woman to have pulled through the wreckage of her husband's death.

But for Agnes, it was the saving grace of God that saw her through. It must be said here that it takes great will to pull through the loss of a very dear one at his prime, especially a beloved spouse. Among the four categories of human abilities: physical, social, intellectual and emotional abilities – the emotional ability is the most crucial in life because a very serious emotional distress is capable of overwhelming and upsetting the other three. This is why it requires great capacity to rally again after a strongly felt emotional trauma.

It was true that Agnes had recovered from the shock of her husband's sudden death, as she had regained and stabilized herself. One thing that accounted for this was her nature. Agnes was a woman of great phlegm. Besides her firm belief in the salvation of Jesus Christ in her growing up, her father always told her that she should always be willing to adapt to changing situations of life while trying to make the most of every circumstance, for a worthier living, as the journey of life was never even and smooth.

'Life is not fixed – it comes in different colours. Be prepared to face each and live through it to tell the story which makes you a stronger and wiser person,' explained Rev. Uloho to Agnes one day as she was about to leave for her university.

This struck hard in her memory and had taken a big place in her attitude towards life. Being a daughter of a pastor, she was brought up and kept on a tight rein around the church, so her life was strictly guided by rectitude. When she left the home for college, as expected, her father ensured that she attended their missionary college, where he handed her over to the college chaplain to watch over, so strict discipline was all she knew in her growing up which eventually took its rigid form in her adult life.

Although, Agnes had fully recovered, there was one aspect she would have to struggle with for a long time. Robert had left a deep vacuum in her life, that irreparable relationship with him would remain a huge void in her life. There were moments when she needed to talk to somebody who understood her heartbeats and her depth of feeling – her agonies, worries, pains and challenges. At such moments, she realized, not her children, not Sarah or any other close fellows, not even the Bible were helpful. At such times, the thought of Robert would overwhelm her and the memories of her past would come to occupy the space. On such occasions, loneliness and a strong sense of helplessness was all she could feel and she would become bitter. *Life can be so unkind and hapless,* she would reflect. This often happened at night in her bed she used to share with her late husband. There was a particular night she woke up, it was windy and raining outside. The sky was rumbling with thunder. She took a pillow and fondly folded herself with it. She did so for some time in her bedroom without having any particular thought on her mind, as she imagined the rain drops on her rooftop at such time of the night. The rain looked set to fall for a long time and the sky seemed to be gathering more clouds for greater intensity of the rain. The sky was shooting out lightning and thunder every second. The rain was dropping harder after sometime on the roof and Agnes could hear the dropping of water from the rooftop onto their compound. She could feel the coldness of the atmosphere outside through her bedroom window, which let the cold wind in, with the flying of the curtains, as one quarter of the window was open. The cold wind of the rain came into her bedroom as a sweet gentle breeze to refresh her. She got out of her bed at that moment, walked to the window and slid it open fully, to have a more refreshing breeze of the rain. She stood there basking herself in the breeze as it rushed in. She remained there for a while without any real purpose. The rain became stormy after a while. It was blowing from one side to the other. Some other times, it reversed itself and increased its intensity. Often, it whistled along as if in a solo, then suddenly, sounds of thunders and lightning would be heard again. It looked as if they wanted to tear the sky to pieces. Heavens appeared angry and was venting its anger upon the earth. Agnes was watching all these and at the same time refreshing herself. It came to a point when she became satiated and would like to go back to bed. But there was something inside her that was resisting her leaving, so she remained at the window, reflecting upon the heavy rain outside. After a little while, some consciousness of distant imagination came to her as she looked out of the window, now imagining the rain in distraction. Her face lowered, her eyes softened suddenly and she became glum. She left the window to her bed and began to sob upon her pillow. She wished Robert was there with her in the bedroom. She remembered when they both sometimes stayed awake in the night like this, and poured out their souls to each other, with some loving stroking amidst laughter and smile. At some other times, it was an occasion for resolving their differences and restored their love and affection. But now there was nobody to talk to, at such a time of the night when she might need to pour out her feelings to somebody that cared and understood her. She became heart-broken at that moment. She had tried to forget Robert by reading the Bible at such times or engage in some kind of chores in the home. But at times when the feeling was so strong, they would not help and she just could not help thinking of him. Sometimes, the more she tried to forget Robert, the more she missed him.

There was a particular night she missed Robert so dearly that she found herself not being able to overcome it, and did not know what to do to help herself, after she had tried several options that used to work for her. She felt for some activity she could use to relieve herself. Agnes walked out of her room that night to the toilet and desired to pass urine or faeces. But neither of them came out of her. She pressed for either as she sat on the toilet in anticipation. While she was still there, an idea came to her. She left the toilet to the living room and went straight for Robert's most presentable portrait in the home. Took it to her bedroom and began to look at it intently with great sense of admiration and devotion. The more she looked at the photograph, the more she admired her late husband. Agnes saw that her husband was looking very handsome and lovely in the picture. She looked at it more intently, searching for some deeper things to admire in Robert. She was now reflecting on several of his conducts and qualities and how he gave her so much love and affection as a husband. She remembered the time Robert proposed marriage to her. She was in her final year in the university then. It was late Friday afternoon when she had just had her siesta after a marathon lecture in 'Adult Psychology.' The first semester examination was just three weeks ahead. Some lecturers who had been lagging behind in their lectures were fixing extra hours now and then to cover their courses before the examination while students in their terminal classes were glued to their studies to ensure that they did not fail any of their courses to warrant extra year in the university – it was a year of anxiety and impatience – many of them were not certain about their lives after graduation, so they were very worried. One thing that many female final year students were most conscious of, at that time, as far as Agnes could remember was marriage. They were of age and would like to settle down to marriage life as soon as possible after graduation, rather than living with their parents again. While she was still on her bed in her hostel that afternoon, contemplating whether to have her bath and prepare to go to the library or should still remain in her bed for some time, all her room mates had left the room, for one engagement or the other. At that moment, she heard a strange knock on the door. She thought it was Joyce, her course mate with whom she studied. *She might have come to fetch me for private studies*, she thought. 'It's too early in the day,' she said to herself as she took a turn on her bed, without making any effort to open the door. She was expecting Joyce to burst in as usual – all female students usually did that. The door was ajar, the knocking was repeated twice hesitantly. It dawned on her immediately that the person at the door must either be a visitor or a male student.

'A minute please,' she answered.

She pulled off her transparent night dress at once and smartly put on a more presentable attire as she could find, rubbed her face smoothly with her hands before walking to the door. She screamed with joy at once, on opening the door the visitor was an ex-president of her Christian campus fellowship. She leaped forward to embrace him spontaneously and eventually led him into the room. There was no time. Robert wanted her to dress up quickly so that they could go to one of the restaurants on the campus, after making enquiries about some persons in their Christian fellowship. He wanted to have some quiet time with Agnes. Agnes quickly dusted herself up – rubbed her lips a little with her lipstick, brushed her hair and quickly traced her eye brows with an eye liner after some powder on her face and they left.

When they came out, Robert led her to a car parked in front of her hostel.

'Your car?' said Agnes excitedly.

Robert nodded his head and smiled. As Robert drove the car into one of the campus lanes and finally pulled up in front of a restaurant, Agnes was full of joy and excitement for being with the president of their Christian fellowship in the university three years ago. She thought life after graduation could really be good, as she noticed great improvement in Robert. He was looking more polished and had added more weight, making him more gentlemanly with an air of good living which evidently showed in his entire appearance. She wished she had already graduated with that kind of relaxed look. When they were seated over a small round table in the restaurant, Robert with the air of someone in charge signalled the waitress. He told Agnes to request for anything she liked. He was prepared to give Agnes a special treat. But she only requested for a mineral water. Robert was not surprised as he knew Agnes to be very modest and discreet in her conduct, though he felt disappointed, as he desired to give Agnes a good treat and make her very happy there. However, this was one of the good qualities he admired in her.

While he was the president of the Christian fellowship in the university, Agnes was the secretary of the union, though she was just in her second year then. By reason of her lower level she was least likely to be considered for executive position. But she had some exceptional qualities that recommended her. Apart from being very active in all their activities, she was very responsible and matured in her conduct, having deep knowledge of the word of God. Besides, her radiant look and warm disposition towards every member endeared her to everyone in the fellowship, so it did not take long before she became very popular in the fellowship. She often led the song ministration in their worship and she inspired everyone to participate in it actively. Agnes was also brilliant – she was among the top three in her class. All these qualities put her in a class of her own in the Christian fellowship yet she conducted herself very modestly. While Robert was the president, he worked closely with Agnes and saw Agnes as a special person among them. A lady, they, the male members, thought, none of them, was worthy to marry – her aspect was fair and arresting _ As far as all the young men in the fellowship were concerned, Agnes' graceful and amiable personality only recommended her to good men in the upper-class of the society, so none of them ever thought in the least of proposing marriage to her. Every one of them believed Agnes was too good for them. Though she was adored among the boys in the fellowship none of them ever betrayed such feeling to her. Back home in her father's residence within their church, she hardly went out. Agnes was always present in the weekly activities of the church. She was a chorister and the youth secretary of the church. Besides helping her mother in domestic chores, her other engagements were in the church. The highest standard of propriety was expected from the pulpit, as a result, her parents kept her and her two siblings on a tight rein, to keep them from misbehaving. There are times when every promising young man around sees a very fine young lady like Agnes with excellent upbringing, as too good for him to marry, turning her advantage to disadvantage, and she might probably end up marrying the most disagreeable man.

After two years of working with Ansco Company, Robert was able to rent and furnished a three-bedroom apartment for himself. He also bought a fairly used second-hand car, immediately after that. The thought of having a family of his own had become his latest pre-occupation. He wanted to marry as soon as possible and raise his own children. He believed that was the best way to live a responsible life. But he had no serious relationship with any lady at that time, and could hardly find any ladies around him that fitted into the personality of his dreamed wife. He surveyed in his mind the ones in the church with whom he had some intimacy and others whom he just had formal acquaintanceship. None of them appealed to him. The more he thought about his marriage, the more his mind went to Agnes. But he tried as he could to resist such feeling because he thought, Agnes whom he saw as a thoroughly bred high-class lady with a punctilious pedigree would not accept to marry a poor peasant farmer's child like him, his education notwithstanding. But there was a night Robert had a dream in which he saw himself marrying to Agnes in a very colourful ceremony in a big church. That dream turned out to be the propeller. He was convinced immediately that the dream was a divine revelation, and Agnes was God's choice for him. Through out that week Agnes became everything to him. Robert could hardly wait to propose to Agnes that weekend. He fasted and prayed through out that week for God's mercy to favour his proposal. The first sign of success as he thought, was when he was granted the permission to leave his work at mid-day on that week Friday, which was rare in his company.

'Nice to see you again after three years,' enthused Agnes barely after sitting down in the restaurant. 'So how has it been with you?'

'Fine.' answered Robert.

'What about you?' inquired him with much enthusiasm.

'You know it quite well – campus stress here and there – assignments, tutorials, seminar, of course, the long essay, then the final exam - all these to be carried out by this small body of mine.' Agnes thrust her two arms forward as she looked at herself to demonstrate how small she seemed to be. 'It's a whole lot of stress, effort and money. You don't know how I envied you when I first saw you at my hostel a few minutes ago – totally different and completely free from all the campus troubles,' sighed Agnes.

'O, poor you,' smiled Robert with a well-felt sympathy. 'But it'll be over very soon – you're counting days now,' he encouraged.

'Let the days run fast. I can't wait any longer. Everything I see now is life after graduation – in my sleep, in my thought and in my breath – In fact, everything in me sees life after graduation.'

'So what are your plans after graduation?' asked Robert trying to test the depth of his water.

'My plans?' repeated Agnes excitedly. Just then, it struck her that she had not really had a clear thought on it. 'Well, well...of course, get a job after National Service, and..,' she reflected with a smile for a second, 'what else will a young lady like me be wishing for? Get married, of course,' she added and smiled without really being conscious of any motive behind the question.

'So, who is the lucky guy?' said Robert with a betrayed curiosity and concern, though trying hard to hide his intention by looking sideway to avoid Agnes' eyes.

'The lucky guy is yet to show up. Probably, still groping around, looking for the way to find his better half,' sniggered Agnes. She laughed louder.

'That was before. The man has eventually found his way and he's now here!' returned Robert with a smile.

At that moment, Agnes' eyes flashed like a torch-light towards Robert's and she became serious at once. The message in her eyes was clear *I hope this is a joke!* Robert became serious too. He took a deep breath and recomposed himself. 'My dear Agnes,' he said calmly, 'truly, I'm here to see you, and to sincerely express a feeling that I have been struggling with since I first met you. A feeling? No, a conquering fire that has been burning inside me these four years. Yet I found it extremely hard to say – I didn't know why – Agnes, you're my love. My heart burns for you,' said Robert almost in a broken voice as his eyes were pleading for sympathy and understanding.

Agnes went silent. She really did not know what to say – her thought was not clear. She was least prepared for Robert's marriage proposal. She never expected this kind of feeling from Robert whom she simply saw as a brother in the Lord while he was the president of the campus Christian fellowship.

'My dear Agnes, it has come to the point where I can no longer do without you – you're always in my mind – I just cannot sleep again. That's why I'm here to let you know how I feel about you. You'll certainly kill me if you refuse me. Believe me, Agnes, I can't help it anymore,' pleaded Robert earnestly when he observed that Agnes was finding it difficult to make up her mind.

'Have you prayed over it?' said Agnes thoughtfully after some interval of silence.

'Pray? I've gone beyond praying. The good Lord has shown you to me,' returned Robert.

'As your wife?' said Agnes inquisitively.

'Yes,' Robert nodded his head.

Agnes gave a virginal blush and was speechless for a moment. She was quite unsettled and confused. 'Give me some time to think about it and equally inquire from the good Lord,' said her reluctantly after the interval of silence.

When they had exhausted their drinks and they had nothing else to say, Robert paid for the drinks and they left. Agnes alighted from his car when they got to her hostel. As she was walking away, Robert called her back.

'I've some things in the boot for you. I felt you might need them.'

Agnes hesitated for a while, 'What are they?' she asked reluctantly.

'Come and have a look!' answered Robert.

Robert came out of the car to open the boot quickly, and Agnes peeped in and saw a lot of provisions and fruits. She eyed Robert suspiciously, not knowing whether to accept them or not.

'Please, read no meaning to it,' pleaded Robert.

Agnes took one of the two packages, 'thanks,' she muttered as she was leaving.

Robert took the second one and followed her to the hostel. A few minutes later they were back to where the car was. 'Bye,' said Agnes softly with a little blush of shyness in her voice when Robert was about to start the car. Robert waved at her and started driving out of the hostel premises. Agnes turned her face, she could not resist her impulse to take a final look at Robert again, a look that followed Robert until he was out of sight.

Not too long after, Agnes realized that she was already falling in love with Robert.

'Ha, what's happening to me?' she muttered to her soul. She found that she could not sleep or do anything else that night – all her thought was now on Robert and the prospect of getting married to him and Robert became everything in her world - Her entire world had collapsed – Robert had taken over everything. The grip was so strong on her that she thought she had taken some drugs that had twisted her mind and she could no longer think clearly.

The following Saturday, Robert came to see Agnes again in her hostel. He had been very anxious to know Agnes' mind towards his marriage proposal. This time, Agnes received him with a more relaxed manner and had a more agreeable disposition towards Robert. She seemed to have appreciated better Robert's feeling towards her after the few days interval.

'Hi!,' she greeted, smiled at Robert, immediately she opened the door of her room to receive him. 'You're welcome,' she added as she led him into the room.

'Wini, meet Robert, a very good friend of mine. Though, you might not have met him, he graduated from here three years ago, in Civil Engineering,' she introduced Robert to a roommate of hers who was in the room then. Winifred looked at Robert, 'Welcome, sir,' she and smiled.

'My room mate and friend,' Agnes said to Robert.

'Don't mind Agnes, we quarrel and fight everyday in this room,' returned Winifred jokingly and they all began to laugh.

Few minutes later, Agnes and Robert left the hostel for the same restaurant they visited the previous Friday on the campus. Agnes agreed to eat rice and chicken with Robert which they washed down with a chilled wine, while they conversed very warmly amidst laughter, without touching the real crucial issue that had been burning in their minds. When they had exhausted their meals and drink, and felt satisfied that they had had enough time together, Robert wanted to go back. He could observe from Agnes' body language that she had acquiesced to his proposal. But he wanted to be certain.

'What do you say about what I told you last week?' he asked when Agnes was just getting out of the car in front of her hostel.

'Why are you worried about that? Leave it to time. Time'll tell!' returned Agnes with an exciting smile all over her face.

'It's okay, I'll abide by whatever rules you apply,' Robert smiled back.

'I dictate the pace and terms – I'm in control,' teased Agnes.

'And I'm ever willing to comply ma, as long as you're mine,' said Robert and they both burst into laughter. Since that day, exchange of visits and letters began to flow between them and their intimacy grew rapidly to the point where they could hardly do without seeing each other for one week. Immediately Agnes completed her compulsory National Service after graduation, they agreed to marry as they both came to believe that they were meant for each other. And their marriage eventually made them soul-mates – always in their best understanding whenever they were together.

She wished he was alive now to tell him how much she loved him. Agnes kept looking her husband in the photograph until she did not know when she started talking to it. 'I long to see you again. I long to hold you tight to myself and kiss your lips and be by your side again. When is it going to be, Robert?' At that moment her eyes blinked with tears and her spirit was breaking. She began to cry. Her eyes were dripping down tears freely. She lost completely the ability to hold back the tears, and she kept weeping. From time to time, she wiped her tears from her face with her wrapper. Saturated with sorrow and pain in her agony, her nose began to run too, as she could not help herself in this emotional outpouring.

After thirty minutes, she rose from her bed, wiped away her tears and her running nose, and reached for her Bible, and began to read. But she still felt the agony in her. In her pain and bitterness she exploded at once: 'I will pull myself out of this dark vale. I'll push myself through this dark tunnel. I'll certainly drag myself out this pitfall. Though its weight is so heavy on me, I'll never crumble under it in Jesus' name! Amen.'

When she opened her eyes finally, she discovered to her amazement that the agony that was almost shattering her to pieces was gone. She sighed for some minutes with great relief, not knowing what to feel – she was just sitting in one of the arm-chairs in the living room motionless, like someone who had just woken-up from a dreadful dream. She went back to her bed later and before she could reflect on the wonder of her prayer, she fell into deep sleep and slept like a baby. The voice of her first daughter woke her up the next morning, 'Mum, you slept so late – it's already seven.' Though, she was late in her preparation that day, she was very happy that the whole agony of the previous night was completely gone out of her, and was feeling rather very refreshed.

So when Agnes radiated that warmth of love and joy in the church, members looked at her with admiration of having an uncommon ability to overcome such devastating grief. But just like every human being, Agnes still had some cross to bear in her beaming and radiating smile.

CHAPTER TWENTY

Agnes' food vending had flourished to where she thought she could open a restaurant in the city centre in addition to her shed in front of the school. Many residents in the neighbourhood of Kuta College also came to buy her jollof rice which was generally considered to be very delicious and cheap. She had redoubled the quantity to meet the increasing demand, yet by 2.00 p.m. her food had been exhausted. Even then, customers kept coming to buy. This had dramatically increased her income and had decided to stop cultivating her vegetable farms, giving all her attention to her food business. These days, she could pay her house rents and her children's school fees without severity. She had bought more new clothes for her children and they had been making steady progress in their education. Two were already in college and were doing very well in their studies. Agnes was greatly encouraged by the boom in her food business and began to see the need to expand her food vending beyond the current level – she was thinking ahead – her children would soon be in the university and the cost of their trainings would go beyond what her food vending could support, so the idea of opening a good restaurant for the executive class in the business district of the city began to dawn on her. She thought she needed to start it early, so that, by the time her children began their university, the restaurant might have stabilised. She had started reading several books on cookery to equip her for the task. She was also consulting some established restaurant managers to have proper understanding of the challenges of managing a quality restaurant that would attract the executive class. Agnes had also decided to open a deposit account in a bank, completely dedicated to this venture. Every week she paid into the account every excess income of her food vending. She was very determined towards this pursuit and had been working very hard to see her dream come true before her children started their university. Having been totally committed to this course for two years, she had been able to raise a considerable amount of money to rent a space in the city business centre.

In spite of her gruelling business effort, Agnes still found time to attend to her children. She was balancing the two. Agnes quite appreciated the enormity of raising children by a single parent. She also appreciated the dream and standards of her late husband in the upbringing of his children and she was determined to do all she could to see that her husband's dream concerning them, was realised after his demise - the greatest debt she thought she owed Robert, her late husband – In this consciousness, Agnes ensured that she gave adequate attention to her children despite her demanding food vending. Her entire house chores were scheduled. She prepared a time-table for each of the activity with a roster, so everyone in the home knew what to do and when. This had reduced supervision and argument over who performed a particular duty in the home. At the outset, Agnes knew that for the time-table and duty roster to be followed strictly, she had to be there at home until everyone of them was accustomed to them.

Her food vending usually terminated before the close of school when her children would return home, but she had to hurry to the market immediately after sale to buy the food items and ingredients for the next day's business. That actually took some time. But once she returned from the market, preparation for tomorrow would begin in earnest till late night. 4 a.m. in the following morning, she was up again to complete the final cooking and preparation. Nevertheless, Agnes ensured that her children were carried along. For her to adequately handle the two important functions in the home, she had to be time conscious with the use of the time-table. There were times when following the time-table might be difficult but she would make every effort to ensure compliance, so that the children could get used to it. She never allowed excuses from the children. She wanted the culture of working with time to sink into them, which her own father taught her. After sometime, the children became used to the time-table and they learnt to work without supervision, however, where they had difficulty in a task, they would come to Agnes for guidance. There were times also when Agnes would leave her own task to see how they were performing their own and she would explain or direct them where she was not satisfied. Agnes particularly focused her attention on the two older ones. She particularly involved them a lot in the home chores – after they had completed their school home works. This was to ensure that she groomed them up very well in the home chores and inherently imbibed the culture of hard work, having the understanding that the youngest child behind could take a cue from them. This had helped the home a lot. There were times when Agnes would go to weekly church activities and she would direct the children on what to do while she was away. In that case, the oldest child, Oro, would take charge of seeing the various tasks through before her return and Oro had been very effective in doing so.

There was a day Agnes returned from 'prayer meeting' late. On her way home, she was very concerned for keeping the children waiting, as it was customary for her to serve their meals for them, and she felt so sorry that they must have been starving at home. She was really pained especially for Oke, the last child who was too tender for such experience.

'Oh, my children, I know you must be very hungry! I'm so sorry,' announced Agnes immediately she came home. She hurried to the kitchen at once to serve their meals. As she looked at the dishes in the kitchen, she observed that the children had eaten. There was some *eba* in a bowl which she presumed was left for her. She immediately dashed back to the sitting room where the children were watching television.

'You've eaten?' Agnes inquired with her eyes darting from one child to another in surprise.

'Oro prepared us food when you weren't coming,' answered the youngest child, Oke, who was just nine years old while the older two simply nodded their heads in the affirmative, not wanting to miss any of the quiz show they were watching.

'The remaining eba is mine, I suppose,' added Agnes.

'Yes,' answered Oro, her first daughter with some air of responsibility without really losing her attention from the television quiz.

Agnes quickly left for the kitchen, seeing that the children might not want to be disturbed from watching the riveting programme on the television. She was so full of satisfaction and joy in realizing that her children could take care of themselves very well in her absence. She would have really wanted to commend them, especially Oro for her initiative and proactiveness but for their devoted interest in the television show. She hoped to do that later when the programme was over.

She hurried over her dinner and took her plates to the sink in the kitchen. After that, Agnes took out the meat and chickens from the freezer to prepare them for her tomorrow's vending. She had earlier ground a large quantity of raw tomatoes which she braised that night. Agnes got all other food items ready that night for early morning preparation in the following day – measured the right quantity of rice in a basket, washed all the plates and dishes for her vending, and arranged them in different bowls that night. All these arrangements were to ensure that the next day's early morning preparation was without looking for one item or the other. That was how she had been doing it. Two hours after her dinner that day, she had all of these tasks completed. She then had her bath and was ready to plunge herself into sleep in anticipation of early morning rise for the completion of the whole preparation next day. By then her children had all gone to sleep. Agnes never allowed them to keep late night watching television. They were already used to her refrain, 'Early to bed, early to rise.' Agnes often thought over the preparation of her business food in her mind in the night before the actual preparation the next morning which made her effort quicker than expected.

Managing her food vending with all its preparations and house-keeping, including raising her children properly, were daunting and nerve-racking. But Agnes had developed a strong appetite for hard work that she never buckled under the strain. Her children began to take over the domestic chores from her gradually as they were growing up. But Agnes never allowed them to be involved in her business – she took absolute charge of that herself. Besides Sarah who exchanged phone calls with her and sometimes paid visits, she had no other companion other than her children, with whom she shared her struggles in the home. They were her friends and companions. Agnes was satisfied with that, bonded by common lot they had come to understand the challenges they had to grapple with as they moved on with life. This had wrought a cord of affection in the home which strung them together with much fondness and tenderness that could hardly be found elsewhere. And their home became a fortress of warmth and cordiality which had safeguarded them against all their daunting challenges of living.

There were times when they would all sit in the living room in the late evenings, after all the day's activities enjoying jokes and laughter; sometimes, one of them could be the object of their banter. But this did not mean that there were no differences sometimes in the home — it was not always laughter. There were times of serious disputations among the children, especially when their mother was away. It was often caused by disagreement which occurred when they were performing some activities together. It could be, for example, who would take the first turn in such an engagement. The shout of 'I first' in a simple matter could eventually lead to a serious disagreement. Although they had time-table and roster and the person assigned to do a particular task in the home, there were several other activities that could not be accommodated in the roster. These became the source of the disagreements.

Oftentimes, Ovo, the second child and the only boy in the family would want to bully Oro, his immediate elder sister and the first child. But Oro would always want to assert herself as the eldest child who should exercise the authority of their mother in her absence. Most often, the other girl, Oke, would want to take sides with her elder sister, making it two sisters versus one brother, and Ovo believed that as a boy he could dominate both girls, notwithstanding they were two. The disputation might end up in a fight and the entire home chores assigned to them that day might be left undone until their mother's return. Expectedly, each side always believed that their mother, who had the final say in matters of the home, would rule in its favour.

Once Agnes returned home, Oke, the youngest, would embrace her with the report of the disputation in her absence, usually from her angle. Then, Ovo would cut in to disagree and the entire matter would be presented immediately before Agnes.

Besides this kind of disputation, playing prangs on one other was another source of quarrels among the three children. Ovo the boy, liked playing pranks on his two sisters. Initially, they always cried to their mother to see that Ovo was punished, and they would be happy when their mother upbraided or spanked Ovo. But such punishment hardly changed Ovo's attitude, rather he would be more angry and preferred to do some nasty thing to the person that reported the matter to their mother, by way of retaliating — he would be angrier and more vindictive causing more trouble. So Agnes often received another report of what Ovo had done again immediately after the first one. In such circumstance, Agnes would resort to chastening Ovo who usually came to her with a scowled and forbidding look when he was called to answer the accusation against him after the earlier one, knowing very well that he had no good explanation, but merely reacting in his inclining bad temper.

'Why are you so troublesome and difficult...I don't like this thing you're doing...Be nice to Oro and Oke. They're your sisters,' Agnes would tell Ovo.

'They make me angry,' returned Ovo in a crumbling voice which often led to his crying. Then, Agnes would be short of what to say. She always ended by counselling Ovo to be kind to his sisters. One day, while Agnes was chastening him, the boy broke down in endless cry. He felt very bad and thought his mother was not being fair to him, as she always adjudged him guilty in the home – a grudge that had made him more bad-tempered and malicious towards his sisters. Agnes was just watching the boy crying. After some time, she attempted to hold him to herself. She wiped his tears away and cuddled him.

'Please, that's okay, stop crying. I only wanted you to be nice to your sisters, okay?'

But Ovo rebuffed her.

'Leave me alone!' he howled at his mother and disengaged himself from her and began to cry louder.

'Ovo! Why?' returned Agnes in a most disappointing and shocking voice.

'You always take side with them,' ventilated Ovo grudgingly, as he pointed in the direction of his two sisters within the home.

'I blame you 'cos you're at fault. I'm not partial. I'm the mother of you three. I can't be partial. If they're at fault, I'll blame them as well, and you know I do sometimes blame them when they are wrong,' said Agnes appeasingly while drawing him close to herself again and started patting him on his back. She wiped off the tears in his face and eventually sat him on her laps.

'Ovo, I love you as well as your sisters. I want each of you to be nice to one another. Love one another, okay?' She rocked him a bit on her laps like a baby while Ovo was gradually yielding to her placatory entreaty. He felt for once being showered with tenderness against his two sisters by her mother and was savouring it like a little baby enjoying the sweetness of sucking its mother's breast milk in a dreaming half-sleep. Ovo eventually became calm before his mother left him.

As time went by, Agnes observed that he was gradually becoming less troubling to her two sisters and this gradual change in Ovo gave Agnes much ease of mind. And she encouraged Ovo by always commending him highly whenever he did something good. As the children grew into full adolescence they began to behave more maturely. They had also shown great promise, performing excellently well in their academics – this had gladdened and encouraged Agnes, as she saw the children's development as a positive sign of a great future.

This had hugely rekindled her spirit. She was working so hard both in her business and in the children to see them into university. Agnes had been brooding and working on her dream of owning a good restaurant in the centre of the town. She had been able to save a considerable amount of money after few years for the venture.

When the children were in their full adolescent stage, Agnes also felt that it was time to bring into their consciousness the challenges they might face when they were out of the home and the possible ways to tackle them. One of her mantras to the children these days was: *Whatever you do, depend on your heavenly Lord, the arms of fresh will fail you.* At every given opportunity, she always reiterated this to them so that it could sink into their psyche. Agnes believed that only the heavenly Lord was wise because He was all knowing – 'He knows the end of situation from the beginning. But no human, no matter his knowledge, can fathom what happens in the next second, so trust and depend upon Him that beholdeth and knoweth all things,' she would admonish. To Agnes, this belief was the foundation of successful living. She believed that, 'It takes the guide of the Almighty God to navigate the turbulent journey of life on earth.'

A year later, Oro the first child completed her college with a very good grade. She also passed the entrance examination to the university that year. It was a great celebration in the home. However, there was a challenge. Agnes had not been able to set up the restaurant and if all the financial requirements for Oro's admission were met, what would remain would not be enough for Ovo and Oke's school fees at the college and for the general upkeep of the home. Besides, the annual rent for their apartment would be due in two months' time. This was another nerve-racking period for Agnes. But there was a kind of confidence in Agnes that kept her from worrying too much. She was calm and hopeful, believing that all the difficulties would just blow away like the wind at their due times. She had a strong feeling of some unexpected favour coming her way.

Surprisingly, she received a registered mail, a parcel, via Ansco Company, a week after. The letter piqued Agnes' curiosity immediately she saw that it was from overseas, Canada. She ripped it open at once. Behold, she saw a bundle of brand new Canadian dollar notes. Instantly, Agnes was enveloped with wild excitement and her eyes raced straight to the sender's name at the bottom of the letter. 'Lea, you're forever a friend of Robert!' she screamed with great excitement. Agnes looked at the bundle of the crisp dollar notes with great admiration for a while and exclaimed, 'What a friend! What a friend! What a friend, indeed!' She thought of other words to say, but she had none coming because she was too excited to think, too overwhelmed with joy, as she tried to recollect some flashes of memory of this 'God's angel' while he was in Ansco company. She could still remember Lea's warm smile when he came to bid them goodbye two days before leaving finally for Europe to join his family. She saw that friendly smile of his now as they shook hands at that particular moment of time. Agnes could hear his lyrical voice afresh, telling her as he looked into her eyes and said finally with beaming smile, 'Agnes, you're a wonderful woman. Please, take care of Robert, my only African friend, as you've always been doing.' 'You can always be sure of that, Lea,' smiled back Agnes. She was about to sob as she relived that last moment with Lea at his parting but she resisted her emotion. 'No, I won't cry, I should rather be happy,' she said to herself. She went back to the letter at once and began to read:

Dearest Agnes,

It came to me like a thunderstorm; a landslide. It was unbelievable and I was crushed out of my breath for days. My entire family were grieved by the news of Robert's death. There was no way to link up with you and your children by phone, which heightened my anxiety and I was worried sick. Robert's death was confirmed to me by some Ansco's old staff members I hooked up to, later.

What pained me most was that, I got the shocking news six years after his death! I could have been there at his funeral to pay Robert my last respects and compliments. Oh, what a pain! I remember he was always entreating me to join the Christian faith, which I often laughed at. But now, I believe the only way to honour Robert, a dear professional colleague and friend who made my stay in Africa a very pleasurable and memorable one, is to turn to his faith, which he so desired of me. My family and I are now Christians and of his denomination. We're Baptists!

Agnes, how are you and the kids? Just wondering how tough it must have been for you. How're you coping? It must be terrible without Robert – just can't imagine it – I believe God's doing His miracle. Enclosed is $50,000 to meet some of your challenges.

Nancy, my love, and our two lovely daughters send their greetings. My very kind and warmest regard to you all, cheers.

Best Wishes

Lea

CHAPTER TWENTY-ONE

The lifeline of fifty thousand Canadian dollars from Lea was a huge lever for Agnes. With it she was able to settle Oro's university fees in her first year and set up a high quality restaurant in the business centre of Otu. Three weeks after Agnes had begun her restaurant, the chief inspector of education in the town, came one early morning to Kuta College with a bulldozer, to demolish all the sheds in front of the school and warned the college management against allowing any sheds in front of the college from then onwards. And all the women that used to vend there were stopped from bringing their wares. Agnes received the news with thanksgiving to God, for saving her from the crisis into which the drastic measure would have thrown her.

Oro went to her university to study medicine. While she was in her third year Ovo gained admission to university, to read Electronic Engineering. By the time, Oro was doing her internship with a specialist hospital, Oke the last child was in her first year in university, studying Economics.

Agnes' restaurant had been flourishing. The first year was a great challenge as patronage was very low. In the second year, she was able to break even and from then the business began to rise as Agnes worked with greater zeal and grit. She went round some firms and companies within the business district to propose direct supplies of lunch to their executives who hardly had the time to leave their offices for repast, an innovation that was welcomed by many executives in the district. In the third year, several more companies and firms became more interested in her service. Agnes had to employ several more hands especially for outdoor services. She purchased a fairly used second hand van for quick delivery of her foods to their various destinations. Her outdoor patrons had also begun to request for ceremonial repasts in her restaurant whenever they had special occasions like seminars, conference and other occasions where special delicacies where required.

Demand for her out-door services became very high in the fifth year of her restaurant. She decided to establish a big catering outfit with a special unit for outdoor services in the business district. It had been a boom all the way since then and Agnes never knew any lack in her world again. Two years after, she bought a brand new Toyota four-wheel drive. A year later, she was able to buy a bungalow for herself in the most exclusive and premium residential area of the town, where the super-rich preferred to live in and her entire life was completely changed. Agnes now wore a patrician look, quite amiable and graceful in her appearance and manner with the dignified comportment of an established life. No single trace of her previous troubled world was seen in her life any more.

Six years after, eminent dignitaries from all walks of life gathered together for the opening ceremony of an ultra-modern superstore of three-storeys in the business district. It was a superstructure with the latest architectural innovation of very elegant physiognomy. It stood out as the latest architectural master-piece in the district, with marble exterior, having its front view in gold glass. The special guest of honour at the ceremony was the Minister of Commerce and Industry who was to declare the superstore open officially for business. Pastor Onokurhefe and his wife, Sarah, were in the front row with the minister. They were brimming with smiles. Their hearts beat with joy as they beheld the edifice with admiration and thanksgiving to God, for His wonderful blessing upon Agnes and they saw themselves as part of the success story. It was a gratifying moment for them. Several prominent members of the pastor's church were equally present to witness the occasion.

Also present at the opening ceremony were members of late Robert's consanguinity. Two among them were also in the front row, having a great sense of pride in the superstore, about to be declared open. Oro, Ovo and Oke were there, seeing to every arrangement of the occasion. They were now grown-ups. Oro who was now working with a public hospital as a medical doctor celebrated her child's birthday a week ago after two-year marriage. Ovo had just got a job with a reputable multi-national petroleum company. He had been scheduled to travel to Holland for a six-month intensive training on the job while Oke, the last was in her third year in the university. The three were poised to make the occasion a success. They moved and worked together with kindred spirit, consulting and cross-checking with one another. They had told their mother to leave everything in their hands and were prepared to let their mother know that they had come of age.

Agnes was fully relaxed trusting that her children would be able to prove themselves. Her air was one of fulfilment as she sat by a specially unique family whom she considered as not just friends but part of her family, without whom, the whole inspiring success-story of Agnes who was now the toast among women would not have been realized. Lea and his family who flew in from Canada the previous day, were quite thrilled to meet with the family of late Robert Onoyoma, and were wild with ecstasy to discover that their 'mustard seed' of fifty thousand Canadian dollars which was intended for upkeep had turned Agnes' family into a millionaire. Agnes had earnestly entreated Lea to be present at the ceremony, to personally witness the wonder the Almighty God, had wrought in her life and family through him. Lea made the journey with his family. Agnes and her children were the happiest on earth that day they received Lea and his family at their international airport. They were like angels, descending from heaven in their eyes.

The business of declaring the ultra-modern superstore open had just begun. It was time for the chairman of the occasion to make his introductory speech. Lea looked at the gathering of eminent persons, look at the edifice about to be declared open – how magnificent it was – and he remembered his fifty thousand dollars as the germinating seed of what had become a business conglomerate. He looked at Agnes, the lady behind all the business wonder. He also gave further thought to her challenge of raising her children single-handedly and was silent for some moment, completely speechless. He was putting everyone in suspense as the gathering was waiting for him to make his speech.

'Distinguished ladies and gentlemen, this is my proudest moment
in all my life. I'm so happy to be here to witness the opening ceremony
of this masterpiece,' he pointed at the superstore. 'I feel so fulfilled in it.
I'm not here to tell this august gathering the story behind it. But let me
seize this opportunity to say that, in all my life, I had never seen a
woman like Mrs. Agnes Onoyoma – she is a woman that has convinced
me that the whole earth will turn to gold if women are entrusted with
the biggest political and economic fortunes across the globe. I had
never seen an enduring and determined spirit like hers,' he touched
Agnes who was beside him and a resonant applause came from the
audience. 'I tell you, Mrs. Agnes Onoyoma will ever remain an
inspiration to all generations of women. With that, I welcome you all
especially our very special guest of honour the Minister of Commerce
and Industry, who is equally a woman, to the opening ceremony of this
ultra-modern superstore - my honour, madam,' Lea gave her a bow.
'Please do have a wonderful and pleasant opening ceremony of this
spectacular edifice,' he pointed at the superstore again. 'It is my firm
belief that it will certainly add value to the economy of this great city.
Once more, I welcome you all.'

And Lea took his seat while his audience applauded him.

Next to address the occasion was the owner of the superstore, Mrs.
Agnes Onoyoma. The master of ceremonies did not mince words when
he said, 'Honour should be given to whom honour is due. With this, I
earnestly request everyone in this gathering to give a standing ovation
to this great woman, Mrs. Agnes Onoyoma, in appreciation of her
sterling personality and immense contribution to the business of this
city.' And it was done with all pleasure and admiration. When Agnes
had picked the microphone, she looked at her audience and saw that
they were all eager to hear her, as if her address was of great value to
them. She could see the awe with which every eye beheld her,
passionately waiting to hear her, and she was overwhelmed with joy –
not really knowing how to begin – she felt so honoured by their high
regard. She thought for a moment and smiled to her audience and

everyone smiled back and applauded her excitedly. *Now, I know that faith can move mountain.*

And her audience clapped again in appreciation, while her pastor and his wife, Sarah, nodded their heads, in appreciation of her opening remark which they considered as a window into her full address.

'My distinguished guests, ladies and gentlemen, the M.C. and the chairman of the occasion, my very dear Mr. Lea Alan, to whom I owe everything,' she touched Lea to identify him to her audience,' have showered me with some high accolades that might make some of you think I am extraordinary. Sincerely speaking, there is nothing extraordinary about me. The glory goes to our Almighty God who owns the heaven and the earth and all their resources and wealth. Please join me to appreciate the good Lord in a standing ovation.'

And everyone stood up and clapped with her.

'Thank you very much. The good Lord will richly bless you for that. Let me also use this opportunity to share with you my own definition of success, using my own experience of life. For me, success or fulfilment comes from the will to rise over and above every challenge and trial that confronts us in our lives and such will requires great forbearance and tenacity, which comes from absolute and resolute faith in the Almighty God and in ourselves too. Some of us are not properly well-informed and guided: We look up to the gracious Almighty God to do things for us, not knowing that the good Lord has already equipped us with the capacity to do those things ourselves. It only takes a step of faith to make them happen,' affirmed she, and many nodded their heads in appreciation.

Pastor Onokurhefe was wishing for more. He firmly believed that successful people like Agnes who had experienced the goodness of God exceedingly were in a better position to make people had faith in God and His living words.

'Tell them,' he urged Agnes on, and everyone applauded spontaneously.

Agnes reflected for a moment as she rolled her eyes for other things that made it possible for her to pull through her most trying times in the past.

'My distinguished guests, I owe my late parents so much. When I was growing up I thought I was passing through steep narrow pathway, without any little space for my own feeling and desire which I bemoaned and resented as a child. But as I look back now, I have come to know better – if not for that stiff pathway, I would not have been able to withstand the excruciating, demoralising and frustrating experience I had in my later life. Truly, the matrix of that strong character was formed in my upbringing. Indeed, I'm very proud of that background now,' smiled she and everyone gave a resounding applause. 'I believe the Almighty God knew what I was to face in my later life, that was why He allowed me to pass through my disciplinarian parents. On the whole, I can say with certainty, reflecting backwards now, that the road to success is strewn with bumps and pot holes. It requires a lot of efforts and care to pull through it, and that demands discipline from the outset. Let me also seize this occasion to appreciate my local church that rallied me up in my darkest hour of difficulty and trial. Without them, probably, there wouldn't have been this turn-around we're celebrating here today!'

And a round of applause reeled out of the gathering in appreciation.

'Now, talking about this complex, this architectural beauty,' she pointed to the superstore, 'I'm devoting and dedicating it to the service of widows and orphans, anywhere they could be found in our society. By His Grace, every proceeds from this business shall go to them,' said she emphatically and a standing ovation rent the air for a prolonged time.

True to her word, Agnes used the profit from the superstore at the end of that year to offer foodstuff to several orphanages, gave capital funds to some widows to start small scale businesses of their own and used the remaining part to give scholarship to few orphans who displayed exceptional brilliance in their schools. In the following year, she saw to her great delight that the profit from the superstore had tripled and she decided to put up a foundation which she christened 'Robert foundation For Widows and Orphans.'

CHAPTER TWENTY-TWO

Elaborate preparations were being made for Oke's marriage. For Agnes, the marriage was to be used to show how the gracious heavenly Father had turned the hopeless life of the family to one of celebration and envy. Oke was particularly fortunate, not only for being the last child of the family, having all the attention of the rest members, her marriage was also coming at a time when the family was well established financially, so every of their good event was an occasion for celebration; an opportunity to express their great joy and thanksgiving both to the society and to their gracious God.

Just before the marriage of Oro, Agnes' first child, Agnes thought it necessary to reunite and reconcile with her late husband's family. Culturally, her children belonged to that family as lineage was by paternity. So before Shadrach, Oro's suitor, was introduced to the Onoyoma's family at Okah, Agnes drove down one weekend with her three children. Then, things had started getting better for them – Agnes had just bought her first personal car. She drove straight to Okome's house. None of the family members of Onoyoma could recognise her and her children who were now grown-ups. They all thought Agnes and her children were strangers from the city who wanted to make some enquiry. When Agnes and her children alighted from the car, curiosity tinged with some hesitation was what they could notice from those who came to them, probably to find out whom they wanted to see. First to come, were several children who were playing in the compound. They were immediately attracted by the exquisite car that pulled up near where they gathered. The children greeted them in their language, as they looked at the good-looking strangers with great interest and admiration. Then, several women, believed to be the wives of late Robert's siblings came forward to greet them, with intention of finding out what the city-looking strangers wanted in their compound.

Agnes recognised two among the four that came. Though they were now older, they were among those that jeered at her when she was asked to come and explain to the family how her husband died. Agnes looked towards them and smiled.

'My dear sisters, is Papa in?' Agnes inquired, pointing towards the main door of Okome's house.

'Yes, Madam, you can go in,' the elderly among them answered. She was the wife of Okome.

'Thanks,' Agnes replied and she walked straight with the children towards Okome's main door. 'Is papa in the house,' announced Agnes as she tapped the door with much animation, waiting to hear the voice of Okome.

'Who's there?' asked Okome.

'Papa, your daughter in Otu,' answered Agnes.

'My daughter in Otu? My daughter in Otu?' repeated Okome to himself, who was now very old. He thought for some seconds but could not remember having anybody he knew in Otu.

'Okay, come in and let me see you,' Okome added, and Agnes with her children walked in. Okome peered at each of them intently, trying to recognise them, as they greeted him. He took a closer look and examined them, one after the other, trying harder. But they were not familiar to him. Agnes beamed with smile, laughing at Okome's fruitless determination to identify them was producing.

'My daughter, please don't laugh. You know I'm old, my memory and my sight are now failing me,' said he amusingly while still making all effort to identify them. 'My daughter, give me your name. I think I'll remember that if truly you're close to me as you have said,' persuaded Okome.

'Agnes, late Robert's wife.'

'Oh, oh, oh, my Goodness, late Robert's wife!' Okome exclaimed as his face suddenly shone with surprise and elation. 'And who are these ones?' he pointed at the children with curious speculative attention.

'Robert's children, of course,' answered Agnes with a smile.

'Onoyoma, my blessed late father! May your soul leap for joy in your resting place. These are Robert's children! Our own children!' exclaimed Okome.

He embraced them warmly one after the other.

'I'm so glad to see you, my children,' he said excitedly. 'You're all welcome, my dear children. Please sit down,' pointing at the old benches in his living room and shambled towards the main door of the living room. 'Hey, who's there? You people should come, we have guests in our midst,' he shouted as soon as he reached the main entrance into his house. 'All of you, come and receive your beloved siblings from the city,' he announced.

And many members of the large Onoyoma family began to come in one by one, including the women and children, as Okome's house was surrounded by the houses of his siblings. Within few minutes, Okome's house was filled with his extended family members, their faces were alight with joy and excitement for the return of those they thought were lost forever. More so, when they were wearing very impressive looks, having very impressive good living in their appearance.

At once, drinks and kola nuts were brought in for their guests, and after prayer for good health, long life and prosperity for everyone who would share in the drinks and kola nuts, Okome directed that they should be passed to everyone present, after he had particularly prayed for each of their guests. All of them drank with jubilation. And after a while, Okome thought there was need to be more particular. He had just remembered the last incident between the family and Agnes which left behind strong animosity. More unpleasant was the dispossession of Agnes and her children of late Robert's important belongings. Now, seeing Agnes and her children looking much better and seemed not to bear any grudge against them, Okome and the rest Onoyomas were filled with great sense of compunction. So behind their smiling faces and the celebration was a hurting remorse in their minds – a shame they were just struggling with in the presence of Agnes and her children, who appeared not to have remembered anything about their wrong. This even made their guilt more tormenting to them – so there was no pizzazz in their entire laughter and celebration. It was hollow and artificial.

Old Okome was just thinking of how to mend fences with their guests, so that the celebration would be complete and true.

'Our dear wife, I really want to thank you so much for your coming, especially your coming with the children. They've grown so quickly,' Okome smiled and took a second look at them. 'You've actually been taking good care of them. We thank you so much!' said he. 'Our beloved wife,' he took a thoughtful look at Agnes who seemed to know the direction to which Okome was heading and became sober at once, 'We wouldn't want to pretend to you.'

He paused for a moment, as his eyes were fixed on Agnes, trying to assess her feeling vis-a-vis how to say what was in his mind.

'Let me put it plainly, my dear, we've offended you in the past. Please forgive us as a family,' he appealed and the faces of all the Onoyoma family members in the house became drawn with sadness, including the women and they nodded their heads in admission of their guilt.

'Please, we're sorry, forgive us,' they all added their voices to Okome's.

Agnes was silent, while the entire house was anxiously waiting to hear from her. The sad memory of those ugly incidents were rushing back to her at that moment. Her eyes softened and began to well up. She bent her head down in tears.

Okome and the rest members of the Onoyoma family became deeply touched and were completely speechless in their own pain.

'Well, I've nothing to forgive. I bear you no grudge,' said Agnes at last in a broken voice after wiping her tears. 'My late husband's people, God Almighty knows I bear no rancour against you. That's why I'm here. I understand the custom which you were applying in my circumstance. But I feel we should be open to reason in applying old traditions. You dispossessed me and your children the belongings your late brother left for us when he died and we were left with nothing to cope with. It was really, really painful. But we thank the Almighty God for His mercies,' said Agnes as she raised her two hands up.

'It was indeed painful, our beloved wife. That's why we're truly sorry for those actions we took against you. Please forgive us,' Old Okome pleaded again.

Every one of them in the house focused their attention on Agnes, searching her eyes for a sign of what all of them longed to see – forgiveness – all their eyes were pleading for it as they all looked at her intensely for this and only this, which seemed to be the antidote of that which tormented their souls at that moment.

Agnes's children were touched by their singular act of penitence and they looked at their mother too, with an eye full of sympathy and compassion for their kin. *Mum, it's time to let go of the whole pain of the past*, they seemed to say with their look. Agnes heaved a sigh of temporary relief and wiped her eyes and her running nose. By her very nature, she did not need their intense pleading for forgiveness. In her very heart, she had already forgiven them. But deep emotional pain of the past can be very hurtful when one is confronted with it afresh. It is like going through the whole pain all over again and that was exactly what Agnes was going through at the moment. She lifted her face and wiped it with her cloth again and looked at everybody in the house.

'Please excuse my emotion. I couldn't help it,' said she as she was struggling to overcome her feeling. 'Sincerely, I quite understand the fact that you were only following a practice that has been there for years. But it was really painful on my side.'

At that moment a flood of emotion overwhelmed her again and she began to cry aloud — a gut-wrenching experience she never anticipated from herself.

Many of them in the house wanted to console her but Old Okome stopped them. He wanted her to cry the pain out and free herself from the deep hurt, locked up in her mind over the years. And Agnes wept openly and profusely like a baby for a while, every one of them gazing at her with compassion and were thoroughly sorry.

Agnes regained herself and directed her children to go to her car and bring all the drinks in the boot. She had come with three cartons of soft drinks including a carton of wine. When the drinks were deposited in the centre of the sitting room, Agnes requested for a flat plate. She put some money on it while the entire persons in the house gazed at what she was doing with awe. They were waiting patiently to understand the meaning of her action.

'My husband's people, my children's family and my family or have you cast me away?' said Agnes with a smile.

'No!' the house chorused.

'So my people, I am happy to be with you today. I'm here with your children,' he pointed at her children sitting beside her, 'to assure you that we are still part of you, especially now that they've grown up. Whatever misunderstanding we might have had in the past is already by-gone. Thank God, Papa has said it all,' she pointed at Old Okome. 'Well, if you look at the table and around it, you'll see some presentations. When we were about coming, I thought it necessary to come with them. There's a token sum of money attached to the drinks as our culture requires. It is for us all,' she waved her hand round the house. 'Papa,' she directed her attention to Old Okome, 'we need your prayers,' she smiled and there was a general laughter. 'My children and I greet you all, *isie aguare*,'* she shouted finally to end her presentation.

'*Iyah!*'⁺ responded the entire house excitedly and there was a general laughter of satisfaction, while Old Okome brimmed with smile. He was overjoyed with what was happening. He never expected Agnes to turn out in this manner, after their ill-treatment of her. He was too amazed with Agnes display of magnanimity. Intermittently, his eyes roved between Agnes and what she had presented and chuckled, totally lost in his admiration for her.

'I don't know what to say,' he shook his head, still looking at the drinks and money on the table with disbelief.

---

* I greet every one
⁺ An acclamation to a speech at a meeting by those present

After the drinks and the money had been accepted, it was time for Old Okome to pray. Old Okome looked at Agnes with great smile as he held a glass of drink towards her - His joy knew no bound.

'Our good wife, I really don't know how to thank you for your benevolent spirit. You're a rare woman to find. I think you're specially created with extra-ordinary good nature. We, the Onoyoma family, is uniquely blessed to have you as a wife in the family. May the Almighty God be with you always. I say may the Almighty Creator of heaven and earth who sees the hearts of humans and rewards them accordingly, continue to lift you up.'

'Amen!' answered Agnes while kneeling before him and the 'amen' was re-echoed by the entire house.

'May you live long with good health and greater prosperity. As the head of the Onoyoma family today, I pronounce you a mother in the family – you're no longer a wife but a mother.'

'Amen,' the entire house chorused.

'May God bless you. I say may the Almighty Creator of the whole universe bless you and bless you and bless you!'

'Amen!' chorused the entire house again including Agnes.

'You shall be blessed and you'll remain blessed,' emphasized Old Okome.

'Amen!' the house chorused once more as Agnes stood up to receive her drink from Old Okome. Old Okome also prayed for Oro, Ovo and Oke, saying that each of them would stand out in the society for their great deeds. Throughout that day, there was a great celebration in the family of Onoyoma.

And since then Agnes had been visiting the family from time to time and had fully reunited with them. Whenever she went to Okah, the family members were sure of some fabulous gifts – bags of rice and expensive township clothes for the women while choice wines and good money for the men to share. She had been taking care of most of their financial needs as her husband used to do, which brought great joy to the Onoyomas at Okah.

Preparations towards Oke's marriage had just begun. Oro and Ovo had fully settled down in their marriages. Ovo married two years earlier and his marriage had been blessed with a male child, Kevwe, a year ago. His birth was highly celebrated in the family. Ovo's wife, Christabel, a nurse by profession, was with her mother-in-law, Agnes, for a whole month immediately after Kevwe was born. Agnes felt particularly joyful – Kevwe was her first grand male child. She personally wanted to nurse and nurture mother and child with all the joy and tenderness of a loving grand-mother who felt so privileged of gradually becoming an established 'Granny.' At the expiration of that one month with 'Granny,' Christabel and her baby, Kevwe, were glowing so much that Christabel wished she could stay with her mother-in-law for a longer time, particularly when she found Oke who was about her age a welcoming and loving companion in the home. And 'Granny' who was so fondly attached to the baby made the family home, a real comfort for Christabel. At her leaving Christabel vowed to come back in her second child-bearing.

Oke was looking forward to a good and relaxed marriage, just like her two siblings. And being the last child and the pet of the Robert's family, she was enjoying the attention of her mother and her two older siblings - she relished her special place in the family. This was why getting Oke's hand in marriage was a daunting challenge for any young man. Having all the care and attention of her family made it difficult for any of her potential suitors to please her with enough attention and affection — It was like a race with the wind. Yet many promising young men were never tired of trying. Oke was uniquely favoured with beauty, her magnetic physical appeal and her good background made Oke a priceless gem among young ladies.

Of all the determined suitors, Fred eventually won Oke's heart. Fred was good looking, dandy and which predisposed him towards philandering and was very clever at his game. He was a young man with the gift of the gab — full of blandishments, so he found girls very easy to have. Perhaps, that was the reason why he was able to win Oke who was a hard nut to crack. Fred came across Oke the first time at her mother's superstore. He drove a glitzy sports car to the superstore to collect some items. Immediately Fred saw Oke, he was swept off his feet, a predilection that possessed him to the point of wanting to do anything to win her. He went straight to Oke at once. Oke was very busy with stock-taking in the superstore that evening. He wanted to speak with her but Oke appeared too busy for such frivolity.

'Good evening, are you one of the sales staff here?' started Fred.

At that moment, Oke raised her eyes to see who was addressing her.

'Not really, but what do you want? I can assist,' returned Oke with much business inclination.

'Really, I've got all I wanted,' answered Fred with a smile. He considered Oke for some seconds with a kind of admiration that was pleading for a little attention. Oke looked at him, expecting to attend to his need. But she observed that the young man seemed to be confused or not knowing what he wanted to say, so she focused her attention on what she was doing. But she noticed that Fred was still trailing behind her as she was taking inventory.

'Please, what do you want? Why are you hanging around me?' said Oke impatiently.

'Like to have a tête-à-tête with you,' smiled Fred.

'That's all?'

'That's all.'

'Not now,' Oke shook her head in the negative, 'you can see that I'm very busy. But I'm always here in the evening.'

'That's okay, I'm Fred, nice to meet you,' he stretched out his hand for a handshake.

'Nice to meet you, too,' returned Oke.

And they shook hands. Fred left almost immediately. When he got home, he dropped his purchased items on the floor of his bedroom and slumped into his bed. He was completely lost in thought. He wished he had more time with Oke at the superstore. He could hear her sweet voice again as he reflected on the brief encounter he had with her at the superstore. That encounter filled every space in Fred's heart. 'So beautiful!' he kept telling himself in his admiration for Oke that night. He had never felt like this before. The following evening he went back to the superstore as he could not free himself from the thought of wanting to see Oke again.

The second day of their meeting at the superstore was more cordial. Fred came there when Oke was just arriving, so they met at the superstore entrance.

'Good evening. Hope you still recognise me.'

Oke looked at him with some interest for some seconds, trying to recollect.

'Oh yes! We met yesterday evening, here at the store, right?'

'Yes,' answered Fred with all interest.

'So, how're you?'

'Fine,' said Fred as he shook hands with her. 'I know you're here to do some work, so I wouldn't want to take your time,' Fred said with great courtesy.

'Yes, you're right.'

'I'd like to chat with you on phone, probably in the late evening today when you're less busy.'

'Why do you want to chat with me?'

'Really, I find you very interesting and would like to know you better,' answered Fred.

Oke took a thorough look at Fred for some seconds, considering whether to grant him his request. She immediately remembered her mother's word – 'Be careful with a stranger.'

'I'm sorry, I can't give you my phone number. I don't know you.'

'I mean no harm,' laughed Fred. 'Please you can trust me,' added he almost swearing with his words.

'It's okay – Let me give you the benefit of the doubt.'

And they exchanged telephone numbers. Fred thanked her and drove back home that evening feeling very happy, having passed the first hurdle. Late that evening, he phoned Oke. At first, he was not so particular. He spoke on general matters, just trying to create some interesting stories which did excite Oke and they both found themselves laughing. Fred repeated the telephone call on two other occasions, usually in the evening. In his third calling, Fred requested Oke to visit him in one of the evenings after her inventory.

'Where?'

'At my home. Good, you know where I live.'

'I don't have that time, please. Besides, my mum won't allow me visit anyone we have not really known, let alone at such odd hours.'

Fred thought for some seconds.

'What about weekend at a restaurant?'

'Not so free at weekends either. My mum, most often, will have me do one thing or the other in the house. So, I'm sorry, I can't afford such a luxury.'

After Fred dropped the telephone that night, it occurred to him that winning Oke's heart was not going to be easy. He realized that though Oke was quite polite and civil, she was only being tactful. He realized that the more effort he made to bring Oke close to him, the more she seemed to be more distant. This began to worry him as he desired her by all means.

After several phone calls without making any headway, Fred thought it necessary to see her again at the superstore. One evening, he went to the superstore. He knew she would be there in the evening. Before he left, he tried as much as he could to look his best in his casual but ritzy clothes.

'Good evening, Oke,' a smiling Fred greeted immediately he met her.

'Oh, good evening, sir,' answered Oke.

'Nice to see you again. How's your day?'

'Just as usual – doing my routine evening job here – you can see it,' returned Oke officiously.

Fred thought for a moment as he looked at Oke taking records of items in the store. He was trying to be careful lest he annoyed Oke. Not really having any clear idea of what to say, Fred hung by in the superstore watching Oke do her work. After a few minutes, he walked straight to her with some measure of confidence.

'Excuse me please.'

Oke looked up and gave him attention.

'I came to this superstore this evening for one singular purpose.'

He drew closer and whistled, 'My queen, just to tell you that I love you, I love you – just can't do anything without you. You occupy the whole world inside me. I can't do anything anymore without saying this to you. Please believe me, you're just everything to me, right now,' pleaded Fred.

'Well, I quite appreciate how you feel about me but I think what you consider to be love might just be a mere lust. I think you're merely lusting after me. You've not known me to express a genuine love for me,' returned Oke and she looked at him in the face and added, 'Let me tell you, for love to be true, it must be mutual, okay? I don't feel the way you feel. You're still a stranger to me.'

Immediately Oke had finished expressing herself, she went about her work in a manner that suggested that she did not want to be disturbed further and Fred left.

Fred felt very demoralized by the reaction of Oke at the superstore that evening. He had always felt very confident of himself – he was suave and from a comfortable family, always with some good money in his pocket. Hitherto, he had the luxury of having his way with girls. He had never been rapped down by any girls the way Oke did that evening, as she made him looked like an irresponsible teenage boy who could not tell the difference between love and lust, and his castle of pompous carriage was completely destroyed. He felt really deflated that evening. Immediately he arrived home, he slumped on his bed without thinking of his dinner. As he lay in his bed, Oke's word kept ringing in his mind – 'I think you're merely lusting after me.' To be very sure, he looked the two words up in the dictionary and tried to distinguish them as they applied to him. *Have I really been lusting after women or loving them?* After some period of introspection vis-à-vis his past and present love affairs, it dawned on him that Oke might be right after all. *Why am I always changing girls after a brief spell of time with each? And after a while, all I see are things that put me off, and wanting to avoid them.* Ironically, that's when they show much interest in the relationship. *Does it mean I can't keep a relationship? Is that the lust Oke is talking about? Does it mean I merely lusted after all the girls that I have left?* These and several other nagging posers relating to his love life were what pre-occupied Fred that depressing night.

Two days later, after a deeper reflection on the matter, he sent a telephone message to Oke:

Thanks for making me have a deeper appreciation of what love is.
I've not really known you enough to love you truly.
I had seen love come and go several times in my life.
But I'd never felt love like this before - I know how I feel
about you. Quite convinced that I've eventually found what
I've been searching for in you. Please don't ignore it –
it's real. Give me the chance to prove that what I have is love – not lust.
    Cheers, Fred.

When Oke received the text in her cell telephone, she went through the text several times as she was deeply moved by it and she replied Fred:

Got your text. Know what love is really? Love is investing tolerance
– investing your life in someone else – Ready to invest your whole
life in me and tolerate all my nonsenses? Then, let us see again at
the superstore, tomorrow.

The following evening they both met again at the superstore. This time, Fred was welcomed and ushered into an office in the superstore, where he was offered a drink to relax himself while Oke was taking the inventory of items after the superstore had closed to customers. Oke spent three good hours in doing her stock-taking and going through the day's sales records to balance her accounts. As soon as she completed her records, she hurried to meet Fred who was already bored with waiting. But he was prepared to wait for any length of time to have audience with Oke that evening.

'Oh Fred, I'm really, very sorry for keeping you waiting for so long. I know you must have been bored. I just couldn't help it. I hope one of the staff brought you a drink,' said Oke when she came in.

'Oh yes, and that was very kind and thoughtful of you. It made my waiting quite relaxing.'

It was already getting dark. All the staff of the superstore had all left saved the security men. It was quite obvious that the circumstance was not favourable for further stay at the superstore, so they decided to drive to a nearby restaurant, in order to have a more sociable atmosphere for their meeting.

That day, Oke returned home very late. Her mother became anxious when she did not return home at the expected time. She eventually came back home two hours later than usual. By then, Agnes was almost freezing to death with anxiety, praying and looking at the clock as every minute ticked away. She almost leaped with joy when Oke eventually came in, as all the storm of anxiety she had borne quickly ceased and she did heave a sigh of great relief, though she was very angry. She did not react at first. Oke knew as she was returning home that night that she would be greeted with fireworks at home and she was fully gripped with fear of what her mother would do to her. Immediately she stepped into their home, Oke went straight to her bedroom. She greeted her mother without looking at her, as she walked past her in the living room to her room.

Agnes did not answer her. She was just too angry, her face flushed with reproach.

It was then it became clear to Oke that her late return that day would not be taken lightly. She undressed herself, took her bath and quietly went to her bed, without daring to go to the kitchen for her dinner that night, although she was very hungry. She thought that would give her mother who was already burning with anger, the chance to explode. She lay on her bed that night expecting the worst from her mother.

Meanwhile, Agnes was waiting for Oke to come to the kitchen to take her meal to the dining table in the living room where she was prepared to pour out her venom on her that night. When she had waited for a long time without seeing Oke, her only companion in the home, she decided to go to her room. Getting there, she saw that Oke was already fast asleep. She stared at her for moment, considering whether to wake her or not. She discerned that her daughter was very tired and exhausted and decided not to wake her up. She went back to the living room wondering what might have delayed Oke that night. She thought over it for quite a while without reaching any tangible reason. Agnes eventually concluded that she would open the matter the following day.

The succeeding evening after Oke had returned from her routine inventory at the superstore, her mother raised the matter of her coming home late the previous night. By then, all the intensity of her anger had fizzled out. She was calm and soft, and spoke with understanding. That close bond that exists between a mother and her grown-up daughter which makes them see each other as friend and confidant was what was left. So there was nothing to hide or pretend about, and Oke told her mother about the doting Fred. After Agnes had heard everything from Oke, she ruminated and laughed.

'Why are you laughing, mum? Does my story sound so funny?'

Her mother laughed again.

'My dear, don't mind my laughter. Your story only reminds me of how your late father started with me – so I was only recalling those good memories, okay?' said Agnes as she cuddled her daughter.

'So tell me how did you both start?' returned Oke with exciting curiosity.

'My dear, let's forget about it lest old sweet memory brings me back to the pit of sorrow, which by His grace I've overcome, okay?' answered her mother with some tenderness in her voice, as she caressed her daughter's cheek with her soft hand of fondness and love.

'I understand, mum. But can't I just hear the gist – I mean the underlining attitude?' said Oke who very much wanted her mother to share her courtship experience with her.

'Oke, do you want to see me cry?' asked her mother with some alarm and Oke shook her head in the negative, in full appreciation of her mother's caution. But on a second thought, Agnes sensed that her daughter was only being curious because there might be one or two lessons she wanted to learn from her experience, so she decided to offer something that might be a guide to her daughter, without really sharing her courtship experience.

'In my growing up as a girl,' began Agnes, 'there was a constant refrain my father wanted to plant in my consciousness. *Always think of a man with pride!* At first, I didn't understand what he meant until one day when I summoned courage to ask him to make his message clear to me. My mother, who was sitting by, laughed with full understanding. So before my father could say anything, she took it upon herself to do the explanation – those two people they understood each other so perfectly that if my father expressed an opinion on a particular matter in the absence of any mother, be sure that when my mother returned, she would certainly have the same opinion, without knowing what my father had earlier said. May God bless their souls.

"Agnes what your daddy's saying is that, when your time to decide who to marry comes, you should think more of a man with a high sense of pride. Listen carefully here", my mother emphasized strongly, "we're not talking about a man who prides himself in his achievements or in his special asset or natural favour. Such a man is arrogant and very likely to be selfish. We're talking about a man whose pride is in his personality – a man with self-respect – such a man avoids any act that's capable of bringing him shame and embarrassment. He decently works hard to avoid poverty as poverty brings embarrassment and loss of dignity. He'll also not want to act disgracefully to avoid loss of face. And because he has self-respect he treats others with respect. That's the man that can bring honour and dignity to himself and his family," explained my mother and my father nodded his head in absolute satisfaction of his wife's explanation. 'It was just then that mantra sank into me and it became the guiding principle in my assessment of every young man who came my way,' said Agnes finally.

'And my father certainly met the requirement,' smiled Oke interestingly with an air of pride and her mother nodded her head, beaming with smile.

'How many of them came before you picked my dad?'

'Several,' Agnes tried to figure out. 'I can't really remember all of them now – some were serious, others were not so serious and some others were just out to catch fun – you know the philanderers are always around. Incidentally, they're the ones with courage,' and they both burst into laughter. 'Somehow, as a daughter of a pastor, the sanctity of the pulpit was always following me, and most of the men were stymied by that. If not, I would have been most probably swallowed by a deluge of pressure from men. I could see very many others burning with desire but they couldn't come near,' narrated Agnes.

The meeting between Fred and Oke at a restaurant did strike home, after all. Fred had an ample time to ventilate his feelings in a much relaxed atmosphere. He and Oke had a lot of time talking to each other and Oke began to open her heart to Fred. After that day, Fred did everything to consolidate the relationship. Besides daily phone call, he also paid frequent visits to her at the superstore in the evening. As they kept talking and seeing, they were becoming very intimate. After sometime, Oke agreed to pay Fred a visit. Also Fred began to see her at her home. At first, Fred did so with great caution, as he had understood that Oke came from a family with a good sense of propriety.

The first time Agnes saw Fred in her residence, quite typical of her, she treated him with utmost courtesy and made him feel welcomed, even though Fred's personality appeared disagreeable. Fred was glitzy and suave-looking as usual, which gave him away as someone who was deep in worldly living. But Agnes did not want to appear priggish and sanctimonious, so she received him warmly, without showing the least reservation. This quite pleased Fred and encouraged him to pay more visits to Oke at home. However, when Fred kept coming to see Oke, Agnes was compelled to interrogate her daughter on the extent of her relation with Fred.

'Mum, initially the relationship didn't mean anything to me. But somehow, it's getting serious. I find myself not wanting to leave his presence lately,' said Oke hesitantly.

'Is he a Christian?'

'Not a very serious one but he promises to be if that'll please me.'

'Because of you?' goggled her mother. 'That means he's not. One can't be a Christian for someone else's sake. He'll certainly renege and that'll be a lot of trouble for you later, my daughter. Christianity is a matter of conviction, conviction from the depth of your soul. I think before you go further with him, we really need to find out who he is,' cautioned Agnes and her daughter agreed with her totally.

Agnes took the matter so seriously that she involved her other two children. In his effort to conform to true Christian standards and demonstrate to Oke that he truly loved her, Fred had begun to keep away from his several girlfriends. He began to attend his church regularly, including the weekly activities and suddenly became one of the devotees. He also became very active in the youth activities of the church. Hitherto, he only attended Sunday service sometimes. He had also been keeping away from his company of friends with whom he attended pubs and night clubs. The time he used to spend with them, drinking and frolicking, at their meeting joints, was now being spent in the church, nowadays. Sometimes, he would go with Oke to her church to attend weekly activities. When Oke saw his seriousness, she was quite convinced that Fred would definitely turn out to be a better Christian. Attending church together had brought them very close. Agnes had seen Oke and Fred together in their local church many times and was watching them from a distance.

One day, Fred's closest friend with whom he usually went out, Charles, came to see him one evening after him and the rest of their associates had complained about Fred's constant absence from their meeting joints lately. When Charles visited Fred that evening, he saw him reading the Bible with great interest. Fred showed little interest in his coming, unlike before. At first, there was a hush, 'What's the matter Fred. We've not been seeing you?' queried Charles.

'Well, it has to be so, Charles,' a smiling Fred replied. 'When light appears suddenly, one sees things clearly. I'm now in the light of God. I'd been in darkness and those things I used to do when I was in darkness, I certainly can't do them anymore 'cos I can see things very clearly now.'

'What darkness are you talking about?' retorted Charles.

'Drinking and womanizing are not the ways of our Creator. Those things are of Mephistopheles — I don't want to live in sin anymore with the author of sin. Lest I forget, Charles, that thing we call love, which we say to any lady that catches our fancy, is not love but lust. I've been enlightened. True love comes from God and for you to love, you must be in Christ, our Saviour and Redeemer, who gave His life away for all of us to be saved from sin, which the number one enemy of human — the devil — has brought upon the world. Charles, you need to come to God and be in the light and abandon those things we thought are enjoyment. The devil is a liar – he is deceiving the world to think so, in order to remove the glory of God from us. Charles, enough of Satan deceit! Come with me to the church this evening and the good Lord will visit you and show you the light and you'll see clearly what I'm talking about. Come with me! I'm inviting you to our youth activity. Be there with me Charles. Will you?' persuaded Fred as he was looking at Charles beseechingly.

'Fred, what has possessed you? Are you the one talking like this? I can't believe my eyes and ears,' said Charles with some disdain. Fred looked at Charles with pity and shook his head, 'Ignorance, Charles, is a great curse. I pray you come out of this curse. It is only then you can see clearly!' Charles gazed at Fred his very good friend in utter amazement. Completely shocked he decided to leave him alone.

Agnes' dragnet of consultation and investigation on Fred came with a shocking revelation — that Fred was an incurable libertine, having pleasure in taking girls for a ride.

'Thank God, I found this out in time,' said Agnes with some relief. 'My daughter will not marry a philanderer,' she sighed after some reflection. Agnes summoned a meeting of her three children the following Sunday afternoon, for the purpose of addressing the 'ill-advised courtship' between Oke and Fred. She knew telling Oke to quit the relationship might not be easy as she had observed that Oke was already deeply in love with Fred. But winning the rest family members to her side in total rejection of Fred would definitely snatch Oke away from Fred. On that fateful Sunday, Agnes presented the nature of Fred to Oro and Ovo. It did not take much debate before they reached a decision that Oke would have to quit her relationship with Fred. But Oke was quite unwilling, entreating her two siblings and mother to realize that Fred had changed from his old ways. Unfortunately, none of them was prepared to listen to her and that made her very upset. In unanimity, they warned Oke never to have anything to do with Fred again, as the family would never support their engagement.

Oke could not imagine leaving Fred on account of her family neither could she contemplate being engaged to someone her family rejected outright. Herein lay her dilemma. That Sunday, she was confused over the issue. She wished her family took its decision when she had not fallen in love with Fred. Besides being in love with Fred, she was quite convinced that Fred had actually become a Christian lately and had completely shed his old ways. But how was she going to convince her own family?

That night Oke related the shocking decision of her family over their engagement to Fred on phone. Fred could not believe what he heard at first.

'What are you saying?' returned he in a shocking voice. 'They say they won't have me engaged to a philanderer, which they believe you are. That's what they found out about you. Fred, be honest with me, are you still a philanderer?' asked Oke in a crying voice.

At first, Fred was just too disturbed to speak.

'But that was before,' said he after he had found his voice again. 'You know I've left all that! You should have told them so.'

'I did but they wouldn't listen.'

'What're we going to do now?' rejoined Fred, in a lamenting and frustrating voice.

'My dear, I don't know. I'm just too upset,' returned Oke.

When Fred dropped his cell phone after the conversation, he was clearly distressed. He could not contemplate the prospect of losing Oke – losing Oke was losing the better part of him. She was all he treasured in the world now.

That night Fred could not wait to see the dawn of the following day — He was too agitated. He could not sleep throughout the night. He wanted to see Oke's mother at once. The night seemed too long. Once the light of day began, Fred took his bath quickly and literally fled his home. He was driving straight to Oke's. The morning was cold and lonely on the roads. He seemed to be alone on the road. His headlights cut through the dark-grey dawn of heavy dew like a searching light, peering into the distance for a very precious object. One or two vehicles drove past him on the other lane after a while. Unusual of him, when he was driving, he did not remember to put on music or tune the radio. Fred was too disturbed to think of such mundane things presently. So many different kinds of negative thought were just running through his mind as he was driving, and he became nervous. Not long, he was at the gate of Oke's home. He honked several times but nobody answered. He kept on like that for a while.

'Who's there?' came a deep loud voice from inside. It was the gate-keeper of the residence. Fred immediately came out of his car and announced, 'Fred, Oke's friend!'

'Want to see her this early hour?'

'Yes, very urgent!'

'Too early to wake her up. Her mother won't like your early morning call.'

And Fred decided to wait outside in front of the gate.

Some minutes to seven, Oke sauntered reluctantly to the gate to see the early visitor. She was surprised it was Fred. He was dozing on his car steering.

'Ah, Fred, you're here?'

Fred raised up his head wearily.

Oke observed that he had not had a sleep in the night.

'Why Fred?' Oke demanded with much concern.

'Just want to see Mama,' returned Fred in a sombre voice.

It was very evident that he was completely ruffled in spirit. Immediately Oke understood the cause of Fred's anxiety and sorrow, she quickly ran back to the house.

'Mother, come and see how shattered and wretched Fred is, when he learnt of our decision. Only God knows since when he has been at our gate,' lamented Oke in a most solicitous and heart-rending voice, as soon as she met her mother.

'Fred at the gate?' asked Agnes and she walked straight to the gate with Oke.

'Mum, I know I'd been living an irresponsible and wayward life,' cried Fred tearfully immediately the three of them were in the living room. 'I've changed! I'm now a Christian,' he announced with all emotion and knelt down before Agnes. 'Please mum, accept me for what I am now. Don't look back! That's gone for good! Please ma.'

He suddenly broke down in tears, as his emotion got the better of him.

Agnes was completely speechless. She did not know what to say. Oke could no longer stand Fred's effusive importunity. She went to her room and allowed her pillow to absorb her tears.

Ten months later, Oke and Fred were to be pronounced 'husband and wife' by Pastor Onokurhefe. The preparation had been a flaming passion for the intending couple. Fred and Oke had been very busy with their shopping and preparing for the great day. By this time, they were so attached to each other that they hardly separated. Oke missed Fred so intensely whenever he was not around her. She always wanted to be by his side, while Fred had this delightful and appreciative attitude towards her, giving the impression that he was so glad to know her and be part of her life. He glowed with joy and satisfaction as the day drew near, wanting the day to come expressly and hear Pastor Onokurhefe declaring them husband and wife. He was anxiously looking forward to the great day – he dreamt it, breathed it, felt it and was seeing it as the days were counting down. These days, whenever he looked at Oke, his damsel, he could see the beauty of the whole world in her face. Oftentimes, he thought the sun rose in her eyes. She had become everything to him.

That early morning of the wedding, the house of Agnes was a beehive of people: family friends, close church members and very close business patrons were in the house to wish the amiable Oke a very blissful marriage. A bevy of young beautiful girls had been with the bride since last night. A very special delegate from the Onoyoma family in Okah was also in the house that morning to represent the extended family at the wedding, after the traditional aspect of the marriage had taken place at Okah a week earlier. It was the most exciting and intriguing period for Oke. Since a fortnight ago, she had been experiencing all manner of attention and interest. Every now and then, and everywhere, she often saw people come around her, saying 'Hey, getting married?' stretching their hands forward with a smile for a handshake. Some others simply nudged her suddenly and smiled, 'congratulations!' Most surprisingly, many of them were people she thought she had never met before. Oke was a very private person, so, most times she flushed at such encounters. But for people, she knew very well or had some acquaintance with, it was always a welcome gesture. All these mesmeric attention sometimes made her feel like an idol with so many admirers and well-wishers in the street. Hitherto, she never knew that she was very well known in the town.

In the morning of her wedding, her very intimate friends were with her – all wanting to see that she had the most winning look at her wedding. One of the most outstanding beauticians in the town was hired by Fred to glam Oke up, yet her friends were there, inside one of the rooms, watching the beautician closely, making one suggestion or the other.

By ten that morning, the 'princess' was set to go to her place of 'coronation.' Oke stepped out of the house to a waiting, well-decorated, most elegant car outside, admirers and well-wishers both within the house and outside, waiting to join her motorcade to the church rushed forward, to have a good look at her and they gave a resounding acclamation of adulation to signify: 'Behold! here comes the queen of brides.'

Fred came to the church that morning in a grand style. He came with a retinue of peers, all looking gorgeous and stylish. Many invitees and well-wishers were already seated, the entire church was set for the wedding. As Fred stepped out of his car, smartly followed by his company of friends lining behind him into the church, he found himself swept up in a whirling excitement and he suddenly realized that his steps had changed. He was not really sure, he was the one moving his feet as soon as he strutted on the aisle with all eyes trying to catch a glimpse of him – the man of the moment — while three beautifully dressed female ushers came forward to welcome them to their special seats in front of the church. Fred was feeling being on top of the world.

Not long, Oke and her bridal train followed. Her little flower girl was leading the way and the marriage ceremony began immediately. It started with a hymn of worship, which was followed by Pastor Onokurhefe's marriage sermon, which he titled 'Where One Plus One Equals Three.' In the sermon, he proved that, in marriage, one plus one could become three. 'Marriage is not Mathematics, where one plus one must equals two,' began he. He drew his idea from Gen. 2:18: in the Bible. Pastor Onokurhefe saw marriage as a synergy between two persons. 'God in his infinite wisdom endows man with some special abilities. He also gives the woman her own special abilities, different from that of man. And for both to produce maximum achievement of God's goodness in their lives, they must come together as one and assist each other, so they complement each other for a greater accomplishment – herein lies the essence of marriage besides procreation. So any man or woman who has failed to marry or refused to marry the opposite sex will definitely not be accomplished in life,' he explained before a rapt audience who seemed to have discovered one major secret of life success.

While the sermon was going on, Fred took a survey of the congregation, out of sheer curiosity, to find out whether some persons he was expecting were present. At once, he saw two of his ex-girlfriends sitting together, whispering and nodding their heads to each other in a pew. He also saw a man who was a regular caller at the inn he and his old associates used to drink and smoke together with their girlfriends. The man looked at him with a revealing smirk in his mouth and seemed to be saying to him, 'You're most undeserving of that lady — She's too prim and proper for you!' At that moment, Fred's jaw dropped and goose-pimples came all over him at once. He wiped his face with his hand unconsciously and bowed his head, 'Oh Lord, I run into your arms. Deliver me,' he muttered to himself. His heart fell to his mouth and was completely lost in thought.

'Now, before we go into the litany of "Yes, I do", is there anyone in the congregation who has good reason why the bride and the groom should not be joined together in holy matrimony?' announced Pastor Onokurhefe in a high-pitched voice. Immediately, a thick silence fell upon the church. If a pin dropped down in the congregation that moment, it would be heard. At the drop of the pastor's announcement, Fred became too nervous and could not breathe. The pastor cast his eyes across the church that was full to capacity. Some other curious invitees also looked round. Fred's relatives and friends held their breaths and refused to look up. Suddenly, Oke began a whimper. All eyes were now on her and there was some confusion. Fred thought someone had raised his hand up and had wrecked the marriage ceremony. Agnes and a few other close persons ran to Oke at once.

A sudden whim of remembrance had just hit Oke when the officiating pastor made his last announcement to the congregation. She remembered what her late father who was very fond of her used to tell her when she was much younger. 'My lovely daughter, on your wedding day, which is your very special day, you shall marvel what your Dad will give to you as a present. It's my secret,' he would beam a smile to Oke. 'I pray the Almighty God will see us all to that day. On that day, I'll dress like a king to give my treasured daughter away to her lucky husband. I know you won't disappoint me — you'll marry a man that we all shall be proud of, in this family,' the late Robert would pat her in the back with all tenderness. But seeing that her father was not at her wedding, Oke began to sob.

'Oke, what's the matter?' whispered her mother as soon as she came close, bringing her face very close to Oke's.

'Daddy is not here,' Oke cried.

'My sweet daughter,' Agnes hugged her, 'your Daddy is in a better place. He's supping and dining with the King of Kings in paradise. Today is your day, my dear, enjoy it! Don't spoil it with his remembrance, okay?' entreated her mother, she patted Oke's shoulder and dusted her forehead with her handkerchief, and the bride regained her spirit. Thereafter, the marriage ceremony went on smoothly with all its excitement. Fred was the happiest for it.

After the wedding and reception, the couple enjoyed a blissful marriage, with three children to celebrate, and Fred never went back to his old ways. He lived happily with his most treasured Oke, as he had vowed, celebrating their life together each day, to the glory of God.

Printed in the United States
By Bookmasters